MAKE YOU MINE

Claire Kendal was born in America and educated in England, where she has spent all of her adult life. She teaches English Literature and Creative Writing and lives in the South West with her family. She writes page-turning psychological thrillers including *The Book of You*, which was a *Sunday Times* bestseller and has been translated into over twenty languages.

📷 @clairekendalnovelist

Also by Claire Kendal

The Book of You
The Second Sister
I Spy

MAKE YOU MINE

CLAIRE KENDAL

HEMLOCK
PRESS

Hemlock Press
an imprint of HarperCollins*Publishers* Ltd
1 London Bridge Street,
London SE1 9GF

www.harpercollins.co.uk

HarperCollins*Publishers*
Macken House,
39/40 Mayor Street Upper,
Dublin 1
D01 C9W8
Ireland

First published by HarperCollins*Publishers* Ltd 2026
1

A catalogue record for this book is available from the British Library.

ISBN: 978-0-00-825687-6

This novel is entirely a work of fiction.
The names, characters and incidents portrayed in it are
the work of the author's imagination. Any resemblance to
actual persons, living or dead, events or localities is
entirely coincidental.

Set in Lomba Book by Palimpsest Book Production Ltd, Falkirk, Stirlingshire

Printed and bound in the UK using 100% Renewable Electricity
by CPI Group (UK) Ltd

This book is produced from independently certified FSC™ paper
to ensure responsible forest management.

For more information visit: www.harpercollins.co.uk/green

To my own hummingbirds,
Imogen, Violet, Lily, and Charlotte, with love.

And in memory of another hummingbird,
my beautiful cousin Karen.

Contents

Part I: Persephone

. . . the stranger's eye detects what the familiar unsuspecting eye leaves unnoticed.

George Eliot, *Adam Bede*

SEPTEMBER 1991

The Finding of Harriet Sapphire

When Helena's foot crashed through the floorboards during a rehearsal for the autumn musical, something made her want to see what was underneath. The others pulled her back from the hole, but Helena broke away from them and lowered herself onto her stomach. Careful to keep her body on solid ground, she looked down.

It was too dark to see anything. 'Get the torch,' she said. 'It's in the little cupboard by the door.' As a teacher, Helena always noticed the locations of things like that – first-aid kits, emergency exits, fire extinguishers. Someone put the torch in her hand, and she switched it on. The beam revealed a passageway lined with shelves. On those shelves were coffins, some with their lids half-off.

The village chapel where the amateur dramatics society rehearsed was near the site of an eighteenth-century mansion that had been destroyed by bombs in 1941. A labyrinth of underground passages had once linked the two buildings, and Helena realised that she was looking into an old burial vault. It was paved with stones and scattered with bones that appeared to have been tossed there in some crazed subterranean game.

'Ugh. The stench.' The voice belonged to Sam, a fellow actor. He was gripping Helena's legs as an extra safety measure. 'Are you okay?'

'Fine,' she said, although there really was something fetid in the air, wafting up at her from below as she continued to look.

The coffins on the shelves appeared ancient, so the flesh on the bodies that occupied them must have long turned to dust, leaving only skeletons. But lying on the ground, face-down, was a man wearing a short-sleeve shirt, so she could see that the skin on his arms was grey-white. Something thick and dark that Helena couldn't quite make out but thought might be dried blood covered his hair. Had he slipped and hit his head, or had somebody done this to him?

She moved the torch beam, peering so hard her corneas were burning, but the more she stared, the more certain she became. Curled on the pale stones, in a foetal position, was a young girl.

Helena simply couldn't assimilate what she was seeing. Ancient coffins, human bones of those who lived centuries ago, and two newly dead bodies. She peered harder at the girl, thinking that what she saw next was simply a trick of the light. But there was no doubt about it. The girl's chest was moving. She was breathing.

'Someone call 999.' Helena was surprised by the calm of her own voice. 'Tell them we need an ambulance and firefighters with ladders and rescue equipment. There are vaults below,' she said, 'and there's a young girl in them. She's alive, but I think she's hurt.'

'Could it be Harriet?' Sam's voice was hoarse with fear and hope.

For the last four months, the case of the missing fifteen-year-old girl, Harriet Sapphire, had gripped the whole country. She had disappeared, along with her bike, while travelling to school on a beautiful sunny morning, just as spring was turning to summer.

The tragedy intensified when Harriet's mother died of cancer, never knowing what had happened to her daughter. But the father was still everywhere. Helena had seen him on a chat show only the week before, talking about the deathbed promise he'd made to his wife not to waste time grieving, and instead to devote his every waking minute to maintaining public awareness and finding Harriet. When he said that Harriet was his sole reason for getting out of bed each morning, Helena had been a bit teary-eyed.

Harriet had become the nation's child. Her Year 9 photo was everywhere, a slight smile on her closed lips, unaware of her own beauty in the way that teenaged girls so often are.

'What colour is her hair?' Sam said.

The missing girl's was an unusual dark red. Helena moved the torch's beam to check, but could see only a long, matted tangle. 'It's hard to be sure.'

There was a faint cry, and the figure trembled so slightly Helena wasn't sure if she'd imagined it. Then, the face turned a little, and the new angle was undeni-able. Helena had studied the missing poster, her love of children, her teacher's duty, making her look and look, just in case. But she never really imagined she would see the girl with her own eyes.

'I think,' she said, knowing they were all waiting for her next words, 'that we really have found her.'

TWENTY-THREE YEARS LATER –
FRIDAY, 26 SEPTEMBER 2014

Areas of Concern

Esmeralda Avelar was sleep-deprived. She'd spent the night worrying about her police vetting interview, and now that the moment had arrived, she was tripping over her words and her own feet as she invited the officers to make themselves comfortable at her kitchen table. While her guests took out their A4-sized files and laptops, Esmeralda arranged the coffee things, nearly losing her grip on a jug of hot milk.

Bob, the Head of Police Vetting, was a former sergeant. He was short, stooped, and exceedingly hairy, with skin that seemed to be covered in light brown fur. 'You said when the appointment was arranged that your father would be out and your daughter at school?'

'We have complete privacy. My dad's playing golf after he drops Líria,' she said.

Sophie, the case officer, brought to mind a prickly maiden aunt from one of the old black and white films Esmeralda's dad liked to watch. 'Is he good?' Sophie said.

Esmeralda hesitated, losing the thread. 'Is he a good person?'

'Is your father good at golf?' Sophie spoke as if she were addressing a child.

'Oh, I see – sorry! Of course that's what you meant.' Esmeralda laughed, though Sophie did not. 'I think I need more coffee. He says he isn't, but I'm not sure that's true – he's quite a self-effacing person, my dad. He keeps going on about how his handicap is going up as he gets older, but he still loves to be out there. So that's all that matters.'

Esmeralda thought of the instructions on the vetting questionnaire she'd completed a few months earlier. And the videos she'd watched, with an actress's cheery voice struggling against the incessant, tinny background music.

We want to know all about you . . .

'So,' said Bob. 'I believe you understand that occasionally we have to have a face-to-face when we come across any areas of concern?'

See the vetting interview as an opportunity for you to clarify any issues that might be considered compromising or concerning . . .

'I see it as an opportunity to clarify any issues,' Esmeralda said, trying not to look as if she were reading an autocue.

Sophie took a sip of her coffee, which she'd taken black. 'Do you have any idea, then, as to why we requested this face-to-face?'

Please be honest regarding your current and previous situation.

'Because I was once a high-profile victim, so I have

personal experience of adverse contact with the police.'
Adverse contact with the police. 'What happened to me
was a long time ago,' she added. 'I hope I did the right
thing in disclosing it in the vetting questionnaire.'

'You did absolutely the right thing,' said Bob, smoothing
his beard. Was he good cop to Sophie's bad? So far, that
seemed to be the direction this was headed in.

'I realise,' Esmeralda said, 'that you need to make sure
there's nothing in my past, or my current life, that can
present a risk to the force.'

'Exactly so.' Bob leafed through the thick stack of pages
that comprised Esmeralda's responses to the vetting questionnaire. 'Birthdate 29 February 1976. So you're nine
and a half – sorry, bet you've heard that before. I know
you're thirty-eight.'

She smiled, or tried to. 'I'm probably the oldest person
in history to apply to be a detective.'

He smiled too. 'The direct entry programme's relatively
new, so there isn't a lot of data yet, but you're definitely
not the oldest.'

'My mum always said that being a leap year baby had
its advantages.'

Bob placed the document on the table. 'Your mum was
Portuguese, yes?' he said.

'Yes,' Esmeralda said, 'and British, after she and my
dad were married.' She gestured towards the pile of original documents she'd set out the night before. 'Her
certificate of naturalisation is there. Líria and I have both
nationalities too. My mum died of cancer while – Hugo
Green – was holding me.' She still struggled to say his
name without stumbling.

'You were fifteen?' Bob said. 'And you and your dad moved here from the other side of the city, after you were found?'

'Yes.' She guessed that the newspapers had had two headlines lying in wait during those long months when she was missing. They must have all expected to run *Kidnapped Girl Found Dead* rather than *Kidnapped Girl Alive*. She made a visible effort to sit straighter. 'It was a long time ago.'

Bob topped up his coffee. 'So . . . You are co-resident in this property with your eight-year-old daughter, Líria Helena Avelar – Líria in honour of your mother – and with your father, Isaac Ernest Avelar? And you work as a language teacher in a secondary school?'

'That's all correct,' she said.

Bob added a spoonful of sugar to his coffee, then a second. 'Don't tell my wife.' He went on, 'Your dad explained the steps he took to protect your privacy after you were found. The house. Your education. The name changes for both of you.'

'Sapphire does stand out a bit,' she said, 'and there were all these stories in the press calling me a lost treasure, or a rare bird who'd been stolen from its nest.'

'Because sapphires are a type of hummingbird, yes?' said Sophie.

'Yes,' said Esmeralda. She wasn't about to elaborate. They didn't need to know that her parents had fallen in love with hummingbirds during their honeymoon in Mexico, where she was conceived. Hummingbird had been her nickname before and after Hugo Green. It was the part of her that had always been and always would be, since the time she began and until the moment she ended. She loved that her dad still called her Hummingbird, and that he called Líria the Mini Hummingbird, saying his daughter and granddaughter were bright warriors like those magical birds.

'So your original name was Harriet Esmeralda Sapphire,' said Bob.

'It was. But let me show you something.' Esmeralda extracted her birth certificate from the pile of documents. 'Avelar is there.' She pointed to the box with her mother's name, then slid her finger to her father's. 'And there's Sapphire. If my parents had gone by the Portuguese naming traditions, instead of the English, I'd have been Harriet Esmeralda Avelar Sapphire. It's a bit of a mouthful, I know. But my dad likes to say that we cut out the brackets and kept what was inside them. All those names are me.'

'The press were calling you Crypt Girl.' Sophie's voice had almost no discernible inflection, as if it were auto-generated by an artificial intelligence programme.

'That was probably the one that caught on most strongly,' said Esmeralda. 'But there were others.'

'Yes,' said Sophie, startling Esmeralda by suddenly looking faintly interested. 'They were quite literary, weren't they? Princess Persephone. Harriet Hades. Lady Lazarus.'

'Exactly.' Esmeralda went on, 'My dad didn't want the other kids pointing at me, saying, there goes that girl who was held in those tombs by that serial killer.'

'You sound quite detached,' said Sophie. 'As if you're talking about someone else.'

Esmeralda hesitated, then wondered what damage the

truth could do. 'I should probably confess that it isn't very easy for me to talk about all this. I've never made a habit of drawing attention to what happened to me as a teenager.'

'The question we really need to ask,' said Sophie, 'is whether this is a vulnerability for you. What if someone found out about your past and threatened to make it public that you aren't Esmeralda Avelar? That you're Harriet Sapphire, the girl from that infamous case?'

This form provides us with a clear indicator of your honesty and integrity.

'I *am* Esmeralda Avelar,' she couldn't help but say, then quickly added, 'I'd prefer not to face that kind of threat, but there's no vulnerability. I'd deal with it openly.'

'What about your daughter?' Sophie adjusted her already-perfectly adjusted grey hair, which was chin-length, cut in a sharp bob and the same colour as her eyes. 'Because we need to safeguard police assets. We need to ensure you aren't susceptible to blackmail.'

'She's only eight.' Esmeralda did her best to mask how the idea made her feel. 'It's too dark a story to tell her when she's so young, but in a few years, in a simple way, I will explain. And sooner, if circumstances emerged and I had to.'

'My understanding,' said Sophie, 'is that you may have delivered the blow to the head that killed Hugo Green, though they were never able to determine that with absolute certainty. Will you share that possibility with your daughter?'

Esmeralda managed to keep her voice calm. 'I know you were sent a medical report. My GP will have said that I can't remember anything about the time I was being held.'

'Yes,' Sophie said slowly. 'Dissociative amnesia, he called it. He said you have the selective form, relating only to those events, and that it seems to be permanent.'

'He used the word retrograde,' Bob said, 'which concerns your inability to access any old memories of what happened to you when you were fifteen.'

'That's right. My other memories aren't affected, and I have no problem forming new ones. I have none of the other symptoms or behaviours or traits that can be associated with dissociative amnesia. It's a defence mechanism to protect you from trauma.' She added quietly, 'So I don't remember what he did to me. Or what I might have done to him.'

'To be frank, Esmeralda,' said Bob, 'it's doubtful you'd be alive now if you – or something else, say, a lucky accident – hadn't taken him out. It's a wonder you're here at all.'

Esmeralda was a walking talking miracle and she knew it. In fact, a day seldom passed when she didn't feel this truth. But she knew also that there were plenty of other miracles in the world. All she could think to say was, 'What happened to me doesn't define me. I want my daughter to know that when the time comes. And it will come. I know that it will. But I'm fit to be a police detective. The amnesia doesn't make me unfit.'

'Right,' said Sophie, making it sound like the opposite. 'I see,' she said, looking at the form, 'that you don't have a current partner, and no previous long-term relationships.'

Please disclose only significant relationships. You need not list casual encounters.

Esmeralda had laughed out loud at that one, given how differently every person understood those two categories. Now, she was amazed she'd been able to find it amusing.

Sophie adjusted her spectacles and peered hard at Esmeralda. 'We realise,' she continued, 'that the questionnaire doesn't ask for the name of a child's other parent.'

'But,' said Bob, looking sideways at Sophie, 'in keeping with your evident thoroughness, you supplied it in the additional information section. Arthur Dalloway.'

'Yes,' Esmeralda said, guessing that they had already checked Líria's birth certificate.

If in doubt, disclose. Better to tell us too much than too little.

'How long,' Sophie asked, 'were you and Mr Dalloway seeing each other?'

'Three months.' Esmeralda's voice was cool but polite. 'Arthur and his parents and sister were killed in a car crash on their way back from a Boxing Day lunch. It was a drunk driver.'

'What a lot of bad luck you've had,' said Sophie, looking narrowly at her.

'Or good,' said Esmeralda, 'depending on how you look at it. I'm alive. I survived what happened when I was fifteen. I lost Arthur and my mum, but I have Líria and my dad.'

As if he knew she needed rescuing, the thin high notes of a bird came from behind her. She twisted around in her chair to look through the wall of glass into the back garden. 'That robin thinks he's our family pet,' she said. 'He likes the berries on my dad's rowan tree.'

'Beautiful little creature,' said Bob. 'I bet that garden is amazing in spring.'

Esmeralda smiled. 'My dad's flowers would win awards if he only put them in competitions.' She got back on point. 'I put the date of Arthur's death in the questionnaire.'

Bob stroked his beard. 'We found several stories about the accident. A real tragedy.'

'Perhaps if he'd lived you'd have been able to sustain a relationship,' said Sophie.

A wave of heat went through Esmeralda's body and she took a sip of coffee to steady herself. If she lost her temper she'd fail vetting, no question. Was Sophie deliberately provoking her, to test her ability to stay composed under pressure?

When Esmeralda spoke, her voice was deliberately calm. 'Are you here because you think my failure to have a long-term partner makes me unfit to be a police detective?' She looked straight at Sophie. 'Do you think Hugo Green left me so damaged I couldn't conceivably pass police vetting?' There. She'd said his name without flinching.

Sophie remained still, her grey eyes boring into Esmeralda's green, but Bob shook his head and surprised her by smiling. 'There are plenty of police detectives who haven't done great with long-term relationships. If that were grounds for a vetting failure there wouldn't be many of us. We just need to get a sense of you. Your past, in your own words, and your temperament.'

'And how you handle yourself when someone asks you

hard questions,' Sophie said. 'Because that's what will happen, most likely every day, if you're accepted for police work.'

Bob nodded. 'Very true.' He pushed his chair a little away from the table. 'It's getting to be time we left you to get on with your day. Anything final you'd like to tell us about why you want to be a detective?'

Esmeralda turned this over in her head. She looked between Bob and Sophie, who were watching her not unkindly or without trust, but with the focus, she thought, of wanting to do a job well, and get to the right answer. 'I have empathy for victims,' she said, 'and I have a kind of mission to locate missing women, to give them back to their families.'

'Do you think you're driven by survivor's guilt?' Sophie's manner had changed. The question was neutral, delivered even-handedly, but with a hint of warmth that had not been there before.

'Probably. At least a bit.' Esmeralda didn't see the point of pretending otherwise. 'It's quite personal, but I really do understand the impact of losing someone you love, of not knowing what happened to them. My mum died before they found me alive, as you probably know.'

'I'm sure she would be proud of you,' Sophie said quietly, so that once again Esmeralda found herself taken by surprise.

The pair were quick to gather their things, smiling as they waved goodbye, so that instead of the stern features Esmeralda had found in Sophie's face over the course of the morning, she saw a woman who didn't make up her mind until all of the evidence was in.

THREE YEARS LATER – MONDAY, 11 SEPTEMBER 2017

The Girl Who Lived

The escaped serial killer otherwise known as Jason Thorne waited on the opposite side of Ella Brooke's street. He had parked beside a hornbeam tree, to make himself less visible, and was sitting in one of the SUVs he'd put away nine years ago, before he went to prison. Jason was nothing if not organised.

And nothing if not faithful. He held the view that true loves could be multiple, as long as he gave his best and most devoted self to only one true love at a time, and the total could be counted on one hand. Each true love had helped Jason to move on from her predecessor, and because he was extremely choosy, he still had two fingers to spare.

Ella was the third in Jason's sequence. It had been ten long months since he last saw her, when she visited him at the secure psychiatric hospital. There, he had given her the clues she needed to find her sister, who'd been missing for over a decade. Only the sister's bones remained, buried beneath an apple tree in the garden of the man who'd kidnapped and murdered her.

Jason did not like to think that Ella had only visited him because of her incorrect suspicion that he'd been responsible for her sister's disappearance. Of course she'd found their conversations as fascinating as he had. Of course she'd visited him because she secretly adored him, and found him as charismatic as he found her. Of course she hadn't simply wanted to pump him for information. Jason liked to reflect upon Ella's gratitude for his assistance in finally learning her sister's fate, and to imagine how she would show her thanks.

Now, at last, he was about to see Ella again. That was why, in spite of the drizzly grey sky, Jason was glowing. Ella's beloved nephew, who'd been a tiny baby when his mother was kidnapped and murdered, left the house first. His dark head was bent against the spit of rain while he checked his phone, a habit Jason had observed in so many young people since his escape from custody ten months earlier. Jason knew that the nephew was called Luke, that he'd turned eleven the previous month, that he had just begun Year 7 of secondary school, and that he was one of the youngest in his class due to his August birthday, as Jason himself had been.

Luke crossed the road, then headed in the opposite direction from where Jason had parked. The boy had grown so much in the nine years since Jason had last seen him. He'd been a toddler then, and Jason had enjoyed spying on Ella as she pushed her little nephew on the swings, or read to him, cradled on her lap in the children's section of the local library, or chased him through the little lanes near her parents' house, the two of them laughing and singing. What Jason saw on those reconnaissance missions cemented a growing resolution not to risk bereaving any future children, and this was against his own interests, because it meant refraining from killing any more women. In the end, though, it wasn't a resolution he had to keep for long, because the police found the bodies in his basement freezers and promptly locked him up in the secure psychiatric hospital.

Jason tried hard to imagine what Ella would feel so that he could plan the things he would do to please and help her. He wanted to make himself better for her, so he spent a lot of time practising his empathy, a skill that did not come naturally to him but he cultivated nonetheless. He had certainly found empathy to be a useful tool with the women he used to target. How easy it was to say what they wanted to hear, so they fluttered their eyelashes as he slipped his magic potion into a drink, as he had with Claudia Bertrum. Or stabbed a syringe of tranquilliser into a thigh, as he had with Julia Smithlin and Penelope Hastings. Claudia had laughed and sipped, then strolled with him, arm in arm, smiling and chattering, towards his car and the last journey she would ever take.

He tapped his fingers on the dashboard. Clearly, Luke was walking to school alone. This was disappointing, as Jason had hoped to glimpse Ella with him. Still, he knew that Ella went for a run each morning, so he was hopeful she'd be out the door for that soon. Ten months earlier, Jason had experienced Ella's fitness first-hand. During her final visit to the secure psychiatric hospital she'd brought him to the ground with one precisely aimed kick. Still, touching her had been worth a fractured kneecap.

Not to mention the fact that the injury had resulted in an unforeseen trip to the orthopaedic unit. What an unasked-for gift that had been, giving Jason an unexpected opportunity to flee, helped by the fact that the pain had been dulled at that moment by the medications and brace they'd given him. If he hadn't left then, they would have returned him to the secure hospital and thrown away the key, then resumed the drugs that made him dull and docile and slow-moving, so that the man Jason glimpsed in their shatterproof mirrors was a fun house distortion he barely recognised.

He glanced at his watch, which was held in a strap of his own devising, studded with the jewelled corpses of beetles. The symmetry was so pleasing. He'd given the places of honour to two rose chafers, arranging them above 12 and below 6, so they appeared to be guarding the timepiece between them. He loved the way their iridescent green set off the gold. Radiating out from each rose chafer was a rosemary beetle with its stripes of metallic green and purple, then a rainbow leaf, then a black and yellow wasp beetle, then a tiger beetle, beaming its green gleam.

One of the many advantages of being free was that Jason was no longer limited to catching flies and moths for his art projects. Those hospital offerings were always falling apart, turning him into a kind of Gothic version of Hansel and Gretel, but one who trailed desiccated antennae and wings instead of breadcrumbs.

Jason continued to look at his watch. Two minutes

passed, then three, then four. If Ella didn't leave for her run soon he'd lose his chance of seeing her face and knowing that he was responsible for the shining joy that had replaced the grief and rage. Since his escape, it had become Jason's mission to punish those who hurt the ones he loved, women with children in particular. On Saturday morning, the man who'd murdered Ella's sister, making Luke an orphan, and assaulted Ella herself had – how to put it – stopped being alive. This change in Adam Holderness's breathing status boosted Jason's pleasure in the new moral code he was living by.

Jason had made the arrangements with Greg, an old friend of his from the secure psychiatric hospital. Greg had been deemed well enough to move to a normal prison and ended up in reach of Holderness. Given that Greg's multiple sentences were longer than the likely span of his remaining life, he'd had nothing to lose. Surely Ella had already been told the wonderful news, and would guess that Jason had masterminded the execution.

Jason had followed Holderness's trial earlier that year, and although Ella had not been identified in court, it was obvious that she was the unnamed Witness X. She'd had to listen to that scumbag say her sister's death had been an accident. Even worse, she would have heard Holderness's silky-smug voice telling the jury that he and Ella were lovers, and that Ella had pursued him because she was in the grip of some pathological sibling rivalry.

Jason's only regret was that he hadn't been able to torture and kill Holderness with his own hands. That, unfortunately, had been out of the question, but there was still so much good he could do, so much to clean up in this dirty world where punishments for the vile were not meted out to his satisfaction. Jason really was a new man.

What a beautiful morning it was, so filled with possibilities. He had a mirrorless camera with a zoom lens on the seat beside him, because he hoped to improve the collection of true loves on display by his bed. Ten minutes had passed since her nephew left, but when Ella still hadn't appeared, Jason had to face the fact that the new photo would have to wait. It was too risky to remain on her street any longer.

He was about to start the engine when a black Skoda estate turned into the road and stopped in front of Ella's house. There was a hint of blue LED lights behind the front grille. There were also bright flashes on the dashboard, probably from additional computer and communication devices. The rear of the car was sitting low, no doubt due to extra equipment. All of these details, glimpsed in a few seconds, made Jason certain the car was unmarked police.

Two women emerged. One was slight and spry in a grey trouser suit, with spiky brown hair that stood up as if she'd gelled it that way on purpose, and wire-rimmed glasses. She was of no interest to him. The other woman had a long, dark red ponytail caught at the nape of her neck. She was elegant in her navy trouser suit, lithe and pale.

This woman was strangely familiar, in a snowy-white blouse that Jason couldn't help but imagine ripping open, though his current fidelity to Ella made him scold himself for that. The women were definitely in the non-uniform

uniform of detectives, which wasn't a look that normally inspired Jason with longing. Since the police had captured him nine years earlier for kidnap, rape, and murder, Jason had seen plenty of this dull detective dress, though pony-tail girl wore it well.

The detectives must be there to talk to Ella about Holderness's recent misfortune. Jason leaned forward, as though he could get closer, into tasting distance of that delicious moment. They hadn't yet reached the door when Jason caught sight of a short, slight, furtive-seeming man rounding the opposite corner. The man was heading straight towards them, but at the sight of the two women he did an about-face, backtracked to where he'd come from, and disappeared. But Jason noticed that ponytail girl halted slightly, as if she'd clocked the little man. She put a hand on her companion's arm, but any hesitation she had was overruled by the spiky-haired one, and the two women walked on.

Jason knew who the man was, and why he didn't want to be seen. Little Thomas, as Jason liked to call him. That sad underwear burglar. His presence was irritating, because it meant Little Thomas was figuring things out that Jason had hoped to keep him from, and acting on that intelligence faster than Jason had anticipated. Still, Jason would catch up with Little Thomas to ensure there would be no unforeseen consequences.

His guts clenched with pleasure at the thought. And it was then that the female detective with the dark red ponytail, who wore the blouse he thought again about ripping open, reached Ella's door, pressed the bell, and turned to look behind her. It was as though she had an

29

instinct that eyes were on her. A good one, Jason couldn't help but think, as he dragged his attention up her body and to her face.

Jason was a remarkably visual person. As well as being an expert lip reader, he also possessed a photographic memory that functioned as well as any age progression software, thereby allowing him to accelerate the changes to a face over time. He had no doubt about who this woman was, and the sighting changed *everything*.

She had stolen into his thoughts recently, necessarily, despite the vow he'd made to himself, but seeing her in front of him, almost in touching distance after so long, he felt as if he'd conjured her. Before she turned back to Ella's door, Jason grabbed the camera, aimed, and clicked the shutter button several times. Then he started the engine and drove away, consoling himself that this was a new beginning rather than goodbye.

He had tried and failed not to dream of her, and had always imagined he would come upon her again someday. At last, his patience had been repaid. It had happened. She had materialised into his life once more, the only person who could push Ella Brooke to the margins of his heart and reclaim her place at its centre. His second true love, and the object of his deepest fascination and admiration. The girl who lived.

TUESDAY, 12 SEPTEMBER 2017

The Mistake

Detective Constable Esmeralda Avelar was standing with her back to the wall of the Major Crime Unit briefing room. Her eyes moved over several giant trifold display stands that were plastered with maps and overlaid with photographs of Jason Thorne's victims.

One of the display stands included a blown-up image of a bulletin board that Thorne had kept in his home office. For reasons nobody understood, Thorne had devoted the board to newspaper cuttings of the Hugo Green case, and that meant that the board included, over and over, Esmeralda's former name, Harriet Sapphire, along with her school photo.

The problem wasn't that Esmeralda was worried about her colleagues recognising her all this time later. She guessed that many of them knew already about what had happened to her as a teenager but were sufficiently poker-faced not to let on. The problem was that she hated to see Green's photo next to her own.

Esmeralda sipped from the flask of coffee she'd made

before leaving at six that morning. Yet again, her attention was drawn to the huge whiteboard documenting the escaped serial killer's timeline. Its persistence as a briefing room prop symbolised the team's failure to find him.

Inside a red circle at the board's centre were the words *Jason Thorne, DOB 15-08-1972*. At forty-five, Thorne was only four years older than Esmeralda. Radiating out from the red circle were blue arrows going in all directions, each of them leading to a key point about Thorne's history.

August 1990. Aged 18, moves from mother's into own property. Starts joiner training.

Thorne had used his carpentry skills to convert the basement of that property into a prison where he held the women he kidnapped, engraving their skin with flowers and vines before he killed them. Clearly, he viewed human beings as artist materials he could decorate, or as toys. To Thorne, women were dolls he could rape and torture. Esmeralda took care to keep her expression neutral and went on reading.

June 1991. JT's girlfriend Lucy Reed (aged 19) goes missing.

March 2001. Penelope Hastings disappears. Last seen getting off bus 2 blocks from home.

August 2003. Claudia Bertrum disappears. Last seen leaving Gold-Digger's Nightclub.

June 2005. Julia Smithlin disappears. Last seen entering Georgian Pleasure Gardens.

August 2008. Bodies of PH, CB & JS discovered in JT's basement freezers. JT arrest.

The police had written Lucy off as a runaway until they'd found Penelope, Claudia, and Julia. After that, they'd been convinced Thorne had killed her. But Thorne had known Lucy throughout their school days, and she'd been his girlfriend. The dead women in his basement, on the other hand, had been strangers. This discontinuity troubled Esmeralda.

Multiple questions about the dates also gnawed at her. Why was there a ten-year gap between Lucy vanishing in 1991 and his first victim, Penelope Hastings, in early 2001? Didn't this circumstance raise doubts about whether Thorne was responsible for Lucy?

Esmeralda reasoned also that Thorne had killed roughly every two years, with the time that elapsed between each murder slightly decreasing. So why were there three years between his last victim, Julia Smithlin, in 2005, and his arrest in 2008? Had something made him stop?

February 2009. JT deemed unfit to stand trial. Indefinite detention in secure psych hospital.

17-11-2016. Assaults visitor, Ella Brooke, who fractures his kneecap in self-defence.

18-11-2016. JT absconds from orthopaedic hospital during treatment for knee injury.

09-09-2017. Ella Brooke's assailant, the serial killer Adam Holderness, murdered in prison.

The final point on the board was new, and had occurred a mere three days ago.

A sudden hush made Esmeralda look up. Detective Chief Superintendent Dominic Vane was entering the room, polished as a politician in his well-cut charcoal suit and silky striped tie. Had she imagined that his attention lingered on her for an extra second?

'We are ten months into Operation Leopard,' said DCS Vane, 'and that is ten months too long.'

Esmeralda was certain that Jason Thorne would be pleased to have inspired the name Operation Leopard. He'd consider it a tribute for the way it evoked not just the power and danger of such a beautiful creature, but also the ability to hide so effectively.

Detective Inspector Harold Whistler hurried in, red in the face, then took the seat beside DCS Vane. The DCS's ultra-fit gym slimness appeared exaggerated with DI Whistler beside him. There was something about DI Whistler that made Esmeralda feel sorry for him, but this was only a vague impression given she'd never even spoken to the man.

'As you will now see,' said DCS Vane, 'we have reason to believe that Jason Thorne has been a busy boy.' He pressed the button of an electronic clicker and an image worthy of a horror film lit up a screen that was built into the wall.

'What is left of Adam Holderness,' said the DCS, 'taken in situ in his prison cell three days ago, on Saturday morning.' The DCS clicked through a series of crime scene photos. Holderness was bound with torn sheets. There was a wire around his throat and a gag over his mouth. His eyes were bulging. Carved on his chest was a crude face, a circle with dots for eyes, a frowning mouth, and a long line for a Pinocchio nose.

'Of course Jason Thorne didn't commit this crime with his own hands,' the DCS went on. 'But the person who did was an old friend of Thorne's and appeared to be acting on instructions, right down to the JT engraved on the victim's skin. And let me remind all of you that the JT signature detail has been withheld from the public and press to stop copycats. The drawing itself is the emoji for telling a lie. The likelihood is that Thorne chose it because he was enraged by the lies Holderness told about Ella Brooke during his trial.'

Standing beside Esmeralda was her immediate boss, Detective Sergeant Dinah Methuen, who scoffed. 'I don't buy Thorne's rebrand as a knight in shining armour who wants to defend women,' she said, contempt in her voice.

'I don't buy it either,' said DCS Vane. 'What's clear is that Holderness's murder gives a new urgency to catching Thorne before he kills again. And to figuring out who his next target may be. Thankfully, it looks like we've finally got a break. Over to you, Ben.'

With his black-rimmed glasses and his thick dark hair that wouldn't lie smooth, DS Ben Sachs always made Esmeralda think of a superhero disguised as a geek. There was a generous nature to him too, despite the callousness that so often built up in police stations. It had taken Ben years to work his way up from uniform to Detective Constable, and he'd only recently been promoted to Detective Sergeant, but he didn't seem to resent Esmeralda for fast-tracking into her role. Not everyone felt the same way, but Ben had advised Esmeralda on how to handle herself multiple times in the six months since she'd joined Major Crime.

She smiled as he took to the podium and seemed to look her way, but Ben's eyes glanced off. 'Right,' he said, pressing the clicker to bring up an image that had become iconic. 'This is the last photo we have of Thorne before he absconded, taken in November of last year and circulated to the public.'

Thorne's hair had the deep burnish of a lion's fur. He was wearing jeans and a red lumberjack shirt, peering at the photographer as if they were a potential snack. Whenever Esmeralda saw this picture, she imagined he must hate that shirt. Those famous amber eyes of his were narrowed in scorn.

'Thorne is in no doubt that he's cleverer than everyone else,' Ben said. 'That he outthinks everyone else. He wants to play games with us, prove how much smarter he is than we are.' Ben clicked again and a new photograph popped up. It was a car windscreen, and a man was sitting in the driver's seat. It was like glimpsing a distant relative of someone you knew very well. Though eerily familiar, you couldn't quite place them. 'As we will now see,' Ben said, 'Jason Thorne is not as smart as he thinks.' Ben nodded to a woman at the centre of the table. 'Best if I pass you to DS Armstrong.'

Detective Sergeant Mary Armstrong headed the High Tech Unit. She looked like a super-model, and was also, in Esmeralda's experience, super-nice and super-clever. Her dark hair was loose, because where Esmeralda always felt a pressure to tame her own into control – a knot at the nape of her neck, or a sleek ponytail – DS Armstrong refused to play along with any such set of codes for professional women.

DS Armstrong squared herself, taking over control of the screen. 'What you're looking at is a frame that we've isolated from a ten-second video taken using an iPhone 7 Plus. You'll see the time stamp is for the eleventh of

September at eight fifteen a.m. For those of you who haven't had your coffee yet, that was yesterday morning. Let's rewind to the beginning and watch in full.'

The film opened on a street lined with small Victorian terraced houses similar to Esmeralda's own. It was Nightingale Avenue, where Esmeralda and Dinah had visited Ella Brooke twenty-four hours earlier. The film zeroed in on a dark SUV parked beside a hornbeam tree. It closed in on the car's number plate before moving to its windscreen, then froze on the same image of the man sitting in the driver's seat that Ben had shown them.

Esmeralda could hear her own heart beating in her ears. Dread arrived, hot and awful. Yesterday, she must have walked right past a car containing the man the entire country was looking for.

'Luke Brooke,' said DS Armstrong, 'is Ella Brooke's nephew. He lives with her. Filmed this when he left for school yesterday. Sent it to us as soon as he arrived at form period. Unfortunately, by the time our officers arrived on Ella Brooke's street, the man in the car was gone.'

Esmeralda was calculating. She and Dinah had been with Ella for no more than fifteen minutes. They must have left shortly before those other officers arrived to try to clean up the mess she should have seen and cleaned up herself.

'And he didn't think to send the film to us immediately?' muttered DI Whistler. 'Give us an actual chance of getting there on time?'

DS Armstrong was visibly tight-lipped when she said, 'Our first break in ten months is down to this kid. Each morning, when he leaves for school, he pretends to be looking at his phone but he's actually scanning for anything out of place and filming it.'

Esmeralda agreed with DS Armstrong. Everyone in the room knew that when Luke was a baby his mother had been kidnapped and murdered by Adam Holderness, then buried in Holderness's garden. It had taken ten years for Ella to discover what had happened to her sister, and she ended up being assaulted by Holderness in the process. Soon after her sister's disappearance, Ella won the booby prize of Jason Thorne's so-called love.

Knowing that Thorne was out there, fixated on his aunt, Luke was constantly searching for threats. It was moving, and tragic, and impressive, that the boy included a reconnaissance of his own street as part of a morning routine that for most children was confined to eating their breakfast cereal and grabbing their games kit.

Líria was a month younger than Luke. Not for the first time, Esmeralda wondered what her daughter would feel and do when she discovered that her mother had been involved in such a horrifying criminal case.

DS Armstrong ran the film back to the number plate. 'First, and no surprises here, the registration is unreadable. The driver clearly took advantage of the wet weather by exaggerating the mud splatter.' This was an offence, but they all knew that traffic police rarely saw it as a priority. The driver undoubtedly knew that too.

DS Armstrong switched to the footage from the automatic number plate recognition camera, which offered them a full view of Ella Brooke's street and Thorne's SUV. 'He was guiding the car blind,' DS Armstrong said, 'with his head bent over to hide his face. No other ANPRs picked him up. He knows where they are and how to avoid them. On advice from Vehicle Intelligence, we're looking for a dark grey Ford Kuga, early 2008.'

Esmeralda couldn't let herself be paralysed by the enormity of her mistake. She made herself raise her hand, but then quickly lowered it, thinking that was what schoolgirls did. But DS Armstrong had seen. 'DC Avelar?' Her voice was kind.

'The ANPR camera is at the through-traffic end of Nightingale Avenue. Did we check if there's any CCTV from the end of the street leading into Florence Close? Or from Florence Close itself?'

'No need. We know from the ANPR the man never left his car and never drove into Florence Close, probably because he knows it's a dead end and didn't want to risk being trapped there. He U-turned to exit Nightingale Avenue the same way he entered it.'

DS Armstrong cleared the screen of the ANPR footage, replacing it again with the still of the man sitting in his car, taken by Luke Brooke with his iPhone. 'In the view of one of our facial recognition experts,' she said, 'we can have a high level of confidence that this is Jason Thorne.'

Esmeralda heard somebody whisper, 'Thorne's definitely glowed up.'

'It's certainly fair to say that Mr Thorne appears to enjoy choosing his own clothes again – I'm guessing he wasn't a fan of the hospital's taste for all things lumberjack.' DS Armstrong let the frame advance another fraction. 'This is the first time he's been seen since he escaped ten months ago, and he's dramatically altered his appearance. Thick glasses to hide the eyes. Shaved head. But the most dramatic change by far is the weight loss.' She focused in on Thorne's wrist. 'Incidentally, it seems from the bracelet that our boy still likes to design his own jewellery.'

'He can list that in his Tinder bio,' said DI Whistler. '"I like to have fun with insects." Has anyone checked in with the local beetle community? They might have some complaints.'

Esmeralda was surprised to find herself having to stifle a laugh. DCS Vane remained impassive. His voice was sombre. 'Yesterday, I visited Ella and Luke Brooke. She and her family are flying out of the country today. I won't say where, beyond the fact that they will be well out of reach of Jason Thorne. This is a course of action Ella has resisted for many months and I can tell you she isn't at all happy about it.'

'History there,' said DI Whistler, making it clear that in his view, Ella was an unreasonable pain in the ass.

DCS Vane ignored this. 'We owe it to the Brooke family, and to every person in this country, to capture Jason Thorne. All leave and rest days are cancelled until further notice.'

Tea Tree Oil

The room began to empty immediately but Esmeralda didn't move. She had missed Thorne. And if she hadn't, if she'd just looked around, all of this would have been over. She turned to Dinah, but before she could speak Ben had crossed the room and arrived at their side.

'The DCS wants you in his office in fifteen minutes, Dinah.'

Dinah leaned closer to Ben and sniffed. 'Have you taken a bath in disinfectant?' She teased him with an ease that Esmeralda marvelled at, given that she herself felt as if bands were forming around her throat and chest, squeezing her voice and breath away.

'It's tea tree oil.' Ben's ears had turned slightly red. 'Wouldn't want you to be late for the DCS,' he said.

'Thanks for the concern, Sachs.'

'Be sure to keep that back of yours straight,' Ben said, watching Dinah march towards the door as if she were on parade, though she held up a hand to flip him off without looking back.

'I quite like tea tree oil,' Esmeralda said, though the fumes really were overpowering.

'My nephew stayed with me last night. My sister doused me with the stuff when she picked him up this morning. She'd just treated him for headlice and tea tree's supposed to ward them off. Clearly wards off humans too, especially women.' He stopped, as if replaying what he'd just said.

Was he flirting with her? Dinah had been raising eyebrows and giving Esmeralda meaningful looks lately, whenever Ben was around. As if the question had only just occurred to her, she said, 'Did the DCS have a message for me too, or just Dinah?'

'Oh. Yeah. Be in his office in half an hour.'

Esmeralda nodded. 'Did they tell you? How I messed up?' Her hands were clasped around the coffee cup, self-comforting with the warmth. 'I mean, really, seriously messed up.'

She found she was glad that Ben didn't speak immediately, or try to wash it all away. 'It's not all on you,' he said. 'It's on Dinah, too. We all mess up sometimes.'

'Not on this scale. Not to the point where people might die from your oversight.'

'You'd be surprised.'

She glanced up. There was a bitterness in his voice she'd never heard before. Ben checked his watch. 'Actually, that's twenty minutes, now. Before you have to be in the DCS's office, I mean.' He looked sheepish. 'Don't be too hard on yourself, Esmeralda. It may not be as bad as you think.'

Unsolicited Attention

Set on top of a hill that overlooked the city, the South West Constabulary's main site had formerly belonged to a grand old private school that bore little resemblance to the dilapidated state secondary where Esmeralda once taught. The briefing room that she had just left had been the sixth-form centre in its previous life. DCS Vane's office was in a late-nineteenth-century manor house.

By the time she hurried through the door, Esmeralda was soaked with rain. Dominic Vane's rather imposing domain had previously been a drawing room. The blinds were open in the internal glass windows of his office. Esmeralda could see him sitting at his desk while DI Whistler paced the room, punching a palm with his fist and punctuating each move with a sideways jerk of his head that sent his lank blond hair flying. There was no trace of Dinah, who must have come and gone quickly, and Esmeralda didn't know what to make of this.

The DCS's personal assistant, Sylvie, was at her desk, running her usual interference. Sylvie was a civilian, though with high-level security clearance, and Esmeralda thought that Sylvie knew more about everything than anyone.

'DCS Vane said you'd be coming,' Sylvie said in her musical voice. 'You can go straight in.'

'Thank you.' Esmeralda took a deep breath, as if preparing to dive into a very long pool and swim to the other end without coming up for air.

'Please sit.' DCS Vane gestured for her to take a chair in front of his desk while DI Whistler stood behind his left shoulder and glowered, unseen by his boss.

Why was the DCS smiling at her? Why had he kept quiet about her mistake during the meeting, sparing her the exposure in front of the others? The more she considered it, the more horrified she became. If Jason Thorne killed again, if he hurt anybody, it would be on her.

DI Whistler threw himself into a chair at the side of the DCS's desk. She and the DI had never been properly introduced. She supposed there wasn't much point, now.

'Yesterday morning,' Esmeralda began. 'I understand if you're about to fire me.'

DI Whistler stretched his legs out in front of him. 'It's true to say that you hardly covered yourself in glory.'

'It's a mistake. You're learning.' DCS Vane actually lifted a hand as if to flick away a minor error.

'The DCS is more generous than I'd be,' said DI Whistler, crossing his arms over his chest and leaning back.

'I read your report on yesterday morning's interview with Ella Brooke,' said the DCS. 'Excellent work.'

'Thank you, sir.' She couldn't decide if she was more

astonished by the compliment or the fact that he'd bothered to look at the report at all – or that she might yet keep her job. 'I had DS Methuen's input,' she added.

'How did Ella react to the news of Holderness's death?' the DCS asked. 'I wouldn't blame her if she danced,' he added.

'I would,' said DI Whistler.

'She wasn't gleeful,' Esmeralda said, 'but she didn't pretend to be shedding any tears.'

'She didn't seem surprised?' asked DI Whistler.

'Not surprised, no. But I definitely didn't think she'd been expecting it.'

'You don't think she's in touch with Thorne, inciting him?' asked DI Whistler.

'No, sir. I don't. But I think she understands Thorne better than anyone else.'

'Why?' the DI said, drawing out that single syllable and injecting it with scorn, a teacher fed up with the worst student in his class.

'Because she has had to understand him, to keep herself and her nephew and parents safe,' Esmeralda said. 'And because she spent time with Thorne when she visited him in the secure hospital, and what she learned really did make a difference to finding her dead sister. Thorne wouldn't have helped her if she hadn't given him something of herself in return, if there hadn't been some sort of real emotional exchange and understanding between them.'

DI Whistler pressed further. 'Do you think she's frightened of him?'

Esmeralda shook her head. 'Not frightened enough.'

'You like her, don't you?' He made it sound as if he'd caught Esmeralda in a thought crime.

She paused, not sure how to answer. Esmeralda thought of Ella Brooke as a superhero, a genre she knew intimately thanks to Líria.

At last Esmeralda said, 'I do like her, yes. And I admire her. I'm glad she's finally letting us protect her and her nephew. Ella says Thorne would never hurt a child, that he sees his care and protection of children as his great virtue.' Esmeralda thought of Líria, and was glad Luke was now safely out of Thorne's reach. She shrugged. 'I'm not so convinced.'

DCS Vane nodded his agreement with her. 'Good to have your insight.'

She nearly shook her head in wonder. DI Whistler's hostility was mysteriously excessive, but more comprehensible than DCS Vane's disproportionate solicitude. He was too senior to be paying so much attention to her. *What the hell was going on?*

'Any progress on the cold case search for Lucy Reed?' DCS Vane asked.

'I'm hoping to talk to Jason Thorne's mother, but it's proving a bit tricky to arrange.'

'Ah. Good news,' the DCS said. 'Sylvie's worked her magic and DI Whistler will be going to Mrs Thorne's with you this morning. Given the recent sighting of Jason Thorne, and Adam Holderness's murder, the interview has altered in objective and urgency.'

Esmeralda continued to feel bewildered about why DCS Vane had singled her out and aimed the full beam of his kind tolerance at her. Whatever the reason, she was going to take it. Lucy was a lost girl, as Esmeralda had once been, and Esmeralda couldn't leave her.

'You'll need to tread carefully with Jason's dear mama,' continued DCS Vane. 'Follow DI Whistler's lead.' He paused, putting Esmeralda in mind of a bad actor who'd been waiting for his moment to say a line. 'I nearly forgot to mention it. From this point on we're delegating your reporting to DS Sachs. DS Methuen has other priorities.'

Esmeralda had been lucky to have Dinah to report to. She didn't want to lose her friend and mentor, but it was hardly surprising they were to be separated after neglecting to notice the most wanted man in the country sitting in a car mere metres away.

As far as Ben went, the real source of Esmeralda's secret dismay was that she had been imagining for the first time in forever what it might be like to go out with a man. Now, that man was going to be her boss, so those fantasies of hers would have to go nowhere.

'Right,' said the DCS, making it clear the meeting was over. 'Enjoy your morning coffee with Mrs Thorne.' He smiled. 'I look forward to hearing how it goes.'

DI Whistler was out of his chair and at the door, tilting his head in a wordless order for Esmeralda to follow him that brought to mind an owner commanding his dog.

They passed Sylvie in the outer office, then emerged into the foyer. DI Whistler headed for the men's cloakroom, beyond and to the side of the grand staircase. Without looking back he said, 'Be in that spot in five minutes. We leave then. I won't wait for you.'

She was glad of his brief absence, so she could rush

off to try to dry her hair and clothes before meeting Mrs Thorne. As she stood in front of the looking glass in the nearby women's cloakroom, her phone pinged with a text. She expected a message from Líria, snuck out during morning break.

Instead, Esmeralda saw a string of numbers that weren't known to her, with no name to identify the sender. She stared at the screen. **I know who you really are, Esmeralda Avelar. Ha Ha. That rhymes.**

A second text came almost immediately, making her blink. **Harriet Sapphire. I know what you did when you were a kid! I really am a poet!!**

Before she could react, the phone pinged a third time. **You have no shame. You are shameless.** Then a fourth. **I will tell. Everyone will know.**

Esmeralda's heart was beating fiercely as she thought of Líria.

Her phone pinged with a fifth message from the same sender, but this time she was ready and held herself with determined stillness. **We've got you, bitch. We see you, witch. We know where you are.**

This was the most chilling message of all, because accompanying the words was a photograph. It was a close-up of her own face and Esmeralda could see a small bit of the green background of Ella Brooke's front door framing her from behind. She knew immediately that it had been taken yesterday morning, when she and Dinah visited Ella.

There was only one person who could have captured that image, and she was about to meet his mother.

Triage, Esmeralda told herself. You will inform DI

Whistler about the texts during the drive to Mrs Thorne's and seek his advice. You will take the phone to DS Armstrong in the High Tech Unit as soon as you've finished the interview with Mrs Thorne – it's not as if those texts are going to evaporate. You have no choice but to push those text messages out of your head for the next couple of hours.

To have a plan of action helped, though her hands were still trembling as she slipped the phone into her bag, reminding herself that she had nothing to hide. Not from Jason bloody Thorne and his text messages. Not from her colleagues. And not from the world.

For now, Esmeralda had a job to do, and she intended to do it as well as she could. She'd spent weeks trying to set up this visit. At last, it had fallen into her lap. Lucy Reed and her parents were depending on her, and she wasn't going to let them down.

The Glass House

Elizabeth Thorne ran a finger over one of the many framed photographs of her adored son. They covered the chimney-piece of her drawing room. They clustered on the little oval table, beside a sparkling crystal lamp. They decorated the walls.

When the bell rang just before eleven, Mrs Thorne paused in front of the gilt-framed looking glass that hung in her hallway. Her expression was severe. Wrinkles were never a pleasant thing to contemplate. Nor was the fact that her hair was now silver and age was making her bones shrink. But it couldn't be helped. None of it could be helped.

She brushed a piece of lint from her grey silk blouse, adjusted her pearls, smoothed her wool skirt, and opened the door.

'Detective Inspector Harold Whistler,' the man said. 'We appreciate you seeing us, Mrs Thorne.' She could smell his aftershave, and it was not an enjoyable experience.

The woman standing beside DI Whistler stepped

forward to introduce herself. 'Detective Constable Esmeralda Avelar. As DI Whistler said, we're grateful for your time, Mrs Thorne.'

Mrs Thorne studied this low-ranking and windblown but rather pretty creature. DC Avelar had chosen a skirt to match her suit jacket, and although her white blouse was buttoned in a modest way, the fabric was faintly rumpled and rain-spattered. Mrs Thorne said, 'And your role here is?'

DC Avelar seemed to search for her voice for a few seconds before finding it. 'I'm part of the team trying to find Jason, Mrs Thorne. We want to make sure he gets the medical treatment he needs, and that you and others are kept safe.'

'My son is a danger to no one.' Her darling boy had his faults, but he would never hurt his own mother. Not physically, anyway. Mrs Thorne sighed. 'Come through. I've made tea.'

She led them to the garden room, shaped like an octagon and made entirely of glass. The pot of Earl Grey had steeped nicely, so she poured three cups and gestured towards a plate of shortbread she'd baked herself, set on the low table between her and the detectives.

'Would you consent to our recording this conversation, Mrs Thorne?' asked DI Whistler.

She waved a weary hand. 'Fine.' Although she had been tempted to refuse this request for yet another meeting, she'd learned that it was better to give the police what they wanted and do it on her own terms. If she didn't, they would continue to pester her.

Mrs Thorne knew all too well that the success of

someone who'd escaped from prison depended on at least three things. Having untraceable and lasting resources. Avoiding family and friends who knew them. And staying away from the places they used to frequent. For all of these reasons, the police would always have their eyes on her, hoping that Jason might slip up. She needed to show them that he hadn't. Plus, a part of her couldn't help but be curious as to what these people were after now. Had there been a new development?

DI Whistler positioned a small black device beside the tea tray. 'The question we must ask, then,' he began, 'is whether you've seen your son recently.'

'Clearly not.' She lifted her teacup and took a calming sip. 'I should think this is stating the obvious, but I really do not see the point of this visit.'

'We believe there's been a recent sighting of Jason,' said DI Whistler, 'and we wanted to share this information with you before we alert the public.'

'Did he appear well?'

'We're worried that the treatment for his knee injury was incomplete,' said DC Avelar. 'And there's been no follow-up.'

'You're too quiet,' Mrs Thorne said, though she had heard perfectly. 'Speak up.'

'Of course. Sorry.' DC Avelar swallowed, then said, 'Jason left hospital before the doctors were ready to discharge him. He also appears to have lost a great deal of weight.'

'Well that can only be a good thing. They were practically force-feeding him, from the looks of that dreadful photo they're always showing. It's inhuman.'

Mrs Thorne decided that DC Avelar's technically pleasant face was ruined by a faint scar across her forehead. Nonetheless, she had the sickening thought that the DC was Jason's type.

'I can see how upsetting this is for you,' said DC Avelar.

'It is indeed, and I must bear it all alone. Alexander – my dear husband – died many years ago, when Jason was only a boy, you see.' She wiped a dry eye, delicately, with a black handkerchief. 'I sometimes don't know how to get through one day to the next. Have you any experience of such profound loss, DC Avelar?'

'Yes,' DC Avelar said, and Mrs Thorne was surprised by the admission.

'One never gets over it,' Mrs Thorne said. 'But I made sure to keep everything normal for Jason. He was such a shy boy. Shyness, of course, is a sign of high intelligence and creativity. And so kind and helpful to his mother. He could never do enough for me. Repairs . . . building work . . . trips to the tip.'

'You must have missed him a great deal when he moved out,' DC Avelar said. 'That was a few days after his eighteenth birthday, wasn't it, in August of 1990?'

Mrs Thorne did not appreciate the implication that her son had been eager to get away from her as fast as he was legally able to do so. 'He visited quite regularly,' she said.

'And those visits would have been from 1990' – DC Avelar appeared to be straining at basic mental maths – 'until 2008, when he was arrested?'

'Indeed.'

'Did his arrest come as a shock?' DI Whistler asked.

'Of course it did.' Mrs Thorne shuddered her head. 'My son is not a murdering felon. He was going on to do great things. He is a sensitive and brilliant artist, a natural leader who charms everyone who meets him.'

'Women must have found those qualities attractive,' said DC Avelar.

'My son was extremely serious about his studies as a boy. Top in every subject, so he did not want distractions. But females crave the esteem that comes from being at the side of a man like my son.' She shook her head in disgust. 'Females,' she said. 'They are all toxic, all poison.' Mrs Thorne considered herself a rare exception to this principle.

'I think you said in a previous interview that Jason didn't introduce you to his girlfriends?' said DC Avelar.

'They weren't good enough for him. He knew that. I knew that. He didn't want to bother me with any females until he found one that was worthy of my attention. There was one, though, during his last few years at school. I did meet her once or twice.'

'Ah,' said DC Avelar, who was patently disingenuous. 'Was it Lucy Reed?'

Mrs Thorne thought it prudent to elaborate on how tiresome that creature had been. 'Yes,' she said. 'I thought her a little . . . strange.'

'If I can return you to the question of when you last saw Jason . . .' began DI Whistler.

'Strange?' DC Avelar wondered. 'In what way was Lucy strange?'

DI Whistler glared at DC Avelar and opened his mouth to speak, but Mrs Thorne cut him off. 'Too much chat.'

Mrs Thorne made her affronted revulsion clear by lifting a hand and tapping a line of four fingers against her thumb to mimic a runaway mouth. 'Just chat-chat-chat-chat-chat.' It was a relief to unburden herself. 'I'm told she went to university to study Chemistry, but that was my subject and she really did not have the head for it. She was not intellectual enough for my son. And she treated him like a slave.'

'That must have been saddening for you.' DC Avelar looked quite sad herself.

'It was. Very much so.' Mrs Thorne produced the black handkerchief to wipe another non-existent tear. 'But it is my son's nature to love. He is faithful, very faithful.'

'I believe Lucy disappeared in June of 1991, after completing the first year of her course,' said DC Avelar. 'Your son was living in his own house by then, so he must have felt very alone.'

'My son was tender-hearted even to those who didn't deserve it. She tried to ruin him. It is my strong belief that she disappeared on purpose, to punish and hurt him.'

'Mrs Thorne,' DI Whistler said. 'Have you ever for an instant doubted your son?'

'Certainly not.' She elongated each word. 'Somebody else put those women in that basement. You'd say my son killed Jack the Ripper's victims if you could get away with it.' She sloshed tea into her saucer as she rose from her chair, then almost immediately lowered herself back into it, realising there was more she wanted to say. 'My son is not a sociopath, or a psychopath, or whatever it is you call them. He did not torture small animals, or pull the wings off flies, or drown woodlice in bleach.' In fact, she had observed her son doing all of these things, hence the specificity of her examples.

DC Avelar said quietly, 'I can see you're upset. We can pause, if you would like to.'

'I would not.' Visibly, deliberately, Mrs Thorne regained her composure. She had studied the way the Queen sat, and was careful to press her ankles and calves neatly together, tilted slightly. She rested her hands primly on her lap. 'Whenever you are ready,' she said, showing these people what real dignity looked like.

'There's something that's been puzzling me,' said DC Avelar.

Mrs Thorne narrowed her eyes and was again struck by the thought that this upstart female really was Jason's type. What a weakness her boy had always had for ethereal ghosts, though Mrs Thorne herself utterly failed to see any charm in that look.

'I realise this may be painful,' said the DC, 'but one of the few things Jason did tell us was that he avoided you from the time he left home in 1990. He said he saw you only once, in December of 2000, on Christmas Day, and that the two of you argued.'

'What exactly are you trying to suggest?'

'It occurred to me that perhaps the two of you had been talking about Lucy.'

Mrs Thorne felt her cheeks grow red, and the fact that she'd been provoked into losing control of her own body enraged her still more. 'Certainly not. Why on earth would my son and I waste our precious time together on that?'

'I'm sorry. It's just that Jason said he'd had no contact with you for the decade before that Christmas. The murders began soon after that. Three women died between 2001 and 2005,' she said. 'We're desperate to understand why.'

'Well there was nothing singular about my son's visit that Christmas. There was no argument, and I saw him regularly until his arrest. We never ceased to communicate.'

Mrs Thorne closed her eyes, shook her head, and waved a hand to dismiss the whole business. When she looked up again a few seconds later, making it clear she was still in great pain, she pointed to a sun-lit outbuilding, a chalet of golden stone that resembled a giant's playhouse. 'That was my son's favourite place. He built it with his own hands when he was just fifteen.'

She did not say that Jason slept in that little house until he moved out, rather than in his childhood room, and that he often had company. That immodest creature he'd referred to as his 'girlfriend' had no sense of decency, and made no attempt to hide her presence.

DC Avelar said, 'I've been admiring those orange and crimson roses in front of it.'

DI Whistler leaned forward. 'Can you remember *precisely* when it was you last saw Jason?' he said.

Mrs Thorne looked at the pair, and turned to DI Whistler. 'Of course not. Why would I?'

'Has your son ever spoken to you about a man by the name of Adam Holderness, Mrs Thorne?' the DI said.

'I read about the case in the press – that doctor – all those missing females, buried in his garden. But as I told you already, I haven't seen my son since you people arrested him. There has been no opportunity for him to discuss anything or anyone with me.'

'That makes sense,' DI Whistler said. 'The hospital shared with us all the requests that were made to Jason for visitation. Our understanding is that he refused yours.'

Mrs Thorne resisted an urge to reach across the coffee table and slap the man across his ugly face. He wore no wedding ring. Clearly, there was no female to take care of him, manage his diet, tell him to cut his nose hairs, which were unruly.

'I'd imagine that many of the requests were from females. Proposals of marriage, declarations of love.' She paused briefly, as if what she was about to say next was so horrifying she needed to steel herself first. 'Wanting to have his babies.' Mrs Thorne searched DC Avelar's pale face for the disgust or outrage this last example deserved but saw no trace of a reaction.

'You're right in everything you say, Mrs Thorne,' DC Avelar said. 'Your son received many letters that were exactly as you describe.'

Mrs Thorne leaned forward to peer at DC Avelar's warrant card, then said, 'Your names. They are not English, though your accent is. Where are you from?'

'From here,' said DC Avelar, with that gentle smile that would charm any fool who didn't see the artifice behind it.

Mrs Thorne wiped her nose with the black handkerchief. 'This is intolerable.' She tipped her head back, closed her eyes, and rested her lower arm across her forehead. 'I must insist that you leave this instant. Show yourselves out.'

She could hear DI Whistler murmuring that the interview had concluded and the time, followed by a click and a thud that she guessed was their recording device being switched off.

'Go, I said,' said Mrs Thorne, wanting the last word, though it was clear they were doing exactly that. When Mrs Thorne opened her eyes a few seconds later, they were indeed gone. But having had the last word was not as satisfying as she usually found it.

The Queen's Enchantment

The dark shadow of Elizabeth Thorne's stone mansion loomed behind Esmeralda and DI Whistler as he steered the car along the gravelled drive. The DI braked abruptly in front of the electronically controlled iron gate, then opened his window and punched a button on a post to alert Mrs Thorne that they needed to get out.

While they waited, he tapped the steering wheel with splayed fingers. 'Babysitting,' he said, before visibly startling and grunting when he realised his window was still open. He closed it so that they couldn't be overheard. 'I'm a DI and I'm fucking babysitting a DC on her hobby interview.'

Esmeralda was marvelling that she had planned to inform him about the texts and seek his advice. That preposterous idea had died within minutes of leaving the constabulary. Before meeting DI Whistler, she'd had a kind of sympathetic pity for him that she hadn't been able to account for. Now, she was mystified that she could ever have felt such a thing.

'Nobody should be a detective without time in uniform,' he continued. 'You will fall on your face and this farce of the direct entry programme will be consigned to the dustbin of idiotic ideas, where it belongs.'

'I hope to prove you wrong, sir.' She was determined to show no weakness to him.

'You won't, Esme.'

How many times had he got her name wrong since leaving the DCS's office? 'It's Esmeralda, sir,' she said.

The horrible texts surfaced yet again in her thoughts, leaving her struggling to concentrate on the job at hand. She tried to erase them from her mind so she could work out what was bothering her about the roses in front of Thorne's giant playhouse. They were like looking at the sun, with deep orange petals at their centres, surrounded by a crimson perimeter. It was as if the blood of Thorne's victims had seeped in to give them those extraordinary colours, although Esmeralda's rational self knew this couldn't literally be true. More to the point, Mrs Thorne's house and grounds had been searched back in 2008 when her son was arrested, and no bodies had been found.

'My dad subscribes to all these different horticultural databases, sir,' she said. 'It's a bit of a family habit, identifying plants, but I've been searching since we got in the car and I think I've found the rose in front of the playhouse Thorne built.' She read aloud. '"The floribunda rose, Queen's Enchantment, was hybridised in 1972 in Germany."'

'You don't ever stop, do you?'

It was true that she liked to keep things moving when she was on a case. Momentum was important. But the

DI's rebuke silenced her — she'd been about to observe that 1972 was the year of Jason Thorne's birth, and felt foolish for nearly saying something so obvious.

Esmeralda thought of the briars surrounding Sleeping Beauty's castle. In her old edition of Charles Perrault, the prince's ogre of a mother wants to kill and eat Sleeping Beauty and her twins. The first time Esmeralda read it to Líria, she'd broken off after a few pages because the horror she'd completely forgotten about had flooded back to her. But Líria had made her finish, and demanded the story again and again. Esmeralda had also come across an Italian version of the tale. That one was even more harrowing, and had appeared early in the seventeenth century, about fifty years before Perrault's rendering.

Esmeralda found her voice. 'The Queen's Enchantment Rose isn't easy to maintain in our climate.' She was sure her dad could do it, though. 'It definitely needs lots of sun.'

He sighed. 'Just stop, Esme,' he said. 'You're exhausting me.'

It was bad enough that he kept trying to shut her down and shut her up, but his refusal to get her name right was riling her even more. Still, she knew she needed to control her anger before she spiralled in rage at him, and at Jason Thorne, and at those vile texts.

'You spent too much time in there on Lucy Reed, Esme. Dog with a bone.'

'Esmeralda,' she said, unable to bite back the correction.

The DI looked over at a camera that was almost certainly giving Mrs Thorne a live feed of the car, perched on top of one of the two stone posts supporting the still-closed gate. He huffed in annoyance, then punched the button on the car phone. When Sylvie answered he said, 'Get DS Sachs to speak to Elizabeth Thorne's gardeners. I want to know exactly what they're contracted to do for her, how long she's employed them, and if there've been any changes to the frequency of visits.' He ended the call without a thank you or a goodbye.

At last, the gate swung open. As they finally drove out of Mrs Thorne's mad land of misery, Esmeralda braced herself to raise another point with DI Whistler. 'Sir?' she said.

'What?' The intonation made his impatience with her clear.

'What do you think about Mrs Thorne telling us that her son would take things to the tip for her?'

'If Thorne chucked Lucy in landfill back in 1991 we won't find her.' Esmeralda hated the way he'd used the word chucked, but she had to give him credit for seeing what she was getting at without her having made it explicit. 'Think about the sheer size of it,' he continued, 'and the lack of precise records about where things were being dumped then. Talk about needle in a haystack, the volume of rubbish, the compression of the debris. Not to mention the fact that they're likely to have sealed that landfill some years ago. Nobody's going to want to open it up now and release those methane gases.'

Esmeralda felt stricken, though she couldn't help but be impressed by his knowledge and reasoning. 'Sonar won't work, sir?' she said. 'Or cadaver dogs?'

'Not twenty-six years later.' As if hearing the slight softening of his own tone, he was quick to revert back to his usual form. 'Especially not on the basis of

something as vague as, "They may have visited a tip."'
These last six words were spoken in an imitation of a
silly feminine voice – presumably her own, which
sounded nothing like this.

'Maybe we could look for other places in England with
connections to Thorne's family. Rich people can set up
offshore companies to conceal their ownership.'

'You've been a DC for about a minute and you think
you know it all, don't you?'

Esmeralda's cheeks were hot. 'I don't think that.'

'Is that university-educated brain of yours able to
fathom that we have the Financial Crimes team trying
to uncover any properties the Thornes don't want us to
know about?'

She was at a loss as to how to reply, so she said nothing.
Instead, she tried to think, but all she managed was to
picture that rambling, dark house Thorne's mother had
brought him up in, and this made her feel even more bleak.
The emotional claustrophobia and imaginative impover-
ishment of it all, the woman's utter blindness to any fault
her son might have, left her with an acute pity for Jason
Thorne that took her by surprise. Repelled as she was by
him, furious and shaken as those texts had left her, she
understood a little more of what had made him, and why
he would want little to do with his toxic mother.

Líria had been an unexpected, unasked-for gift.
Esmeralda had thought it wasn't possible to love your
child too much, but she was no longer sure. She
imagined Mrs Thorne wafting through that old mansion
of hers like Miss Havisham, presiding over the Museum
of Jason. She considered the money Thorne donated to

children's hospitals, and wondered if the horribleness of his own childhood was behind his stated mission to protect children.

Thinking about Mrs Thorne, and the oppressiveness of that house, and wondering where Lucy's body was, praying it wasn't lost forever in landfill, made Esmeralda realise that she'd been missing something. It was as if a tiny bubble, buried deep in her brain, had been released by the mysterious process of mental associations, and in particular the haunting idea of Lucy's corpse. The bubble came loose, and floated up, where she could access it.

'There are some photos in the case notes,' she said. 'One is of Mrs Thorne with her son, standing beside her husband's grave on the one-year anniversary of his death.' She did some basic mental maths. 'It would have been taken in 1983, a couple of weeks before Thorne turned eleven. There was a memorial service to unveil the gravestone.'

'Get to the point.'

'It's clearly a place that means something to Jason Thorne. Maybe he went back eight years later and buried Lucy there.'

Esmeralda was thinking about how Hugo Green had put his victims on top of the already-dead, making them share the coffins with those ancient skeletons. But Thorne could not have imitated this, because he couldn't have known about Green back in June of 1991, when Lucy went missing. It wasn't until September of that same year, three months later, that Esmeralda herself was rescued and Green's nightmare playground was discovered.

DI Whistler shook his head and tutted. 'As I said, you really do think you know it all, don't you, Esme?'

A swell of anger overcame her. 'I've told you already, sir. My name is Esmeralda, not Esme.'

'Esme is a nickname. Don't you like it?'

'I prefer to be called by my own name.'

'Well that is surprising,' he said, 'given the evidence to the contrary.'

If those texts hadn't included a photograph that only Jason Thorne could have taken, she'd wonder if Whistler himself had sent them to her. He could easily get hold of her private number and he'd been in the men's cloakroom when they pinged onto her phone. He displayed exactly the same contempt for her that characterised those messages.

She swallowed back her rage and said only, 'What do you mean by that?'

'I think we both know, Esme.'

She needed to get back on topic. It was Lucy who mattered, not DI Whistler. 'I can dig out the photos of the grave. Go to the churchyard to see if it appears to have been upset in any way.'

DI Whistler's only response was a groan. When he braked for a red light, there was a screech of tyres and the furious horn of the car behind them.

'Fuck off,' he said under his breath. Then, 'There's going to be a press conference on Thursday. The DCS wants you there, for mysterious reasons of his own. Ever ask yourself what they are?'

Yes, Esmeralda thought. All the time. But I'm not about to talk about that with you.

Whistler's phone went. He grimaced to see that the display was showing DS Ben Sachs's name, but accepted the call on speaker.

'Mrs Thorne uses a national company, British Gardening Services,' Ben said. 'They do all the heavy work. For the last decade they came each week. Ten months ago, she changed the arrangement to bi-monthly.'

Esmeralda was racing to process this intelligence. Had Mrs Thorne reduced the visits in order to hide her prodigal son in the house? Or – and she thought this more likely – simply in the hope that he would feel safe in turning up there at some point, and sufficiently desperate to put up with being in her presence? She quickly dismissed the idea, knowing that Thorne and his mother were too smart for that.

The DI was looking straight ahead, exaggerating his concentration on the road. 'There are some photos in the Thorne case files of the father's grave, Sachs. Go there. I want to know if there've been any changes to it since . . . When was it, Esme?'

'He was buried in 1982,' she said, 'but the photo was taken in 1983.'

'Thank you, Esmeralda,' Ben said. 'Let's have a catch-up soon.'

'Arrange your social calendar on your own time.' Without another word, DI Whistler pushed the button and cut Ben off.

As soon as Esmeralda and DI Whistler returned to the South West Constabulary site, they abandoned the unmarked car they'd used to travel to Mrs Thorne's and headed in opposite directions.

Esmeralda went straight to the High Tech Unit, which she'd never visited before, though she knew it had been the Chemistry block when the place was a school. It still smelled vaguely of something she couldn't identify, though she had the thought that Lucy Reed would have been able to if she hadn't been stolen out of her life as Esmeralda herself once was.

All but one of the High Tech Unit's team members had already gone home. There was no sign of DS Mary Armstrong, but in the centre of the room sat a man with a shock of rust-red hair, whose back was towards her.

'Hello,' Esmeralda called out. When the man slowly turned his chair so he could look at her, she realised he was familiar to her – she'd seen him joking with Ben – though they'd never been properly introduced. She added, 'Sorry to interrupt. May I come in?'

'I think you already have.' He had the freckles to go with the hair. 'DC Dinsdale,' he said. 'You can call me Mike.'

'DC Avelar,' she said. 'You can call me Esmeralda.'

'I know who you are.' Doesn't everybody, for all the wrong reasons, she thought, as he added, 'What can I do for you, Esmeralda?'

She walked towards him and put her phone in his hand. 'Can you help with this? I think the texts may be from Jason Thorne. They arrived after this morning's briefing, but I had to go straight to an interview so I haven't had a chance to get this to you until now.'

His expression was severe. 'You didn't think to bring the messages here first?'

She shook her head and felt sweat between her shoulder blades. 'I considered it, but I didn't feel able to delay DI Whistler. He was doing the interview with me. I'd planned to tell him as we drove, but he – he had a lot to think about. The interview was with Jason Thorne's mother, so I worried about being late and losing the chance. It wasn't easy to get her to agree to meet with us, actually.' She managed a smile, worrying she was talking too much, but still added, 'Sylvie's magic.'

He was evaluating her so intensely with his pale blue eyes. 'I'm familiar with that magic.' He nodded slowly, then glanced at the phone in his hand. 'Your passcode, please.'

As he read the text messages, then reached the photograph, the freckles on his face grew more distinct in the room's bright but eerily unnatural light.

'Nobody mentioned it at the briefing,' Esmeralda said, 'but DS Methuen and I were at Ella Brooke's yesterday morning at the same time as Thorne. We didn't notice him.' Her voice caught in her throat. 'We didn't stop him. He must have taken that photo of me then.'

'There isn't a single one of us who hasn't had a big fuck-up at some point.' She remembered Ben saying something similar only that morning. 'Ask DI Whistler,' he said, then quickly added, 'but that's a story for another day.' He looked hard at her. 'Are you happy for me to do whatever I need to with your phone?'

'Go ahead,' she said.

'Nothing private you don't want me or anyone else to see?' he asked.

'I'm an open book.'

'I highly doubt that.' He pointed to a small kitchen area to the side. 'Go make yourself a cup of tea. Write up your report on the interview with Mrs Thorne while I play with your phone. Sound good?'

She could only nod yes, then move away to put the kettle on.

Despite or Because

Two hours later, Esmeralda was still in one of the small meeting rooms that rimmed the High Tech Unit's open-plan office. She had been joined there by DCS Vane and Mike's boss, DS Mary Armstrong. Mike was visible on the other side of the interior glass wall, now assisted by others, who she realised must have been called back into work.

'Thanks for bringing your phone in,' the DCS said.

'No problem.' Yet again, she was startled by how nice he was to her, and also puzzled by why that kindness had an unsettling effect. She knew that many would consider the DCS conventionally handsome, but his jewel-blue eyes chilled her. 'Have you found anything to help us track him down, DS Armstrong?' she asked.

DS Armstrong shook her head. 'Nothing so far – and call me Mary. The sender's number is anonymous and encrypted. If he'd used a service to generate it we might have had some luck, but we think he did it himself. He probably used a burner, and one he stowed away some time ago. No doubt he's already destroyed it and has others ready to go. Before you ask, there's no data on the photograph, either. If there ever was any, he wiped it.'

DCS Vane's elbows were on the desk. His chin rested on his steepled hands. 'There are four questions I'd like you to answer.' He didn't alter his position an iota. 'When and where and how and why did you come to Jason Thorne's attention?'

'I know the when and where and how. I'm not so sure about the why, sir. Before I give you my answers, may I please ask a question of my own?'

'Go on,' he said.

'Are you going to fire me?'

'Ah,' he said. 'That's always your assumption.'

DS Armstrong – Mary – cocked an eyebrow. 'Why would he do that?'

'Because I made such a huge mistake yesterday morning, missing Jason Thorne on Ella Brooke's street. And because Thorne's mother sent a list of complaints about the way I conducted her interview today.' An hour earlier, Sylvie had magically appeared to deliver that update, and a distant part of Esmeralda had marvelled at Sylvie's ability to convey bad news so kindly.

Mary crossed her legs with a dancer's grace, which was pretty much how she did everything. 'You certainly make things more interesting around here,' she said.

'But I've become a distraction,' Esmeralda said. 'I'm not just someone helping us to solve the case – I've become a part of it.'

'I will need to think carefully about how we manage

this,' said DCS Vane, 'and the necessary adjustments and safeguards, but we look after our own in this constabulary. Drawing Jason Thorne's attention is no small matter, but you are not being fired. As for his mother . . .' He made a derisory puff of air. 'She complains every time we talk to her, and it's always the female officer she picks on.'

Esmeralda nodded. 'Well, in terms of Jason Thorne I don't think I know much that you couldn't assume. The when was early yesterday morning. The where was in front of Ella Brooke's house, on Nightingale Avenue. The how was that Jason Thorne was parked on Ella's street and must have seen me approach her property – I'm sure he took that photograph then.'

'All of that seems highly probable,' said DCS Vane, his cold blue eyes watching her steadily. 'But we need to be asking ourselves if there's any chance Jason Thorne has met you before.'

'That's not an experience I'd be likely to forget,' Esmeralda said, 'let alone survive.'

'The vetting team disclosed what happened to you as a young girl, as the victim of Hugo Green. I've never thought it necessary to raise it directly with you before.'

'I work on the assumption that everyone here knows.' She looked again through the internal window to watch her colleagues examining her phone, projecting its contents onto screens, downloading her data. 'If they didn't before, they certainly will now.'

'I'm afraid you're correct in that,' Mary said.

'When you met the vetting team before your appointment, you also disclosed,' said DCS Vane, 'quite properly, that you suffered from dissociative amnesia as a result of trauma. The medical report you authorised your GP to make to us confirmed this aspect of your medical history.'

Esmeralda placed her hands in her lap and pressed her palms neatly together. 'I suffered from – I still suffer from – dissociative amnesia. But I have the selective form, so it *only* affects my memories of Hugo Green. I remember everything else as perfectly and imperfectly as *you* do. It doesn't affect my cognition or reasoning in any way.'

After an awkward pause, she went on, 'The only evidence linking me to Thorne is his documented interest in the Hugo Green case. Those news clippings on that bulletin board of his had my school photo, always the one from the missing posters. I think Thorne figured out who I was after he saw me at Ella Brooke's yesterday, and that's why he named me in those texts. We know that he's a super-recogniser. Not many people would identify me from those press photos, but he almost certainly would.'

DCS Vane's face didn't move. She wasn't telling him anything he hadn't already considered. 'I'm afraid there may be more to it,' he said. 'This doesn't leave this room.'

'What?' Esmeralda was too wired not to be blunt.

'There's evidence that Thorne wasn't fixated on Green,' he said, 'but on you.' The DCS took a tablet from his briefcase. 'The disclosure officer scheduled these as highly sensitive, so they're redacted from the Thorne case files because you were under age when Green took you and your new identity is indefinitely protected under a legal order.' He passed the tablet to Esmeralda. 'These drawings of your face were found in a drawer in the basement room where Thorne kept the bulletin board. There were over a dozen of them.'

The drawings had been done in charcoal, and were dramatic and skilful. She had to admit they were accurate – it was recognisably her – but Esmeralda thought they made her look like a teenaged boy's fantasy.

'We think he based the first few drawings on the school photo that was circulated when you were missing,' Mary said. 'The later ones are his predictions of how you'd look as time passed.'

Esmeralda swallowed, though her mouth was dry. She was startled by how Thorne mapped the subtle changes in her face as she grew from a girl into a woman. She scrolled through quickly, and it was like watching an old-fashioned animation, as if someone had taken a photograph of her each year and arranged them in succession.

Her chest was tight, but she tried to keep the fear out of her voice. 'Thorne isn't alone in being obsessed with the Green case, and with me. That's why my dad changed our names and house – and my school, when I finally went back – all of that was to try to hide my old identity.' She scrolled through the drawings again. 'So Thorne did roughly one of these a year, between 1991 and 2005. That means he stopped doing them during the three years before his arrest, which was also when he stopped killing women, at least as far as we know. Why do you think that is? Could there be a link?'

The DCS said nothing, merely studying her. Mary shrugged her bewilderment.

An unwelcome realisation sparked. The force had been in possession of the drawings since they captured Thorne nine years earlier. That meant that they knew when they hired her that she was an object of his interest. Were her disclosures to the vetting unit actually why they wanted her to be a detective? All this time, she'd thought they'd let her in *despite* what happened to her. But maybe they'd let her in *because* of it, wondering if she would give them insight into a connection between Hugo Green and Jason Thorne.

DCS Vane laced his hands together and tapped the side of a bent index finger against his chin several times. 'I'm thinking aloud here. Thorne's a local boy who doesn't like to stray far from home,' he said slowly. 'So was Green. Could be Green involved Thorne, and for Thorne you then became the one who got away, the only one who escaped him.'

Esmeralda felt the weight of his gaze. 'I remember when Green stole me.' Her voice was shaking. She was back in that moment, her bike crashing. A man, so furious and greasy and horrible smelling, so determined as he grabbed her and dragged her into the van, pulling her through the crack between two worlds, out of the light where she and her parents lived and into endless darkness.. 'I – I remember the emergency services rescuing me, after he was dead. But I don't remember anything between those two events. I wouldn't – if Thorne was a party to any of it, I wouldn't be able to say.'

'No, you wouldn't. If Green showed you to Thorne, you buried it.'

'I think that's enough,' said Mary.

But DCS Vane pressed on. 'Thorne was still a boy when Green took the first three girls. There was a gap of five years between the third girl, Sadie Pope, and the fourth – you.'

To the DCS, Sadie was a mere name, a victim from a long-ago case. He didn't have to carry the knowledge that he had spent four months within a few metres of her body, or to live with the shame of not being able to remember anything useful about what Green's victims experienced. When Esmeralda was rescued, the police had asked gentle, persistent questions. And she understood why. For Sadie's family, she was the only person alive who could give them any real answers, any real closure. Except that, as it happened, she couldn't. All Esmeralda could do was stand beside Sadie's mother over the grave where she was finally able to bury her child.

'Sadie went missing in 1986,' DCS Vane continued, 'when Thorne was fourteen years old. It's doubtful he had anything to do with that. If Thorne was involved with Green, my bet is that it was only with you in 1991, when he was nineteen and you were fifteen.'

It had entered Esmeralda's mind that she was in a dangerous situation. She had asked herself – especially over the past few hours as she sat with the sour taste of her interactions with Mrs Thorne and DI Whistler – whether it was odd that she was not being withdrawn from this particular investigation. Or at least given some measure of protection.

But she felt now the pulse of frustration that she suspected DCS Vane shared: she wanted, more than anything else, to find Jason Thorne. And her position might help them to do it. What she said next came without hesitation. 'You could exploit that, sir.'

He narrowed his eyes at her in a question.

'Thorne's forced me into this case, so why run from it?' When the DCS said nothing, she went on. 'Thorne lives by some honour code to protect children – he hates anyone who hurts them. If you release to the public that we're investigating whether he was potentially involved with a man who kidnapped and murdered young girls, he'll go mad. Maybe he'll do something stupid and give us the break that will help us to catch him.'

'I won't take any actions that leave you exposed,' DCS Vane said.

Yeah, right, she thought. 'But I already am,' she said. Esmeralda turned to Mary. 'Since I gave my phone to Mike, I've had a few ideas – questions, really – about those texts.'

'Go on,' Mary said.

'Okay, I know the texts had to come from Thorne, because he's the only one who could have taken that photograph of me at Ella's. But they don't sound like him.' She groped for what she was trying to say. 'To call me a bitch is ill-mannered. Jason Thorne is lots of things, but not that. And to celebrate those idiotic rhymes . . . I would have thought that Jason Thorne would consider it a slur to be accused of writing something that bad.'

'I think you overestimate him,' said DCS Vane.

'That's a safer side to err on than underestimating him,' Esmeralda said. 'Ella Brooke says that Jason Thorne hates ugliness, and impoliteness, and he absolutely detests unintelligence. Those texts were all those things.'

'He does hate those qualities,' said the DCS, 'unless he's carving a picture on your skin. I call that impolite and ugly.'

There was a knock on the door. Esmeralda saw Mike waiting, and Mary nodded to him to come in. He held Esmeralda's phone out to her, but he was looking at Mary. 'Are you going to explain to her?'

'Thank you, Mike,' Mary said. 'Go home and goodnight.' He withdrew and Mary turned back to Esmeralda. 'For your safety, as well as your family's, and to aid the investigation, we'd like to clone your phone. In essence, we want to put spyware on it.'

'Like to or already have?' Esmeralda asked, turning the phone over in her hand.

'Already have, but we can remove it at any time,' Mary said. 'You've only to say.'

'So you can see my texts and emails as they arrive, and listen in on any calls?'

'All of the above,' Mary said. 'Basically, everything and anything on your phone. Apps, social media, whatever you have, we'll see it, so no privacy.'

'We'll also be tracking you through the phone,' said the DCS, 'so if Thorne comes close, the cavalry can swoop in.'

Esmeralda studied the DCS's face, and it came to her that it was like looking at a once-beautiful man who had sold his soul to the devil and lost something. 'Good idea,' she said slowly.

The DCS touched her shoulder, lightly, and she fought the lightning urge to shrug him away. 'Don't worry about anything,' he said. 'We've got your back.'

She thought, I bet you do, but slipped her phone into her bag. At last, she stood up, said a polite goodbye and left the building. As she dragged herself to her car, it felt like the end of the longest day she could remember since becoming a detective, but she was dreading the still-longer night to come.

Bedtime Stories

When Esmeralda finally arrived home, it was nearly ten. Her dad had been listening for her key in the lock and met her at the front door. He looked out into the street, frowning.

'What is it, Dad?' She started to turn.

He shook his head, put a hand on her arm to try to stop her. 'It's only moon shadows and tired eyes, as your mum used to say.' Despite his protest, Esmeralda stepped out again and looked up and down the street, but saw nothing. At last, her dad closed the door behind them and locked it, then said in his quiet way, 'Bad day?'

'Not the best,' she said. 'Líria's still up?'

'Just out of the shower. I told her she needed to get straight into bed but we both know she won't sleep until you say goodnight.'

Esmeralda nodded. 'I'll take a quick shower myself, then go talk to her.'

They were in the kitchen. 'On second thought,' she said, turning to the cupboard to take out a bottle of vodka and slosh a good measure into a glass. She brought it to her mouth, closed her eyes, and downed it neat, tossing her head back for the last drops.

'Like a true Russian,' her father said as she slammed the empty glass onto the counter, 'but it ought to be followed with caviar, which we appear to have run out of.' He knew all too well that Esmeralda rarely drank and was not even a tiny bit Russian. 'What is it, Hummingbird?'

'Tonight is the night, Dad. It's all coming out. I have to tell her.'

Half an hour later, Esmeralda and Líria were lying side by side on Líria's narrow bed, looking up at the ceiling they had decorated with glow-in-the-dark stars.

Their heads were on the same pillow. Esmeralda's hair was still damp, so it looked almost black mixing with Líria's deep gold in the moonlight.

'There's something I need to tell you, Líria,' she said, trying not to think about her father's anxiety that the force weren't protecting her better, and her guilt that she couldn't tell him why. 'Something upsetting that happened to me a long time ago. I was only fifteen, but because of some things that are happening at work, I need you to know about it now.'

Líria's eyes were wide, and Esmeralda couldn't blame her for looking as if she were about to go on an adventure. Still, Esmeralda didn't get far before stumbling over Hugo Green's name and breaking off.

Líria scooted still closer, burying her head in Esmeralda's side. Her voice was muffled when she said, 'It's okay, Mum.'

So Esmeralda forced herself forward. She told the story in little pieces, without too much detail. 'I understand,' she said afterwards, not daring to look at her daughter, 'that this is a big story to hear, and it may make you see me very differently. But you need to know that I'm not ashamed of anything that happened to me, or anything I did.'

'It was him or you.' Líria thought for a second. 'How did you kill him?'

She was unnerved by Líria's certainty about how Green died. 'I can't remember and nobody really knows for sure. He might have slipped and cracked his skull. But yes, there's also the possibility that I hit him in the head with the thigh bone of a dead viscount.'

'Big slay,' Líria said. 'That's defo one way to do it, Mum.'

Esmeralda actually laughed, marvelling at her daughter. 'All the times I played out how I would tell you this, Líria, I never in a million years imagined that you'd make me smile at the part when I have to tell you that I might have taken a human life.'

'Don't say it like that. You saved a human life. You saved yours.'

Esmeralda was drained beyond description, but in awe of her daughter. 'You can ask me anything you want. Now, or any time. The only slightly tricky thing is that I blocked out most of my memories of those months when I was . . . away.'

'Did the man . . . hurt you?'

'I think he probably did. But as I said, I don't remember much. Maybe that's for the best.'

'So . . . what happened to you . . . caused problems with your memory.' Líria reached for the small framed photograph of her father, which she kept on her bedside table. 'Is what that man did to you why you can't remember my dad? Why only Grandad can ever tell me anything about him?'

Esmeralda was startled by this question. 'Something like that. It's connected to loss.'

Líria moved her head closer to Esmeralda's, and squeezed her hand. 'That's sad.'

'I suppose it is.' Esmeralda pushed up the sleeve of Líria's nightdress to tickle her arm. 'But happy too, because I had you.'

Esmeralda explained about her original name and the changes they made to give her privacy.

Líria didn't hesitate. 'Were you famous? Is that why you had to hide who you were?'

'I suppose I was quite famous, but not in a good way. There are always people who get obsessed, who think they know you. Some will even try to meet you.' She thought of the drawings Thorne made of her, tried to push him from her mind. 'The silver lining was that because I was technically a child, the press had to leave me alone after I was rescued.'

'Would I find you, if I searched online for your old name? Harriet Sapphire's pretty.'

'There'd be stories from when I was missing, and after I was found. There are clips of Grandad being interviewed on television – he was a bit of a superstar, you know.'

'Of course he was.' Líria was soon serious again. 'Where were you kept?'

Esmeralda took a deep breath, then said, 'In a kind of underground place, filled with old coffins.'

Líria's whole body stiffened. 'That's terrifying. How did you not die down there?'

'The police said if it hadn't been summer, the cold would have killed me.'

'Were you scared of the dead people?'

'There's nothing to fear from the dead,' she said. 'Talking about the viscount with you made me remember something.' She paused, then said, 'I think I came to believe that the people in those dusty coffins would protect me. That they were my guardians. Maybe they frightened me at first, but not in the end.' They were all I had down there, she thought.

Líria was quiet for some minutes, and Esmeralda thought they both needed to process the conversation. At last Líria said, 'Was it dark?'

'My eyes were sensitive to light for a while after they found me, so I think so.'

'Is that why Grandad always says you're like an owl? Because you see in the dark?'

'Possibly,' she said slowly.

'How did you get air?'

'There was an iron gate at the end of one of the passages that fed into the crypts, so they weren't completely sealed like people thought. It was at the edge of some woods not far from the man's house. The police think he discovered it by accident.'

'But this is pretty intense.' Líria thought for a little while. 'Grandad says we all have our scars. And some you can see, and some you can't.' She traced a light finger over the fine diagonal line on Esmeralda's forehead. 'I love your scar. Did you get it when you were fifteen?'

'Yes, but I don't remember how it happened. It's one of the mysteries.'

'You're still the prettiest of all the mums at the school gates.'

'Are you frightened by what I told you, Líria? Because I'm fine now, mostly.'

'I'm not frightened. I'm angry. Is what happened to you the reason why you wanted to become a detective?'

She smoothed her daughter's silky hair. 'Partly.'

'That's why you're so good at it.'

'I made a really bad mistake yesterday morning,' she said.

'You always tell me everyone makes mistakes,' Líria said, though her voice was drifting now. It was past midnight and she was tired, becoming a dead weight in the bed. 'You say it's learning from them that matters.'

'True. That's what I'm going to try my best to do.'

Esmeralda's dead mother came to her in the night. She was wearing a flowing white dress, just like the one she had sewn many years ago for her little girl to wear in the school nativity play. Her long dark hair was loose, and she was standing at the foot of the bed, her face so radiant Esmeralda wondered if she was an angel.

Her mother reached out a hand, but Esmeralda knew if she moved to take it, that longed-for figure would disappear. She tried to tell her mum how much she needed her, to beg her to stay, to tell her that she wanted to look at her forever. But before Esmeralda could get the words out her eyes opened, and the dream blew away, and her mum was gone again, and the sunlight was pouring into the room through the window, because she'd wanted to look at the moon the night before and hadn't drawn the curtains.

Part II: Eurydice

I can imagine, in some otherworld
Primeval-dumb, far back
In that most awful stillness, that only gasped and
   hummed,
Humming-birds raced down the avenues.

D. H. Lawrence, 'Humming-Bird'

WEDNESDAY, 13 SEPTEMBER 2017

A Breach of Regulations

The blinds were closed in Ella Brooke's house, which was hardly surprising given that DCS Vane had said she and Luke were out of the country. Esmeralda parked a few doors down, then walked to the non-ANPR corner of Nightingale Avenue. This led to Florence Close, the no-through-road that Jason Thorne had avoided on Monday morning.

Although Esmeralda had failed to observe Thorne himself, she had noticed a slight and rather pinched-looking man.

She re-read the notes she'd made about him two days earlier. Halting as soon as he spotted her and Dinah with all the subtlety of someone who'd slammed into a wall, then turning on his heel to round the corner out of Nightingale Avenue into Florence Close, where she guessed he'd originally come from.

So there'd been two men in Nightingale Avenue on Monday morning who hadn't wanted to draw attention. Jason Thorne was on everyone's radar, but the fleeing man was only on Esmeralda's. She thought of the texts once more, and her instinct that they weren't Thorne's voice. From the angle of the photograph, there was no doubt that Thorne had taken it. But could someone else – the man who'd slipped away, perhaps – have sent her the texts, after Thorne supplied him with the image?

Florence Close went on for half a kilometre before it dead-ended, leaving you with the choice of two foot-paths. One led to an old railway line. The other fed into the complex of alleyways that wove behind the neigh-bourhood's tangle of residential streets. Esmeralda could follow at least part of the route the man would likely have taken. And her colleagues could follow her, she thought, thinking of her phone in her bag, pulsing like the beacon it now was as they tracked her. Like Líria, whom she had explained the concept to that morning, she found the idea reassuring and enraging at once.

A third of the way along, she spotted a house with a CCTV camera that pointed outwards. The lens was posi-tioned so that the pavement was in its range. Even if the man had left a car on the street rather than made his whole journey on foot, there was a reasonable chance he'd walked this way to collect it.

She straightened her suit jacket, adjusted her lanyard so that her warrant card was visible, and made her way up the perfectly swept footpath to press the button for the bell.

A short woman with dark hair opened the door. Esmeralda had spent the last six years tuning out the dirty looks from the married women at the school gates who thought that a shy single mum like her, with no visible wedding ring or partner, must be planning to seduce their husbands. The woman evaluated Esmeralda, then gave her just such a look.

Esmeralda introduced herself and held up her warrant card. 'I wonder,' she began, 'if you are aware of the fact that your CCTV camera is recording beyond your property boundary? The lens appears to be pointed at the pavement, which is a public space.'

Esmeralda had been wrong about the woman's complacency. Her mouth trembled. 'Has there been a complaint from someone? We only have the camera because my husband has a lot of expensive equipment in the house. For his work.'

'No complaint,' Esmeralda said.

'The people at number fifteen hate that we leave the lights on in my husband's office all night.' The woman was speaking fast. 'They're always moaning that it shines through their curtains when they're trying to sleep.'

Esmeralda privately sympathised with the people in number fifteen. 'A lot of people aren't aware of the guidelines about CCTV.' This was not true. Pretty much anybody who purchased a personal security system would be informed about the UK laws and regulations. She smiled, though, and added, 'But now you know, so no harm done.'

The woman brushed a curl from her forehead, a nervous gesture, and Esmeralda was startled to be confronted by this evidence of her own new power, especially in light of how helpless the events of the last two days had made her feel.

'I'll make sure to adjust the angle,' the woman said.

'And I'll put up some clear signs to alert people. There won't be any consequences, will there? Like, a fine?'

'No.' Esmeralda shook her head for emphasis. 'Absolutely none. Please don't worry. But I don't suppose you can tell me how long you keep the footage from your camera?'

'Thirty-one days before it's automatically deleted,' the woman said. 'That's what the police say to do, you know. We really do try to follow guidelines, but there are so many . . .'

'There really are,' Esmeralda agreed. 'But your set-up sounds ideal.'

'It's cloud-based storage.' The woman's confidence was plumping back. 'That's what the police recommend, according to the security company we use.'

'Actually,' Esmeralda said, 'would you be happy for me to view your footage from Monday morning? That would have been the eleventh of September. The time frame we're interested in is between eight and nine a.m.'

'Would I be helping you with an actual investigation?'

'You would be,' Esmeralda said. 'And we would really appreciate it.'

'Would you like a coffee while you look?' said the woman, opening the door wider so Esmeralda could come in.

Symbols

Esmeralda was on her way to the constabulary. She had the woman's illicit video footage on a memory stick and was eager to get to the Central Image Investigation Unit to see if they could help her identify the sad little man, who had indeed been caught by the camera.

When her phone rang, she imagined it might be Líria, but the car's display showed that the number was withheld. She answered on speakerphone.

The greeting that returned her own was low and deep and amused. 'Hello, Esmeralda.' He seemed to be tasting her name.

She was in no doubt about who she was talking to. 'Hello, Mr Thorne,' she said. 'You've been busy lately, haven't you?'

'How pleased I am to know that you have been thinking of me,' he said.

'Yes, but not in a good way.'

'Well, I have been thinking of you in a very good way.'

She realised who his voice reminded her of. It had the

resonance of the villain in the end credit scene for one of Líria's favourite superhero films. Líria had made Esmeralda watch that footage too many times to count, screaming in excitement and convinced that the entire future of the cinematic universe had been signalled in those few seconds.

Esmeralda's heart pounded. Somehow, she had to keep Thorne talking. Not because she thought it likely they'd be able to trace the call – he'd have made sure that wasn't possible – but because she had a faint hope they'd hear something that gave away where he was. She managed to pull the car over on a low hill, in front of a row of grand Georgian houses, then said, 'I didn't appreciate your texts.'

'I haven't sent you any texts, Esmeralda.'

'I don't believe you.' She was amazed by the cool calm of her own voice.

'Your lack of belief in me is disappointing and uncharacteristically impolite,' he said.

When she looked up, as if searching for help, she noticed the stone acorns that decorated the parapets of the houses, and she felt as if she'd been given an answer.

In the months after she was freed, her father had bought her a little jewelled trinket box in the shape of an acorn, telling her it was a charm that would keep her rooted and strong and safe. Whenever Líria saw a symbol of something good, she would say, *It's a sign, Mum*, and that was what Esmeralda wanted to believe those stone acorns were.

'I do not lie, Esmeralda,' Thorne added, 'and especially

not to you. Tell me about these texts.' She thought he actually sounded worried.

'That's a no to telling you about the texts, I'm afraid, Mr Thorne. If you sent them, I don't need to tell you about them. And if you didn't, as you say, then I'd rather not share.'

'I like to watch over those I care about *in person*.' His words made her shiver. 'And to communicate with them in person too. Texts are ugly, Esmeralda. They carry an unacceptable risk of misunderstanding. Clarity is of great importance to me.'

'You claim to care about Ella,' she said.

'I care about you too. You're my hero, you know. I'm your biggest fan.'

'Lucky me,' she said, and then regretted it. But he laughed, and that laugh made her think, Why the hell not? 'There's something I'd really like to know,' she said.

'Well,' he said. 'If I can do something for you that you'd like, then – what is the expression?' She could hear him tapping his fingers. 'Ah. Yes. That's the one. *I'm all in*.'

'I met your mother yesterday and tried asking her, but she wasn't inclined to help.'

'I bet she loved you,' Thorne said, and it was clear from his tone that he had the measure of exactly what his mother had made of Esmeralda. 'Ask away.'

'I want to know what you and your mother argued about when you visited her at Christmas, in 2000.' Esmeralda realised she was holding her breath. She was certain everybody listening in on the call was too. It was difficult not to rush in, not to fill the silence. But she held back and waited.

At last Thorne said, 'We argued about Lucy.'

It was as she'd guessed, but she needed more. 'What exactly about Lucy?'

'That is all you get for now, Esmeralda. I will whisper the rest when we are alone. It won't be long.'

'I don't appreciate being threatened,' she said.

'That's a promise, not a threat. Anything I say to you, I mean.'

'How reassuring.'

'I'm your guardian angel, you know,' he said.

She rolled her eyes. 'Where are you, Mr Thorne?'

'Taking steps to help you. In your career, despite its inconvenience to me, and in all other ways too.'

'I'll come to you this minute,' she said, 'if you tell me where I can find you.'

'That's the most enticing offer I've had in a very long time. It pains and astonishes me to have to say this, but I'm afraid I'll need to take a raincheck. For now, I've left you a little present. I would suggest a stroll in the Georgian Pleasure Gardens. Incidentally, Esmeralda, I like your hair loose. Seeing it that way is the next best thing to running my hands through it.'

Her heart began to beat faster. She'd slipped off her hair band after she left the camera woman's house and had planned to put it back when she arrived at work. Had he really seen her?

As she scanned the rather imposing residential street, her eyes were drawn to an ornate carving of a lion's head on the pediment above a front door. If it was a sign, as

Líria liked to say, then this one, with the fierceness and dominance of a dangerous predator, seemed to favour Thorne.

There is no meaning in arbitrary designs, she told herself. Surely if the things that had happened to her had taught her anything, it was that. She needed to stop this way of seeing the world or she'd soon find herself leaping over manhole covers like Líria, who thought the sky would fall if she even touched a toe onto a group of three drains.

She pulled into the road and made a U-turn. 'Where in the gardens, Mr Thorne? They're enormous.'

'Don't you like games, Esmeralda? Hide and seek?'

'I prefer things to be straightforward. What did you leave for me?'

'That would spoil the surprise. Let's just say it will assist you in your ambitions.'

'Mr Thorne,' she started to say, but the line went dead.

She was glad to have Mary Armstrong on speed dial. 'Did you get all that?'

'We're on our way to the gardens,' Mary said. 'He is seriously creepy and provoking, but you kept your head and bought us time by keeping him talking.'

'The real challenge would be to get him to shut the fuck up.' And though she hadn't meant to be funny, Esmeralda heard a split second of laughter before Mary ended the call.

The Pleasure Gardens

The Pleasure Gardens were a kind of hexagonal island bordered by busy main roads on all six of its sides. Esmeralda parked on a sloped street near the tennis courts and entered the park at the top, through its easternmost gate, remembering that this was the very place where Thorne's third victim, Julia Smithlin, was last seen alive.

As Esmeralda hurried down the steps, she imagined Julia flying ahead of her on the early morning run she'd been on when she disappeared all those years ago. Esmeralda pictured Julia glancing behind her, catching her eye and beckoning her forward, as if to say, *Find him, Fix this, Avenge us.* Esmeralda blinked, and the vision blew away like vapour.

'Concentrate,' she said aloud, calculating that Thorne would have been gone before he even phoned her, exiting through any one of the park's multiple openings, all of which spilled directly onto roads where he could have left a car. At the same time, she couldn't help but be struck by the peacefulness of the winding paths. The birdsong overpowered the low hum of endless traffic. The wind in the trees sounded like running water.

She reached an open-sided building that had been designed to offer shelter from the rain, and stepped inside to look around. But there was nothing between its pillars or under its arches or on top of the giant stone slabs that paved it. Nor was there anything beneath the U-shaped wooden bench that curved round the three walls.

She crossed the white iron bridge, pausing to look down to the canal below her, the ripples on its surface dappled by sun. She saw only joggers along the towpath, and dogwalkers, and mums pushing buggies or trying to coax toddlers.

She noticed a rusting gate that allowed access from inside the park to the towpath. Another means of potential escape. There were countless banks he could have climbed to get away, as well as barges he might have jumped on. She moved forward again, along the central path.

Every few minutes came the chug or glide of a train. The latest was squeaking like nails down a chalkboard. When she reached the bridge over the railway line that cut through the park's centre, she saw that the noise was from a cargo train. She studied its carriages, open and filled with grit.

When her phone rang again, she knew who would be at the other end of the withheld number. 'Enjoying your late morning ramble, Esmeralda?'

'Did you enjoy yours, Mr Thorne?'

'Enormously.'

She didn't doubt the truth of that, after his long stay

in the secure hospital followed by ten months of hiding. He'd chosen well in targeting the Pleasure Gardens, which were almost impossible to contain. 'What am I looking for?' she said.

'A beautiful goddess like you cannot help but find it,' he said. 'I wish we could speak longer, but I can see that you've already alerted your friends to my presence. Misplaced loyalty, Esmeralda, but you will learn that sad lesson before long.'

He had told her two things. One was certainly deliberate. The other was probably accidental. Still, Luke's iPhone footage had shown that even Jason Thorne could make mistakes.

DCS Vane was rushing towards her, and she shared with him the thing that Thorne might not have intended to reveal. 'I think he's near the railway line, sir, southern direction. I heard a cargo train pass by here, then the same noise through the phone a few seconds later when he called me.'

The DCS was nodding and lifting his phone to his ear to act on this information the instant she'd finished speaking, then she was off again, her mind racing through Thorne's allusion to a beautiful goddess. That was the thing he'd meant to tell her, she knew, as she rushed towards the Temple of Venus. When she reached it, she nearly collided with Ben Sachs. Each of them held out an arm to steady the other in what was a near-embrace, then stepped quickly back.

Absurdly, she thought of what Thorne had said about her hair, which she could feel was now a tangled mess, blowing everywhere. She'd been waylaid by that phone call, then this stop in the gardens, before she could discipline it back into its ponytail.

Ben's own hair was sticking up as usual. Somebody ought to smooth it down. Her hand lifted a little, as if of its own volition, and she pressed it against her side. What was wrong with her? This really was not the time for her thoughts to run out of control.

She saw that Ben was wearing an earpiece. 'Did you listen in on those calls?'

'Yes.'

The two of them were on the move again when she asked another question. 'When did you find out I'd be reporting to you instead of Dinah?'

'Before the briefing yesterday morning. The DCS made it clear he'd tell you himself.' They were stepping between the Temple's columns. Ben was near enough for her to notice the scent of soap on his skin and clothes. 'Whatever Thorne left will be close to this building,' he said.

They were on the path that led to the children's play-ground in the distance, but followed it for only a few metres before halting in front of a large circle of grass. In the centre of that grass was a tree stump that made a sort of table. Without speaking, she and Ben moved towards it. A pale green envelope sat on top of the stump, alongside a flower.

Esmeralda bent to examine Thorne's little gifts, thinking it was lucky that nobody else had got to them first, and that they hadn't blown away. 'It's a water lily.' She glanced at the nearby pond. He'd obviously decided to ignore the signs asking visitors not to pick the flowers. One of Jason Thorne's more minor infractions. But he had good taste. The outer petals were intensely pink, and the stamen bright orange, the same colours as the Queen's Enchantment Rose, she vaguely realised. But Esmeralda much preferred the lily, which smelled like almonds and looked like fire. 'I think they bloom in the morning and close by late afternoon,' she said. 'More evidence that he's not long gone from here.'

'We'll leave the lily in place for the CSIs to deal with, but we'd better look now at whatever's inside the envelope. You do the honours,' Ben said, as they pulled sealed packets of blue gloves from their pockets. 'It's addressed to you.'

Her name was in that handwriting she knew so well from the case files, perfect as calligraphy. She lifted the envelope with her gloved fingers. Ben studied it along with her, their shoulders touching. They seemed to become aware of the proximity at exactly the same moment, when each of them leaned slightly away from the other.

Thorne hadn't sealed the envelope, but not because he feared leaving DNA, given that he'd made no attempt to disguise where the letter had come from. She slipped out the matching pale green paper, decorated with his signature daisies and vines, and read.

Dear Esmeralda,

I have left a present for you on the slip road. Not the most romantic of offerings and locations. But I am making the world a better place for those I love and for others who deserve help. You are rare in ticking both those boxes.

I realise that the sacred compact between the writer of a letter and the person to whom they address it is not respected by your friends in the force. I am in no doubt that they are reading what should be our intimate correspondence. For this reason, I look forward to being with you face-to-face, where we can have privacy.

JT.

Ben rolled his eyes. 'What a charmer.' He took an evidence bag from a pocket and held it out. 'Old habit from when I was in uniform, carrying one of these at all times.'

'I'll copy you with that one from now on.' While she concentrated on slipping the letter and envelope into the evidence bag, back to back so the writing was visible from either side, she said, 'There's something bothering me. It already was, but now even more.'

'More than being the object of Jason Thorne's affection?' he said.

'That strains any definition of affection I've ever known.' She handed him the evidence bag. 'It's that the texts from yesterday don't sound like Thorne.'

'In what way?'

'Thorne doesn't speak crudely, he doesn't use common insults, and he's too eloquent to have written those stupid rhymes, let alone call attention to them.'

'I'm not prepared to use the word eloquent about Jason Thorne,' Ben said.

'It doesn't help not to be real about what Thorne is.' She held out Thorne's letter. '*This* is what he is. Careful in his words, in whatever form. You heard how he spoke to me during those calls a few minutes ago. You've read the letter. They're nothing like those texts. He said he didn't send them. My instinct is that he was telling the truth.'

'He's a perfect Scout.' As Ben took the letter, something in Esmeralda's expression made him dial back on the sarcasm. 'I'm not saying there's nothing in your idea.'

'Ella Brooke thinks Thorne doesn't lie, but I'm not sure she has that quite right. I think the point is that he isn't very good at lying, so he tries to avoid it as far as he can.'

'If he didn't send the texts, then we're looking at two different people managing to get your private number over the same two days. Mystery Person A messaging you. Jason Thorne calling you.'

'Maybe they know each other – there's something about this we're not getting.'

DI Whistler appeared, flushed and out of breath. 'We're evacuating the park, checking the bins, looking at the CCTV. We've got nothing so far. The man's a magician at avoiding cameras.' He narrowed his eyes at Ben. 'Did you check that grave, Sachs?'

'I'll get to it.' Ben's voice and colour were calm, unlike DI Whistler's, and Esmeralda saw that despite the other man's seniority, Ben had absolutely no fear of speaking against him. 'The DCS has other plans for me today.'

When he saw the DCS himself approaching, DI Whistler swallowed back what Esmeralda was certain would have been a furious response.

Ben passed the letter, protected in the clear evidence bag, to the DCS, who read it quickly with DI Whistler.

'I want search teams on all motorway slip roads in a

twenty-kilometre radius,' the DCS said. 'We start by targeting those with no cameras. If Thorne has left something, he'll have chosen a road where he won't be picked up.'

DI Whistler pointed at Esmeralda, his eyes narrowing. 'She shouldn't be here,' he said. 'She's too close, with him calling and texting and writing her love letters.'

'She's part of Operation Leopard,' said DCS Vane. 'And don't refer to Thorne's tripe as love letters.'

DI Whistler's already flushed face went redder still.

'Walk with me,' DCS Vane said to Esmeralda. They were soon headed towards the eighteenth-century mansion at the front of the gardens. They cut through an arched iron gate, then veered right towards the car park. 'You did well this morning,' he said. 'I know that can't have been easy and I know it's intrusive.'

'I appreciate that, sir,' she said. What she really wanted to say was *Are you using me to get him? Are you using me as bait?* A part of her registered the conflict she was feeling about this, even, if she was honest with herself, her own inconsistency. Like everybody else, she was willing to do almost anything to catch Thorne. But she was still angered by the idea that they had her playing a dangerous game without telling her the rules. Then, she decided she wasn't being fair, because with Jason Thorne there were no rules.

When she looked to her left and saw the little chalet that reminded her of the gingerbread house in 'Hansel and Gretel', her heart gave a small squeeze. Now, the chalet was no more than a storage shed stuffed with dusty box files, but it had previously been a café. Her mother used to take her there when she was a little girl, treating her to a cake and hot chocolate with cream after a push on the swings and a twirl on the roundabout and a whoosh down the slide in the playground. She realised she hadn't let herself come back to the Pleasure Gardens since her mother died. Since Hugo Green. If it weren't for Jason Thorne, perhaps she'd never have returned.

Esmeralda realised another thing too. The chalet was in the style of the playhouse that Thorne had built in the grounds of his mother's house. Had this been a place he too had visited as a child and been happy in, and loved so much he tried to reproduce it? She struggled to imagine Elizabeth Thorne taking him. Had someone else? She shared her thoughts about the little house with the DCS, who made only a thoughtful sound.

They'd reached his car. 'We'll give you back your privacy as soon as we've got him,' he said. 'I'll see you later on site.'

She watched him drive away, then retraced her steps towards the opposite end of the park, where she'd left her own car. Ben was gone, but as she passed the Temple of Venus she saw DI Whistler was still standing inside its pillars, beneath the circular roof. His phone was to his ear as he made the arrangements for the slip road searches, but he rang off and aimed his usual grimace at her. 'You're a trouble magnet, Esme.'

Despite the deliberate refusal to use her correct name, she couldn't help but wonder if Whistler was right. She didn't like it, but she trusted the honesty of his brutal words more than she did the DCS's smooth ones.

The Good Witch

Esmeralda's ponytail was back in place when she walked into the Central Image Investigation Unit. In its former life, the building had been the school's art block. She wondered if she only imagined that there was still a faint scent of oil paint in the air.

When she saw that DC Scarlett Woodfield was at one of the workstations, Esmeralda silently cheered, then felt a little guilty. She knew that Scarlett was spending more time at a desk in CIIU than she really wanted to. This was because Scarlett was seven months pregnant, and had told Esmeralda that she was fed up with being treated like a fragile doll by their managers, who were too obsessed with health and safety.

Esmeralda felt a kinship with Scarlett. Before joining the police, Scarlett had been an artist and photographer. She'd modelled throughout art school to earn money, and there were an untold number of nude paintings of her out there. Fortunately, Scarlett said, they were mostly so bad she wasn't recognisable. Esmeralda had been touched and a little startled that Scarlett had confided in her. 'You're not the only detective with a history,' Scarlett liked to say.

As Esmeralda drew near, she saw that Scarlett was scrolling through photographs on her multiple screens. She looked like a beautiful witch conjuring magic. Her blonde hair was piled messily on top of her head. There was a pencil behind her ear and a charcoal smear on her cheek that made Esmeralda suspect she had woken early to sketch, or perhaps been at it late into the night. Maybe she thought it would be hard to do that after the baby came. Or maybe she'd been too uncomfortable to sleep.

'Hello Esmeralda,' Scarlett said, at last looking up from her screen.

'Hello. Scarlett, you . . .' Esmeralda brushed a finger over her own cheek as a signal to Scarlett, who wiped the smudge away.

That done, Esmeralda explained what she needed and put the memory stick in Scarlett's hand. Five minutes later they were watching the 'squirmy little man', as Scarlett called him with her pinpoint accuracy, hurrying along the pavement and looking truly spooked as he glanced over a shoulder to check if he was being followed.

He didn't notice the CCTV camera until it was too late and he'd already given it a view of his face that was so perfect it might have complied with Home Office passport photo specifications. At that instant he literally slapped a hand over his mouth, ducked his head and practically broke into a run. Esmeralda was certain that if there'd been sound capture they would have heard an audible groan.

She was growing more convinced by the minute that there really was a connection between this man and Jason Thorne. She needed to figure out who he was, what he was doing near Ella Brooke's house at the same time as Thorne, and why he was disturbed when he saw Esmeralda and Dinah. For him to want to avoid them suggested that he was familiar with the police.

Scarlett went forward a few frames with absolute control, then spooled back the tiniest bit. 'That's it. Right there.'

Esmeralda marvelled at the photo Scarlett had isolated. He was pale, with blotchy skin, and appeared not to have shampooed his hair for several days, so it was difficult to make out the colour – something on the spectrum of light to medium brown, she thought. His teeth were chipped and yellowing, and although his T-shirt must have originally been white, it was now the same shade as his teeth. His jeans were stained and far too loose. All in all, he appeared so unloved and uncared for Esmeralda couldn't help but feel sorry for him.

'I'll start by running this through the custody image database, see if we've picked him up before.' Scarlett opened up software that made no sense to Esmeralda. With everything Esmeralda did, she needed to check and double-check each stage of the process, knowing all the time she was probably getting multiple things wrong.

The computer fan began to whizz, and Esmeralda thought the sound was inside her own brain. Without realising it, she put a hand to each side of her head and pressed.

'Esmeralda?' Scarlett broke into her thoughts.

'Yes?'

'If he's been a bad boy it'll make a quick hit more likely, so cross your fingers he's been in custody and they took a photo.'

Scarlett's phone went. She listened for a bit, then said, 'I'll tell her, yeah. I'll send her right over.' She was giving Esmeralda *the look*.

'What?' Esmeralda said.

'Sylvie said the DCS wants you waiting for him in front of his office in ten minutes. You didn't know for sure I was in CIIU today until you came in and saw me, did you?'

'No. How would I?'

Scarlett was frowning. 'Did you mention to anybody that you were coming here?'

'No,' she said again, thinking that absolutely nothing got past Scarlett.

'So what made Sylvie know to ring my desk phone, within a metre of you?'

'They're tracking me,' Esmeralda said. 'They put some kind of spyware on my phone.'

Scarlett shook her head, making clear her outrage. 'Thorne, yes?'

'Yes. Did Sylvie say what the DCS wants?'

'Only that he's taking you off with him somewhere. Field trip fun,' Scarlett said. 'I'm trying not to be jealous. This room is about as dangerous as things ever get.'

'Sorry, Scarlett.'

'Not your fault,' Scarlett said.

'Why on earth does the DCS want me there? I'm way too junior. It makes no sense.'

'*I* know you're a superstar, but I seriously doubt they do. Must be Thorne's bulletin board with the Hugo Green case and your picture on it. It's pretty fucked up.'

Esmeralda thought of telling Scarlett about the drawings Thorne made of her, but realised she couldn't stomach it, so she said only, 'If it helps us get Thorne and take him off the street, maybe it doesn't matter.'

'No, Esmeralda.' Scarlett bit her lip and shook her head. 'It does matter.'

Esmeralda stood. 'I'd better hurry.'

'I'll come back to you if I get a hit on Mr Not-Ready-For-His-Close-Up,' Scarlett said. 'Tomorrow, though, not tonight. I see a long day in your future.'

'Líria is going to kill me for being late again,' Esmeralda said, 'and she's far scarier than Jason Thorne.'

But Scarlett didn't look convinced. 'Few things on this earth are scarier than Jason Thorne. Don't forget that for even a split second.' She looked around the room at the others, all bent over their screens, then lowered her voice. 'Everyone here is a weirdo. Don't you dare fucking get yourself killed and leave me on my own with them.'

The Slip Road

A body had been found on a disused motorway slip road, and DCS Vane wanted Esmeralda to attend the scene. That was why she now found herself in the back seat of an unmarked fleet car. Ben was driving, and she was relieved that DI Whistler was with him in the front rather than next to her. Instead, she had DCS Vane by her side.

The approach to the slip road was already filled with emergency vehicles. Ben parked behind them, and Esmeralda was soon wearing the standard white shoe covers, hooded suit, blue gloves, and face mask. As they made their way on foot along the centre of the slip road, the DCS broke away to speak to the Road Policing Senior Investigating Officer, who was clearly worried about how long the stretch of motorway would need to remain closed.

What had once been a proper slip road was now a mere access road that fed into a defunct toll road as well as narrow lanes to private farmland, so there were few reasons for the public to travel this way. A small number must have, though, given the evidence of the rubbish tangled in what Esmeralda could identify as Sea Fern Grass, with the idle theory that such a plant might thrive there thanks to the icing-salt mixed in with the soil. As Esmeralda stepped over a crisp packet and a plastic bottle, she understood why the place suited Thorne, and how that very local boy would know of it.

The Crime Scene Manager had a tent over the victim, and confirmed to DCS Vane that they'd guessed right about the lack of cameras. Nonetheless, there was at least one piece of good news. Searchers had found a wallet beneath the dense shrubs and bushes, and inside it was a single debit card. They'd already learned that the card hadn't been used for a month. 'In the name of George Rossiter,' the Crime Scene Manager said, 'though we can't be certain that's who this is until the postmortem and formal identification.'

The name was vaguely familiar to Esmeralda. She had the thought that if Jason Thorne had killed this man, the wallet's presence was not a careless oversight. Rather, Thorne wanted his victim easily identified.

The body remained as it had been found, on its back and partially covered in scrubby vegetation, so that the forensic team could take photographs in situ. An anonymously suited man was beckoning them to draw in closer to the overgrown grass verge. Ben told Esmeralda in a low voice this was the chief pathologist. During training, she'd seen countless images of bodies, but this was her first real one at a crime scene.

'I'd say he's been here several weeks,' the chief pathologist was saying. 'Can't be more exact until we get him on the table and run more tests. There's a fair amount of decomposition, but the salt has helped to slow it. Look at this.' He used a long metal hook to move the green-leafed bush aside and they all peered more closely.

Esmeralda was glad that the man's face was hidden by the plants. She studied his naked torso, which was exposed. The skin didn't look like skin any more. It was purple black.

'His hands and arms were bound beneath him,' the chief pathologist said. 'And do you see those marks?'

A circle had been engraved into his skin. A short arrow protruded out of the circle's rim, at what would have been the two o' clock mark on a clock, pointing upwards and towards the right. The lower rim of the circle was just above the man's navel and the top rim was under his nipples. Inside the circle was what appeared to be a wrist that ended in a fist.

It was a symbol that Men's Rights activists used. Esmeralda recognised it immediately, and could hear the pathologist discussing it with DCS Vane. Just beside the symbol, she could make out initials. JT. The mark of Thorne.

She turned away, feeling the blood drain from her own face, and made an effort to stand straight and firm.

Ben was by her side. 'All right?'

'Excellent,' she said, distracted by the water drops on the lenses of his black-rimmed glasses. They made her realise it had started to drizzle before she felt any rain on the top of her own head.

'This is your first body?' Ben said, leaning closer so he wasn't overheard.

'Get a room,' Whistler said in a low voice as he passed.

Ben muttered something that sounded like *Fuck off*, but Esmeralda ignored the DI as she would a bully in the playground.

'First one since joining,' she said. She suspected Ben could work out the unspoken tangle behind those four words.

'You and I are leaving now. Whistler and the DCS will follow later.'

'No.' Esmeralda shook her head. 'Why was I here at all if I'm already going?'

'Between you and me, the DCS wanted to be sure you knew for yourself what we're dealing with when it comes to Jason Thorne. He doesn't want you romanticising him.'

'That's not a lesson I needed. I know what Thorne is.' She was absolutely furious as she gave the body a final look. 'I want to help. What's with the Men's Rights activists symbol?'

'If the victim is George Rossiter, it makes sense.' Ben passed her his tablet. 'I'll drive so you can read this on the way back.'

On Ben's tablet was a file for George Rossiter. As she read, Esmeralda realised why the name was familiar. Twelve years earlier, she had followed the press coverage of Rossiter's trial for the murder of his estranged wife, Monique. But it was Monique's name that had stayed with her, not that of the man who'd killed her.

On a Sunday evening in March of 2005, the then forty-year-old Rossiter left his fourteen-month-old twins with his new girlfriend and drove to Monique's house. Wrapped in a newspaper under his arm was a kitchen knife that he had bought the previous month.

When Monique opened the door, expecting the return of her sons, Rossiter pushed his way in and proceeded to stab her multiple times. He then drove to a nearby forest, where he hid her body. The blood that the police found in the hallway, despite apparent attempts to remove it, made it clear that Monique had come to harm there.

'There can be no doubt that Monique's death was pre-meditated murder,' said the prosecuting barrister at the opening of the trial, emphasising the victim's humanness by repeating her name whenever he possibly could. 'Monique suffered catastrophic injuries to her heart, lungs, and major arteries and veins. Monique had no chance of surviving this.'

Juries, Esmeralda thought, usually reached the right decision. But that did not happen in George Rossiter's case. Those twelve men and women fell for the defence's argument that Rossiter had not *planned* to cause over a dozen sharp force injuries to Monique's face, neck, hands, and upper body with the knife he'd brought along, then wrap her in the sheet he happened to have with him before burying her in the grave he'd prepared months earlier.

Even the defendant's own barrister seemed astonished that the jury had believed this sad tale of provocation by a rich and spoiled wife who was cheating her husband out of his due in a toxic divorce case. The screeching, controlling harridan was treating Rossiter with disrespect, trying to make him homeless, take his children away, and destroy his self-esteem. This was a version of Monique that nobody who actually knew her recognised.

The jury had also swallowed Rossiter's story that he attacked his wife while in the grip of an abnormality of mental function. The defence specified that Rossiter had suffered temporary insanity while experiencing an adjustment disorder. But what the hell was that?

Esmeralda looked up from the tablet. 'Ben?'

'Esmeralda?'

'What's an "adjustment disorder"?'

'A whole load of bullshit,' Ben said. 'Supposedly a destructive overreaction to an acutely stressful event in a person's life. The idea is that their self-control is impaired. The general rule is that this happens within three months of the stress event.'

'So the defence said the stress event for Rossiter was the divorce case?'

'Yeah. But the arguments over the divorce started when the twins were born. That was fourteen months before he killed Monique, so not even close to being inside of three months.'

She was impressed by his recollection of the details. She glanced over at him, hands on the wheel and eyes on the road. 'Thanks.' She turned her attention back to the tablet.

When the jury acquitted Rossiter of murder, the judge had no choice but to downgrade the charge to voluntary manslaughter, but imposed the maximum sentence of twenty-four years. Rossiter served half the sentence, less six months on remand, and was released on licence in March of 2017.

While in prison, Rossiter had exercised his parental right to take part in decisions about his children. Although the boys were living with Monique's mother, Rossiter interfered whenever he could, preventing her from taking them on holiday, insisting on reading their school reports, obstructing every choice she made about their education.

Esmeralda looked up from the file and realised they were back on site and driving into the car park. 'The children are thirteen now?'

'Yes, and they want nothing to do with their father.'

'Do we know when exactly George Rossiter disappeared?' she asked.

'Not sure of the timeline yet, beyond his release from prison six months ago. Investigations are ongoing. We'll know more by tomorrow.'

As Ben turned off the engine, a series of texts pinged on Esmeralda's phone, a succession of five that came so quickly the sender must have had them ready to copy, paste, and fire. The sound made her stomach drop with a kind of dread. She took the phone out of her bag, knowing Mary's team would be reading them too.

Tomorrow will be the worst day of your life, bitch.

Tomorrow the world will see you for what you are, witch. (Ha Ha. More rhymes!)

Tomorrow you will be exposed in every way, whore.

Tomorrow is your starring role, cunt.

Tomorrow your punishment begins, ungrateful murdering slut.

She thought of that old nursery rhyme. *Words shall never hurt me.* How untrue it was. With a shaking hand, she passed her phone to Ben. His face was expressionless as he read.

And then Ben seemed to disappear, and she reached out and gripped what she could, to stop herself from sinking. A faraway part of her knew that something was wrong with her breathing. It was too much and too fast and when the air went in it was making her chest hurt.

Snapshots from the day gone by seemed to flash before her. Her daughter's face. Thorne's voice on the phone, intimate as a lover's. The body on the slip road with its horrifying engraved torso. Everybody looking at her, knowing who she was and what she was and what she might have done, and what had been done to her. Somebody out there, making his ugly threats.

She wasn't sure how much time passed before the colours began to return and everything grew still again. There was a face, the brow wrinkled with what she realised was worry, and a clean scent that she liked, of soap and almonds. There was a hand in hers. She was squeezing it tightly, and saw that the hand belonged to Ben. As if dropping a hot potato, she released her grip.

'I think it will work again, someday,' he said, opening and closing his fist. 'My circulation seems to be coming back.'

'God. I'm so sorry.'

'No harm done, honestly, Esmeralda.'

'I haven't broken any of your bones, have I?'

'Only a finger or two.' He paused, then said, 'You know Thorne's fun will be short-lived, don't you?'

'I do know, yes.' She sat up in her seat, collecting herself. Detectives were supposed to be self-possessed, and clear-sighted, and brave. She, on the other hand, had just experienced a full-blown panic attack.

Ben was her boss. An extremely kind boss, and one who would probably allow any colleague who was visibly melting down to break his fingers, but her boss nonetheless.

It was time to go home. She began to gather her things. Ben's tablet was on her lap. When she picked it up to pass it back to him it slipped from her grip and thumped onto the floor by her feet.

'Crap.' She moved to grab it, but he got there first and they bumped heads. 'Sorry!'

'It's fine.' He held up the tablet to show her the screen was undamaged.

She noticed the five o'clock shadow on his jawline, and was startled by how attractive she found it. Channelling as much composed politeness as she could, and glad that Ben couldn't read her mind, she said, 'Goodnight – and – see you tomorrow.'

Her hand was on the door handle, but when Ben spoke again she halted, wondering if she'd heard him right. Had he really just asked her if she liked ice cream?

Killer Chocolate

'I know a great place,' Ben said. 'And there's an unwritten code that no work-related matters can be discussed there, especially after a bad day.'

'That sounds good.' In the six months since they'd met, Esmeralda had never gone anywhere with Ben that wasn't operationally necessary. 'It will have to be a flying visit, though. I need to get home to my daughter and my dad.'

'Sure,' Ben said, as they got out of the fleet car and headed towards their own. 'We'll have some packed up so you can bring it back for them. Do you want to follow me there?'

The ice cream parlour was tucked away behind the abbey, in an old lane filled with quaint tea rooms and souvenir shops. An old-fashioned sign swung gently above their heads. ICE CREAM DREAMS, it said in large letters, and below, in a smaller font, CREATE YOUR OWN.

Ben pushed open the door, a bell rang to announce them, and they stepped inside.

The tiny room was lovely. An elderly couple was sitting at one of two wrought-iron tables in front of the window, dipping long-handled spoons into tall sundae glasses.

'How have I never noticed this place before?' Esmeralda said.

'It only opened last week,' Ben said, as a woman with dark hair and glasses rushed out from behind the counter to throw her arms around him with such force Ben mock-staggered before hugging her back. 'Amy, this is Esmeralda. Esmeralda, my sister Amy.'

Before anything further could be said, Ben's phone went. He took it from his jacket pocket and glanced at the caller ID, frowning. 'I need to take this one.' He stepped outside with the phone to his ear, and Esmeralda heard him answering as the door swung closed. She could see him through the shop window, shadowy, as he paced.

Amy returned to her place behind the counter. She had the same charcoal-grey eyes as Ben. 'So, are you and my brother seeing each other?'

My, my, aren't you direct, Esmeralda thought. 'No, I'm Ben's . . .' She was moving a hand forward and back, as if the movement would help her answer. 'Colleague-friend. Bit of a miserable day at work. I need an antidote.'

'Well, you've come to the right place.' Amy made her face angelically innocent just as Ben came back in. 'He never brings anyone to meet me, you know.'

Amy's words left Esmeralda part-disbelieving, part-amused, and part-hopeful, though the only response she could manage was to peer studiously into the refrigerated gelato display case, which was what Ben was doing too. The assorted bowls and jugs beneath its curved clear covering were filled with sweets and biscuits and fruits and syrups. Despite the shop's name, she couldn't see any actual ice cream. 'How does this work?' she asked.

'You create your own,' Amy said. 'The idea came from my son. Toby likes what he likes, so we were always designing flavours for him in our kitchen.'

'Home chemistry,' Esmeralda said. 'My daughter and I do that with cakes.'

'Exactly. There's a vanilla base I make myself, in small batches.' Amy pointed to a separate glass-fronted freezer behind her, its shelves lined with rectangular containers of stainless steel. 'Then I mix in whatever you like.'

'Líria will want chocolate. Mixed with chocolate. And then more chocolate.'

Amy laughed. 'Líria's your daughter? What a pretty name – I have a syrup to change the base flavour that I think she'd like. I call that Killer Chocolate.'

'That sounds perfect.' Esmeralda was enchanted by Amy's passion for what she did. 'Four to take away, please. Plain vanilla for my dad – he's a bit of a puritan.'

'Good vanilla is an art,' Amy said. 'You'll have to let me know what he thinks.'

'Definitely.' Esmeralda looked again at the options in the display case. 'Killer Chocolate for me and Líria. Mine with chocolate hazelnut spread mixed in, I think, and Líria's with cookie dough and Oreos, please.'

'What's the fourth?'

Esmeralda turned to Ben, who was examining the fruits. 'What would you like, Ben?'

Amy said, 'He'll pretend to consider, but it'll be strawberries and only strawberries.'

'I'll have cream on top,' he said.

Esmeralda was the only child of two parents who'd doted on her but couldn't give her a sibling because of the cancer her mother had lived with for well over a decade. Líria was the only child of a single mother with zero interest in more children. But as Ben and Amy affectionately teased each other, Esmeralda was unusually wistful about the fact that Líria would never have a brother or sister. Somewhat uncomfortably, Esmeralda had the thought that it would have been good for Líria to share her with a sibling.

Amy scooped four large mounds of the vanilla base, placed them at intervals on a huge white surface, and cut the mix-ins into three of the four piles with what looked like a mezzaluna knife, a curved half-circle with double handles that she rocked from side to side at speed while moving it forwards and backwards. Then she expertly folded each of the separate creations into a container with the shop's name and logo, popped on a lid, and wrote the contents in red letters that stood out against the cup's pale pink background.

When Esmeralda took out her bank card to pay, she discovered Ben had beaten her to it. 'My treat,' he said, as Amy handed him a white bag with the ice creams.

'Family discount,' Amy said. The couple at the little window table had finished their ice cream sundaes and were leaving. Amy lowered her voice to a theatrically confiding whisper. 'You get it too, Esmeralda. Seeing as you're a colleague-friend and all.'

Esmeralda tried to keep a straight face, not knowing how else to arrange her expression as she said thank you and promised she would bring Líria in soon.

'The phone call was the DCS,' Ben said, as the two of them walked. 'You're not going to ask about it?'

Esmeralda shook her head. 'Nope. I've had enough of that place for today.' She hesitated, then asked, 'How does Amy manage the shop with Toby?' She was thinking about how much her father had always helped with Líria. How she could have raised her daughter without him, let alone held down her teaching job, was unfathomable. Working for the police would have been a different level of impossible without his support.

'The shop used to be their sitting room. They live in the floors above it, so Toby's always close by after school. Amy's husband Liam does something in IT, and works mostly from home. The grandparents step in when needed. So do I, when I can.'

The abbey's coloured floodlights made it easy to see in the dark. Quickly, they reached the nearby street where they'd left their cars, but Ben seemed to want to delay saying goodbye. 'Can I ask you an important question?' he said.

She stiffened a little. Ice cream, and then difficult questions. Maybe it would be Thorne, or Hugo Green, or something more complicated about Líria. 'Go on.'

'So when do you celebrate your leap year birthday? February twenty-eighth or March first?'

She had the faraway thought that he must have learned her birthday from her file. 'March first. My mum said that was the closest we could get. She said February twenty-eighth made no sense because I hadn't been born yet.'

'Sounds to me like your mum had the right idea.'

'I think so.'

As she and Ben finally said goodnight, Esmeralda had the oddest sensation that they were parting at the end of a date.

When she arrived home, Esmeralda could see Líria's silhouette in the sitting room window. The front door opened before she reached it. 'What time do you call this, Mum?'

Esmeralda glanced at her watch, squinting a bit under the bright beam of the outside light. 'I call this nine o'clock, Líria. How was your day? Are you going to move out of the way so I can come in and hear about it properly?'

'No.' Líria emphasised the point by spreading out her arms to block the open doorway, which was a little absurd, so that Esmeralda had to be careful to keep her face serious. 'You were supposed to be home two hours ago.'

'Something came up at work. Then I stopped to get you and Grandad a surprise.' That was when Esmeralda realised she'd forgotten to take the ice creams from Ben.

She was still standing on the footpath, empty-handed, with Líria on the other side of the doorframe, when a newly familiar car entered her street and stopped in front of her house. The driver's door opened and Ben got out, holding the white bag as he crossed the pavement towards the footpath.

'Mum?' The word was a question that Esmeralda ignored, though Líria's voice had been low.

Esmeralda blinked. How did Ben know her address? Was it because they were tracking her phone? Or because she was now reporting to him? Maybe the seemingly omniscient Sylvie had given it to him.

As he arrived at her side, Ben answered her unvoiced question. 'I thought you saw that I was driving behind you.' His smile was uncertain, and she realised that she must have appeared visibly anxious, and also how tired and distracted she was not to have noticed that he was following. They'd parked within metres of each other so it would have been easy for him to caravan behind as she drove the traffic-free five minutes home. He added, 'I didn't want your ice creams to melt – I tried your phone but it must have been on silent.'

'Ah,' she said, returning his smile and thanking him. 'That makes sense.'

'Hello,' Líria said, all of her pre-teen grumpiness with her mother locked away, though she was tightly clasping Esmeralda's hand.

'This is Ben,' Esmeralda said. 'We work together.' My *colleague-friend*, she thought. 'Ben, this is Líria.'

Líria wore her gracious smile, as if she spent all of her time studying etiquette books.

'We stopped for ice cream on the way home and I forgot to take it,' Esmeralda added, despite this circumstance already being obvious.

'Made by my sister Amy.' Ben held out the bag of ice

cream and Líria released Esmeralda's hand to take it. 'One for you, one for your mum, and one for your grandfather.'

'That's really kind,' said Líria, and Esmeralda had the eerie sensation of hearing herself, of knowing her daughter modelled her responses on what she saw her mum do.

'Amy just opened an ice cream shop,' Esmeralda said.

'Amazing,' Líria said. 'Grandad's in the bath, Mum.'

'Oh, right. Thanks sweetheart.' Esmeralda turned to Ben. 'I know my dad would want to say hello and thank you himself. He'll be sorry to have missed you.'

'Next time,' Ben said.

Líria was rifling through the ice cream bag. 'There are four in here. Is the one that says strawberries yours, Ben?' she asked.

'How did you know?'

'Lucky guess.' Líria put the lidded pink cup in Ben's hand. 'Won't you come in and have it with us?' she asked, and though Esmeralda doubted anyone else could see it, she knew Líria didn't really want him to.

'That's a tempting invitation, but it's late and I know all three of us have early starts tomorrow. So I'll say goodnight.'

As they watched him climb into his car, Líria whispered, 'Interesting,' elongating the first syllable.

'Why?'

'He likes you, Mum.' Ben was starting the engine. 'As in *really likes* you.'

'Do you think so?' Esmeralda tried to sound casual.

'Well, yeah.' Líria made that last word into two syllables.

Ben opened his window and waved, and they waved back as he pulled out.

'Lots of people fall in love at work.' Líria was searching the bag of ice creams as she spoke.

'Do they, oh wise one?'

'Everyone knows that.' She held out the tub of Killer Chocolate with cookie dough and Oreos. 'Mine?'

'Of course,' Esmeralda said.

'When did you first meet him?'

'Is this an interrogation?' Esmeralda said, laughing.

'Yes.'

'Six months ago. On my first day in Major Crime.'

'And you're not counting, Mum?' As they watched Ben's car turn the corner, out of their sight, Líria said thoughtfully, 'He brought the ice cream to us because you forgot it. That's weird.'

'Why?'

Líria finally allowed her mother to enter the house. 'Because you never usually forget anything.'

THURSDAY, 14 SEPTEMBER 2017

A Private Conversation

Esmeralda trailed behind DCS Vane and other senior detectives from Major Crime, navigating the maze of corridors that would take them to the press conference. Before the South West Constabulary took over the site of the former school, the building where Esmeralda now found herself had housed the theatre.

They were backstage, weaving past windowless dressing rooms with their doors open for air and light. A few had been turned into poky offices for the media team. Others were used to store broadcasting and recording equipment, and various props and displays.

The DCS broke free of the crowd surrounding him and aimed himself at Esmeralda. 'Time for a quick chat?'

She followed him into an empty office, feeling the others watching, including Ben.

'You doing okay?'

She wasn't sure if his question was prompted by the torso engraved with the Men's Rights symbol or by the five new text messages. 'Fine. Thank you,' she said.

'I appreciated your being there yesterday. I wanted to fill you in.'

Why on earth was she, a lowly new Detective Constable, getting a personal, one-to-one update from a Detective Chief Superintendent? None of this made any sense.

'The dead man *is* indeed George Rossiter,' the DCS went on. 'Hasn't been seen for a month. Been living in a bedsit since his release from prison six months ago. Landlord reported him missing in the middle of August, largely because Rossiter was in rent arrears.'

'Poor love.' She was startled by her own bitter sarcasm, her hardness towards a murder victim, but she couldn't let go of her rage at what Rossiter had done to Monique.

'So you know what a charmer he was. Since his release, Rossiter and the mother of the woman he stabbed to death have been engaged in a custody battle. Rossiter was backed by fathers' rights activists from the manosphere. Do you know what that is?'

'The manosphere blames me for Hugo Green's death. So yes, unfortunately.'

He paused, then said, 'So you'll know that the manosphere is made up of different online communities who promote masculinity and misogyny. Rossiter was their perfect victim hero. Lost his job as an architect. Lost the house his dead wife had owned, which went to her mother. Lost his new girlfriend. Lost his children.'

'Any clues yet as to how Jason Thorne got hold of him?' she said. 'I mean, Thorne did lead us to the body, and he has form in using human beings as canvases for his artwork.'

'Rossiter's laptop and phone purged themselves as soon

as we touched them. From something the landlord said, it's looking like he thought he was meeting a woman, someone he'd interacted with online. Likely it was a lure.'

'And someone's talking to Monique's mother?' Esmeralda asked. 'Given she has motive?'

'She's been interviewed. She was in Scotland with her grandchildren in August, when he was last seen in London. Unless she arranged it, but no evidence so far that she did. We know she's been anxious since his release, thinking he'd come after her. What are your thoughts?'

Esmeralda cleared her throat, which felt dry. 'That maybe Thorne's going after bad men now. Making the world a better place, as he put it. Can you imagine anyone who fits the bad man bill as perfectly as Rossiter?'

'He'd be high on anyone's shortlist for pure evil.'

She nodded. 'I'm not justifying Thorne' – secretly, though, she wondered if she was – 'but the damage George Rossiter caused . . .'

The DCS's intensely blue eyes were fixed on her face, giving her the odd impression that he was assessing her as a suspect rather than really listening to her as a detective, but she forced herself on. 'If Thorne went after Rossiter because of what he did to Monique and the children, then he's changing his victim pool.'

'It's obvious why Thorne targeted Holderness, given what he did to Ella Brooke,' said the DCS, 'but there are plenty of evil bastards out there. Why zero in on George Rossiter out of all of them?'

Esmeralda pressed her lips together, admitting to herself that she'd allowed her hatred of George Rossiter to cloud her ability to think. She needed to remember that the real enemy was Jason Thorne. 'There's something in the selection we're not seeing?'

'Precisely.' DCS Vane glanced at his watch. 'We need to get moving, but I wanted to say you're doing good work on Lucy Reed.'

She was startled, because she assumed everyone thought she was being a pain about this, but she would take support wherever she could find it. 'Thank you, sir.'

'No thanks needed. The whole point of the fast-track programme was bringing in fresh ways of thinking. We set out to recruit from a pool we've neglected and I think we're lucky that landed you here.'

Now this is overkill, Esmeralda thought. 'That's generous of you to say,' she said.

'Better get going.' He moved towards the door. 'The show's about to begin.'

A Public Scene

A few minutes later, Esmeralda was in the wings of the old auditorium. Curved bench tables formed a half-circle around the stage where the DCS's performance would soon take place. At those tables sat scores of journalists. Nothing was happening yet, but they activated their cameras all at once, then stopped all at once, with the mysterious synchronisation of a school of fish. The clicks made Esmeralda remember the noise of the cicadas from the summer visits she and her parents used to make to the Algarve when she was a little girl.

She felt a new presence beside her and saw it was Dinah. Both women turned to watch DCS Vane stride decisively to the centre of the stage. Behind him was a blue backdrop with the constabulary crest and an image of the Queen. The media team were circling the DCS with their video cameras, adjusting his lapel mic, testing the sound as he settled into position like a film star.

'Good afternoon. Thank you for coming.' The DCS's

greeting triggered a fresh wave of lights flashing over his face. 'Three days ago, on Monday morning, we were provided with the first credible sighting of Jason Thorne since he absconded ten months ago.' Like a magician, he gestured to a large screen and the still of Thorne in his car materialised.

'We will shortly be circulating this new photograph, and we are asking for your help in alerting the public to the fact that Mr Thorne has changed his appearance. In particular, he has shed a great deal of weight. This means that we are now searching for a markedly thin man, unusually tall at over one point nine metres, bald, and possibly wearing glasses. In addition,' continued DCS Vane, 'he may walk with a pronounced limp due to an injury to his left knee.'

There was an autocue, but the DCS appeared not to be using it. 'This investigation is fast-moving. We are asking members of the public to be vigilant. But I must stress the need to exercise extreme caution. If you know of an abandoned or derelict building where Jason Thorne may be hiding, do not enter it. If you see someone fitting his description, he should not be approached. Alert the police immediately by dialling 999 or using any of the methods listed here to get in touch with us.'

Someone from the media team pressed a button, and a list of communication channels appeared below Thorne's face. There was the constabulary contact form and telephone number, its Facebook and Twitter private message pages, and the option for ringing Crimestoppers anonymously.

'The police evacuated the Georgian Pleasure Gardens yesterday morning.' The voice belonged to a female journalist. 'And you closed a section of the motorway later that same afternoon. Can you tell us why?'

'I won't be providing operational details. You wouldn't want me jeopardising a live investigation.' The DCS gestured to a second screen and an image immediately appeared there. It was a snapshot Esmeralda knew well, of a young woman at a summer garden party, caught laughing. She was wearing a light blue sundress with tiny pink daisies. Her skin was pale, and her hair long and dark, with the front swept into a sparkling clasp.

'This is the last known photograph of Lucy Reed,' said DCS Vane. 'Lucy went missing on the twenty-fifth of June, 1991, three days after this photo was taken. She was nineteen years old, 163 centimetres tall, and she'd just returned home for the summer after completing her first year at Durham University, where she was enjoying her Chemistry course and doing well.'

Esmeralda had seen the original of that photograph displayed at Lucy's parents' house only a week earlier. She was filled with gratitude to DCS Vane for circulating it.

'On the day she disappeared, Lucy told her mum that she was meeting a friend for coffee but would be back in time for dinner,' continued DCS Vane. 'We don't know where Lucy was going, or how she travelled there. CCTV was in its infancy then. We are now undertaking a major review of Lucy's disappearance, given that she was Jason Thorne's girlfriend during the sixth-form and until the time she was last seen.'

It was another journalist's turn to shout. 'Why was

this major review not undertaken two years after Lucy went missing?'

The DCS answered with his usual calm. 'This case has been assessed every two years, as per schedule. If any members of the public had contact with Lucy during late June of 1991 or afterwards, we would like to hear from you. We would particularly like to trace the unknown friend Lucy said she was meeting.'

Mrs Reed's words from the week before were echoing in Esmeralda's head. 'How can I die in peace, not knowing where Lucy is?' Mrs Reed had not disclosed any serious health condition, but Esmeralda suspected she had one. When she pictured Mrs Reed's hand, so thin and frail, resting on top of her husband's, Esmeralda saw her own mother.

'Finally, I have this to say. Jason, I am talking to you directly. I want to assure you that we will get you the help and medical attention you need, and you will be treated with respect.' The DCS thanked the press, placed the lapel mic on a table, and began to walk off-stage, ignoring the continuing barrage of questions while the media team hurried away in order to prepare the film for release and then react to any responses once it went out.

That was when Esmeralda saw a male journalist in the back row of the auditorium jump to his feet and shout, 'DCS Vane! Wait! You need to hear this.' He was stumbling over the knees and feet of his colleagues to reach the aisle, all the while holding out his phone as if it were an explosive device. He tripped and nearly fell onto a woman's lap. The other journalists paused to observe this unexpected bonus show.

Police officers were speeding towards the journalist while he struggled to do something to his phone before he was intercepted.

A voice filled the room. 'Since, as you say, you are addressing me *directly*, Dominic, and since you have promised to treat me with respect, I will extend the same courtesy.'

Esmeralda knew that voice all too well. It was rich and deep and extremely amused despite the fact that it was being broadcast on a tinny phone in a large auditorium.

DCS Vane pivoted, jumped off the stage, rushed through what was once the orchestra pit, then took the steps two at a time to reach the journalist and take the phone. 'Hello Jason,' said DCS Vane. 'You have my attention.'

Esmeralda thought the hearts of every person in the room had simultaneously skipped a beat when they realised who that voice belonged to.

'Please be advised,' said Jason Thorne, 'that if you take me off speakerphone I will end this call. The sound quality will change and I will know. I see no reason to exile the hard-working members of the press from our conversation, though I realise they will have signed away their rights, and possibly their souls, when it comes to reporting restrictions. My friendly suggestion is that you do not play games with me. Though I do so enjoy games.'

'How about chess?' said DCS Vane. 'Name the location and I'll bring my own set.'

'Very kind of you to offer. Chess is my favourite – *board* game. But let's not rush things, Dom. Do your friends call you Dom?'

'No,' said DCS Vane, 'so feel free. Care to tell me what you want?'

'Oh, but the list of my – *wants* – is far too long for this occasion. And, the nature of my desires, well, they are too intimate to share in such a large crowd.' Thorne's voice went through Esmeralda's skin and into her blood and bones.

'When did you last see Lucy Reed, Jason?'

'There is only one person who will get an answer to that question. Please tell DC EA that I will arrange for the two of us to be alone soon, and that I am very sorry for what is about to happen.' With those words, the line went dead.

She was vaguely aware of journalists muttering, *DCEA?*

Other voices quickly followed. *Detective Constable? EA must be their initials.*

Esmeralda could hear the DCS booming that this was a live investigation and all journalists had signed the South West Constabulary Media Agreement. He went on to spell out the fact that anyone who broke it would face arrest and multiple legal sanctions. All members of the press were under strict instruction to say nothing beyond the official filmed statement he himself had made, which would soon be released to all media outlets.

Esmeralda watched the pandemonium from the wings, half-frozen in the wake of Thorne's phone call. She became aware of a presence at her side. Before she could react, DI Whistler was pulling back the curtain that hid her from the room and the movement attracted a fresh wave of camera flashes. Esmeralda's stomach dropped. She turned to retreat from view, but Whistler blocked her path. He hesitated almost imperceptibly, then took her arm to keep her facing forward. His grasp was so tight she knew it would leave a mark, though he stood as though he were guiding her rather than keeping her restrained.

Hit, pull, strike. That was the training she had been drilled in, and which she had repeatedly practised with Dinah.

Without thinking, she slapped the back of Whistler's forearm to force him to release his grip, then wrenched herself free. She only just stopped herself from completing the third quick action of the sequence and punching him in the chin, though he was visibly reeling from the force of the two moves she had already executed.

'Bitch.' He was scrambling to steady himself. He'd been too enraged to contain that word but was still shrewd enough to hiss it under his breath. He knew very well that the two of them continued to face the audience, and that the journalists were capturing all of it.

'Why the hell did you do that?' she asked. 'What is your problem with me?'

His voice stayed deliberately low, so no microphone would pick it up, but his inexplicable hatred of her remained inflamed. 'You're going to lose everything.'

She wanted only to get away from him and the cameras, so that was what she did, steering herself back into the wings and out of sight. But hiding herself did nothing to alter the fact that instead of helping to solve the case, she was increasingly becoming a part of it. Instead of keeping to her place in the margins of the story, she had become a central character.

She felt for the lanyard around her neck, then looked down and saw that her warrant card was facing outwards for all to see. She lifted it, although she knew exactly what was on it, easily read if you had a half-decent shot and simply zoomed in. Those journalists had been close enough to get the detail they were after.

Exposure

Esmeralda had been caught in a whirlwind when she was fifteen and her body became a living, breathing crime scene. The police medical staff had turned her this way or that to examine a chafed wrist or ankle, or take a swab, or scrape beneath her fingernails, or weigh and measure her, or document an injury with their cameras. The bright lights of their flashes hurt her eyes after so long underground. And although her father had fought to stay by her side, there seemed always to be detectives asking questions in voices that couldn't decide if they were addressing a toddler or a woman.

Now, twenty-six years later, Esmeralda was struck by the quiet stillness that surrounded her in the High Tech Unit, despite the intense activity everywhere else. DS Mary Armstrong's large workstation was covered in monitors and equipment. Too many people were gathered around it for Esmeralda to be able to see what was actually on the screens.

Ben was one of those people, his body tipping forward

as he studied the displays along with Dinah. DI Whistler was superglued to DCS Vane's side as usual, his face frozen in concentration in the way of someone who knew they'd done wrong but was trying to pretend otherwise. Mary was in her chair, examining the journalist's phone which, despite his protests, had been confiscated.

'The journalist is Larry Fawcett,' Ben was saying. 'Part of the police press pool. He has a long record of written pieces and televised interviews on crime in the South West. There's a website with his contact details, including his number. All easy for Thorne to find.'

DCS Vane turned to Mary. 'Anything from the device so far?'

Mary shook her head. 'Thorne used a burner to call Fawcett, just like when he phoned Esmeralda directly. I'm wondering why he did it this way in the middle of the press conference. Why didn't he go straight to her like he did before?'

'He likes an audience,' said DCS Vane.

Ben was eyeing Whistler with the disgust he'd reserve for something horrible on the bottom of his shoe. Esmerelda heard him say her name, but couldn't make out anything else.

Whistler, on the other hand, was loud and clear. 'She brought this on herself,' he said. 'It's called attention-seeking and I'm the wronged party.'

Esmeralda's cheeks were boiling hot. She felt a rush of blood to her head that made her wonder if rage and a sense of injustice could actually make a person faint. Her urge to scream was at odds with her desperation to be invisible. She watched Ben take a step towards

Whistler and grab his shoulder, prompting Whistler to swear and shake him off.

'Cut it, you two.' Mary's voice zinged like an electric current. 'We have a text message from an unknown number coming through to the journalist's phone – it's likely gone to any other devices he has too. I'm going to project it onto my monitors.'

DCS Vane spoke low in Whistler's ear, and Whistler seemed appeased by whatever was said because he nodded, then exited the High Tech Unit as Mary continued.

'Right,' Mary said. 'So Thorne writes, "I'm sure you'll do whatever you can to get this taken down, Dominic." He's sent a link.' She paused. 'It's a media sharing platform and it went live twenty minutes ago. I'm not playing any sound until I know what we're dealing with.' Esmeralda couldn't see Mary's screen for the crowd of detectives. 'It looks to be a trailer for a video game. The quality of the visuals is high. This is *very* professional.'

Seconds went by, and DCS Vane adjusted his position to block the screen even more decisively. Esmeralda could also see Dinah's profile. Her hand was over her mouth. Ben was beside her, both hands in fists that he was clenching and unclenching.

There was a thrumming in Esmeralda's ears, as if she were underwater. She was tired of standing by that filing cabinet in the corner, leaning against it like a woman-sized rag doll. She launched herself forward, pushing her way through the crowd of people gathered around the monitor. Just as she finally glimpsed Mary's screen, it went blank.

'Put it back, Mary.' Esmeralda felt her face go red with fury. 'I have a right to see.'

But Mary only said quietly, 'Not now – not yet,' while Dinah stretched an arm around Esmeralda's waist that she threw off.

'Mike,' said Mary, 'reach out to the platform. Issue an urgent takedown notice, but keep our access. We need to close down the window for the public to see this. Be sure the platform preserves any analytics and sends them to us straightaway.'

Mike was up and moving before Mary finished the sentence.

'The platform is mainstream,' Mary said. 'Normally I'd expect it to be underground or private given how extreme the content is.'

'What is it, Dinah?' Esmeralda said. 'Tell me.'

But Dinah only shook her head, and Esmeralda felt as if she were in a nightmare where she was invisible, where nobody could hear her no matter how loudly she screamed. Dinah was half-sitting, half-standing against the edge of a desk. 'Is the platform likely to agree to our takedown request?' Her voice was uncharacteristically weak.

'They refuse maybe two in every hundred referrals at most,' Mary said. 'From what I've seen so far, they'll say yes and thank us.'

'How long until it's gone?' the DCS said.

'Optimistic would be a matter of minutes,' Mary said. 'Pessimistic would be hours.'

'Esmeralda.' DCS Vane was speaking without looking at her, though she was less than a metre away. 'Go to my office and wait for me there.' He threw a quick side-ways glance at Ben. 'Stay with her until I arrive.' He addressed everyone else. 'Anything you've seen, or will see, doesn't leave this room.'

As Ben drew closer, Esmeralda saw that he was regarding her with an executioner's quiet grimness. She could hear her blood, pumping through her body. It was so loud, like a horse's hooves. Another of those funny memory bubbles broke away and floated to the top of her brain, and she remembered how she used to listen to the drumbeat of her own heart, the only noise there was in that otherwise silent land of the dead.

The Interlude

As soon as she was outside, moving freely and breathing fresh air, Esmeralda thought of a message her mother had left for her. Her father had written her mother's precious words in a small notebook, and read them to the fifteen-year-old Esmeralda while she recovered in hospital. *It isn't the things that are done to you that make you who you are, but how you respond to them.* A message from the land of the dead, for someone who had come back from it. Esmeralda wasn't going to let herself forget that message now.

In front of the late-Victorian building which housed DCS Vane's office was a wooden bench. Esmeralda stood near it with her arms crossed, studying Ben's carefully blank face. 'Are you going to tell me what's going on?'

'Sorry, Esmeralda.' Ben sat down, leaving an empty space beside him. When she remained standing, shaking her head in refusal, he said, 'You heard the DCS.'

'It's not fair that you know something about me that I don't. That lots of you do.'

'If I didn't know the DCS was on his way to update you, I'd tell you now.' Again he gestured towards the bench. 'Please sit down. Take a minute.' This time she relented. Ben raised a hand, as if to touch her, then let it fall.

She'd noticed a gold plaque that was affixed to the centre of the bench's top slat, and turned to read it.

In memory of PC Nicholas Gregory,
May 1973 to August 2001.

A dedicated and professional officer, taken too soon
doing a job he loved.

Always missed, always grateful,
forever in our hearts.

'Do you know anything about PC Gregory?' Esmeralda asked.

'He was my friend,' Ben said. 'We joined together.'

Without thinking, she pressed his hand.

'It was some time ago.' Ben was visibly weighing up what to tell her. 'Nick was working with Whistler,' he said slowly. 'We were all fairly new PCs then. The unofficial version is that Whistler missed a knife on a stop and search and Nick paid the price and bled to death. There's an official version where Whistler's exonerated.'

She remembered Mike telling her to ask Whistler about big fuck-ups. 'Every bad story seems to involve Whistler,' she said, 'and they all end with his blamelessness.'

There was a chill as afternoon edged towards early evening. Esmeralda grabbed her jacket from where she'd dropped it on the bench and slipped it over her blouse, wrapping it tight. She needed to shake Whistler and Thorne out of her head, at least for a few minutes.

She looked up. In the centre of the gravelled roundabout that fronted the building was a pond. 'That dragonfly,' she said, giving Ben time to follow her gaze. 'I think it's a migrant hawker. Do you see the blue and orange flecks?'

Ben studied the dragonfly. 'How did you learn this?'

'I like to be outside.' When Esmeralda and Líria went on a walk, Esmeralda would sometimes lift her face to the sun, close her eyes, and spin in circles until she fell, laughing and dizzy. Líria had grown up thinking this was what everyone did, but the last time, instead of copying Esmeralda as usual, Líria told her mother to stop being so embarrassing. Esmeralda added, 'You see stuff that way.'

'Even at the risk of freezing to death,' Ben said.

'Yes.' The dragonfly was flitting and hovering, posing briefly on a leaf. 'They'll be gone soon. That's probably one of the last we'll see until next summer.'

The bench overlooked the fields and country lanes that sat between the South West Constabulary site and the city below.

'This view's one of the perks of the job.' Ben paused, then said casually, 'A few of us are meeting for a drink tomorrow night, if you're around?'

'I'd love to,' she said, 'but I have a date with Líria after work. Popcorn is involved, and I promised her I'd pick up ice cream from your sister's on my way home.' Since their talk late on Tuesday, Esmeralda had been desperate to spend more time with her daughter.

'Sounds better than beer and crisps,' Ben said.

Esmeralda wondered if Ben was like her, and shared her craving for peace. Maybe he'd had enough chaos and adventure in his life, enough of picking up women and getting drunk with his friends in pubs. She was curious as to how he would respond when she said, 'You don't mean that.' She was also a little startled to hear herself teasing him.

'I do,' he said. 'Mostly.'

The light was draining away quickly. It was already after seven. 'I should text Líria and my dad that I'll be late – I made the mistake of saying I'd be home in time for dinner.' As she took out her phone, she said, 'Did you know Mrs Thorne phoned Sylvie with a long list of grievances about me? She was demanding a word with the DCS, but Sylvie just told her where to find our complaints form.'

'Sylvie told me,' Ben said. 'She likes you, you know.'

Having the Sylvie Seal of Approval made Esmeralda feel a tiny bit better.

'She also gave me the gist of Mrs Thorne's grievances.' Ben shook his head in mock-bewilderment. '*Lack of appropriate awe for her elders and betters. Asks impertinent questions.*'

'Oh dear,' Esmeralda said. 'The injustice wounds me.'

'I forgot to mention *Relentless.*' He made a theatrical gasp. 'And she threw in *Freakishly strong.*' He shook his hand, as if it still hurt. 'Also, *Difficult to refuse.*'

She laughed. 'Mrs Thorne had no trouble refusing me!'

'Maybe I improvised those last ones. But seriously, Esmeralda. You don't need to lose any sleep over Mrs Thorne.'

'I'll try not to.'

'Weren't you going to send a text?'

She gave her phone a comically accusing look, as if surprised to see it in her own hand. 'There was a reason I took this out, wasn't there?!' Quickly, she typed a message to Líria and her dad. **Eat without me. Not sure what time I'll be in. Love you both.** A minute later came a reply from Líria. **Again? :(Can't sleep til ur home.** Instructing Líria not to wait up would be hopeless, so Esmeralda simply wrote, **Look after each other,** then saw Líria was instantly typing another reply, which zinged through mere seconds later. **Grandad made bacalhau com natas. Special treat.** Esmeralda wrote **yum** and a heart emoji, and got back a broken heart from Líria that made her feel guilty and annoyed at once.

She was picturing her dad with her mum's old recipe book, which was in Portuguese. She knew he would have asked Líria to translate, although he could read it perfectly after years of effort to learn the language. The book was extra-precious because her mum had made little pencilled notes in the margins, recording adjustments to ingredients or methods.

As she put the phone away Ben said, 'Líria okay?'

'She's not loving how often I'm late home.'

Ben probably knew this already, given the spyware on her phone, but he simply nodded understandingly and said, 'She's a great kid. I enjoyed meeting her.'

'Likewise,' Esmeralda said, making herself feel better by deciding that she would start to send personal texts to her dad and Líria in Portuguese, and ask them to respond in it too. She smiled to herself to think of her colleagues, Ben included, madly copying and pasting into translation software. She needed to find amusement where she could.

Ben took out his tablet and passed it to her. 'I know you've seen this before, but I thought maybe you'd like another look.'

It was the case file copy of a brief newspaper article published during the summer of 1983, about the ceremony to commemorate Alexander Thorne's gravestone. What especially drew Esmeralda's interest was the accompanying photograph of Thorne at almost eleven, which was not far off Líria's age now. He was so gangly and tall in his dark suit, standing by his mother, and Esmeralda felt a stab of pity for that lost boy, despite her near-hatred for the man. Since meeting Mrs Thorne, Esmeralda understood more about how that child had become the monster who so many called evil.

Mrs Thorne, on the other hand, seemed to be struggling not to appear as if Christmas had come five months early. Still a young woman, she looked ready for her catwalk debut in her black silk coat-dress and elegantly wide-brimmed hat with its net veil, and must have been glad for a chance to bring out her pearl choker and matching earrings.

Esmeralda enlarged the image so she could study it more closely.

'What are you seeing?' Ben asked.

'The roses,' Esmeralda said. 'The breed's called the

Queen's Enchantment. Mrs Thorne has them in her garden too.' Esmeralda was struck by how vivid the petals of crimson and sunburst orange seemed against the pale headstone.

'Interesting,' Ben said. 'Anything else?'

'A bottle of poison with a label saying, "I killed my husband".' Ben laughed and Esmeralda continued. 'Look at Cruella de Vil's hands. Her nails are short and in bad repair, even though she's picture perfect in every other way. Do you see how the earth around the grave appears freshly disturbed?'

'Looks that way, yeah,' he said.

'Maybe she was doing a bit of graveyard gardening, transplanting those flowers so she could oh-so-touchingly memorialise her husband with the Queen's Enchantment. But the thing is, it was summer then, so not the right time of year to move those roses.'

'I'll swing by the grave on my way home tonight,' Ben said. 'Take a look around.'

'Thanks,' Esmeralda said. She didn't want to ambush him, but couldn't help trying again. 'Can I ask you something?' She watched caution shutter his face as if she'd pressed a button that flipped blinds from open to closed, but that didn't stop her from saying, 'It was me, somehow, in that video game trailer, wasn't it?'

'Esmeralda,' he began, and she thought he really was going to tell her, but he cut off at the sound of footsteps, coming from the stone path that twisted its way from the site's maze of buildings towards the former mansion house behind them. 'You're about to get your chance to ask all the questions you want.'

She looked up and saw that Mary, rather than Whistler, was gliding along by the DCS's side. Ben seemed to read her thoughts. As the two of them gathered their things, he said, 'The DCS sent Whistler to talk to the journalist. We want his other devices.'

'Ah,' she said, already moving to join the two senior detectives in their silent procession into the building. 'Thanks for waiting with me, Ben.'

'I enjoyed it.' His voice was quiet, and she knew those words were for her ears only.

Before the door closed behind her, she glanced back a final time. Ben was still standing by the bench, exactly where he was when she last looked. He was watching her, and the grim expression she'd seen for the first time that day was back on his face.

Film Night

Esmeralda was sitting beside Mary Armstrong, trying to maintain her composure as DCS Vane studied her from the other side of his desk. 'What happened earlier today between me and DI Whistler,' she began to say.

The DCS cut her off. 'From what I saw, it looked like he grabbed your wrist when he shouldn't have, and you whacked his arm when you shouldn't have. Let's call it even.'

Esmeralda worried she'd sound like a child if she pointed out that Whistler started it and the altercation was anything but even. 'I've waited as patiently as I can, sir, but if the game trailer Thorne sent was about me, then I should see it like everyone else.'

Mary took off her glasses and let them dangle from the chain she wore around her neck. She pressed a palm to each of her eyes for a few seconds, then said, 'You do need to see it, yes, but I didn't want you to watch it in front of other people.'

She saw Mary's eyes flick to DCS Vane's, then his

almost-imperceptible nod of agreement. He spun his monitor one hundred and eighty degrees, slid his keyboard and mouse along the desk to Mary, then stood up and wheeled his chair to view the screen alongside them.

Film night, thought Esmeralda.

The trailer opened with an aerial shot of a lush jungle. Then came the male voiceover, in a tone of outraged despondency. 'Those feminist bitches are always getting the best games banned.' There was a long pause before the dramatic but hardly surprising proclamation, 'Until now.' The second word was drawn out with ridiculously overplayed emphasis.

The camera drew closer until the specks of what seemed to be two human figures became visible, moving in the deep green. As the pace increased the voice was charged with excitement. '*Men's World* is an immersive, action-packed, role-playing video game like nothing you've ever experienced before.' Esmeralda wondered how the speaker could draw breath after so many adjectives in a row uttered so quickly but still with perfect clarity.

The camera was zeroing in as a different voice, several decibels lower, announced, 'Brought to you by The Actaeon Club.' The trees grew more distinct, as did the two humans, who were weaving their way through the plants, leaping and rushing.

Mary froze the film expertly. 'We've looked at trying to identify the voices,' she said, 'but they're a mix taken from film and game trailers in the public domain. Easy to splice them all together. Lots of off-the-shelf software to do that and achieve professional results.'

'Actaeon's a character from the myths, isn't he?' Esmeralda said.

'He was a hunter,' said Mary, 'who blundered into the woods where the goddess Diana was bathing. She was so enraged that Actaeon saw her naked, she threw water in his face and turned him into a stag. Ended up being torn apart and eaten by his own dogs.'

'Nice. That's definitely the sort of thing Jason Thorne would know,' said Esmeralda as Mary clicked and the film began to unspool again.

The camera was now at ground level and zooming in on the two figures, who could be seen in more detail. A woman was running through the jungle landscape, dark red hair flying as she was chased by a man. Both were seen from behind. They looked astonishingly real and human, as if they were live actors rather than animations.

With a dramatic jump, the camera moved inside the man, so that everything was now seen from his eyes. He, and the viewer, were inhabiting this world and stalking the woman through it.

When the fleeing woman turned to check how close her pursuer was, Esmeralda's heart began to beat faster and she had to work to calm her breathing. Because the face of the woman in the game trailer was her own, superimposed but alive-seeming.

'Harriet Sapphire changed her name to Esmeralda Avelar,' continued the voiceover, 'but The Actaeon Club has found her. No more hiding for this murdering, ungrateful slut. Justice is late but vengeance is swift. And you are the one to carry it out.'

The woman with her face stumbled, cried out as she righted herself, and staggered forward. 'Did you think you could hide from us forever? Harriet Sapphire, we have tried you in absentia, and found you guilty of the vicious murder of Hugo Green. That was how you rewarded him for the attention he paid to you.'

Although Esmeralda was choked with rage and horror, a faraway part of her thought the narrator sounded as absurd as a cartoon villain. The man had caught up to the woman, and as his arms wrapped around her waist and he wrestled her onto the twigs and leaves carpeting the jungle floor, Esmeralda shut her eyes, unable to look.

'Harriet Sapphire was asking for it when Hugo Green took her. She's asking for it from you.' There was a scream, followed by the man's laugh. 'She'll protest. She'll make promises, but you're wise to her lies. She'll try to bargain, but you know not to trust her.'

Esmeralda opened her eyes again, and saw the woman's terrified face, her own face. And though she didn't remember the things that Hugo Green had done to her, she knew that this horror film must be near the truth of those experiences.

She tried to tune it out, but the images and sounds rushed at her in the trailer's final seconds, as if all of the filters she'd been trying to apply failed at once. And she saw that the man's hands were around the woman's throat and her face was blue. And she heard the voice-over again, celebrating what had been done, and what could still be done.

'Not many players get this far, but you are as skilful as they come, a real champion. Now, resume your beautiful journey through the undergrowth. In *Men's World*, justice is served and punishments are true. In *Men's World*, you can take as many as you want. In *Men's World*, you are king, and everything is exactly the way it should be.'

The force's bland, pre-set wallpaper was back on the screen. The contrast of this calm with what had been there a minute before was dizzying.

The key, Esmeralda decided, was both to know and not know at once. To allow a small corner of her mind the realisation that the game trailer existed, but to lock it away in there tightly. Wasn't that what she had been doing since she was fifteen?

'I think I need some water.' Yes, she thought. That is still my voice. I still sound like me. She started to rise to get some only to feel Mary press a bottle into her hand.

'Mike's really good, you know,' Mary said. 'He had it taken down in minutes.'

There was sweat on Esmeralda's brow. She wiped it with the cuff of a sleeve. 'How did they make her have my face?'

'Deep-fake technology,' Mary said. 'They use artificial intelligence to take your image and make it seem like you're saying and doing things you aren't.' She shook her head. 'They're getting better at this stuff. It's harder to spot what's real and what's not.'

Esmeralda was gripping the arm of her chair with

her left hand, and the water with her right. 'How many saw it?'

'There were a dozen views before it was removed,' Mary said. 'Not including us.'

And Ben was part of that us, Esmeralda thought. He'd been in the High Tech Unit a few hours ago, watching those multiple screens on Mary's workstation and clenching his fists. That was how he would always see her, now.

What a good actor he was, sitting beside her on the bench and treating her as if she were a normal person, as if he actually liked her. They'd watched the dragonfly together, and though he never said, and though he acted like her friend, that image of her would have been in his head, and she knew that there was no way to ever get it out.

The Actaeon Club

'Do we know who the viewers were?' Esmeralda wasn't hopeful, but couldn't help but ask.

'No,' Mary said. 'Data protection. We're trying to overcome that but Mike did at least get his contact at the platform to send over the analytics, so we know the viewers were all in the UK, and the video would have landed in their feed through an algorithm.'

'An algorithm looking for what?' Esmeralda asked.

'An algorithm that's wanting to tick at least three boxes,' Mary said. 'Box one would be users who've shown an interest in extreme male rights groups.'

'Such as the Men's Rights activists, the ones whose symbol was engraved on George Rossiter.' She turned to the DCS. 'The manosphere, as we were discussing earlier, sir?'

'Yes,' he said.

'And the other boxes, Mary?' Esmeralda asked.

'Box two would be hard-core misogyny, box three explicit sexual violence.'

'And The Actaeon Club?' Esmeralda asked. 'What do we know about them?'

'One of our contacts at the National Crime Agency has been tracking an extreme male rights group who goes by that name,' Mary said. 'They see Actaeon as a hero who was unfairly punished by a woman.'

'The Actaeon Club is targeting sexual assault victims who've injured or killed their attacker,' said DCS Vane. 'The NCA thinks the club's targets are on what they call *The Diana List* – Diana is to reference the goddess who destroyed Actaeon. The aim is to humiliate and punish these women, to ruin their lives in order to avenge the men.'

'Actaeon are believers,' Mary said. 'They want to be the manosphere's new heroes, rulers of those pathetic little communities of men who hate women. They're trying to discover the anonymous woman behind each of these supposed heroes of theirs and make her identity public. Obviously, it's a set of gruesome couples, linking each of these women to the last man in the world she wants anything to do with.'

'Hugo Green for a start,' said Esmeralda, 'which means me.' She took a small breath, then said, 'We need to make sure they don't discover the identities of any more women. How many members of The Actaeon Club are there in total?'

'The NCA thinks five at most,' said the DCS, 'but more likely only three.'

'The less of them there are,' Mary said, 'the lower their risk of discovery. We think they communicate through encrypted channels. Probably hide their real names even from each other.'

'And Thorne must be one of them,' Esmeralda said, 'if not the founding member.'

'We can be pretty sure from his signature JT that Thorne sent the video to the journalist's phone,' Mary said. 'But we can't assume he made the film himself. To do that takes quite a specific skillset. I mean, Thorne's IT skills are impressive but they're not *that* impressive. We also can't assume that Thorne was the one who actually uploaded the video to the platform. He knew where it would be, and when it would be released, because he sent us the link immediately after it went live. That doesn't mean he put it there.'

'But isn't that odd?' Esmeralda said. 'Because he knew when he sent it that we'd take it down as fast as we could to reduce the impact. So why not just allow it to go live without telling us? It could have done a lot more damage that way, spread further, entrenched itself too deeply for us to unpick.'

Mary nodded. 'We have to allow for the possibility that he doesn't want to damage you.' She broke off, thought briefly, then said, 'He knew the content of that film would hurt you. Did he want to make sure you didn't encounter it alone?'

The DCS scoffed.

Mary shrugged. 'It's a puzzle. Why did Thorne use Esmeralda's initials during the press conference? Why didn't he expose her then, in public, in front of all those journalists?' She shook her head. 'He chose not to. And yet we know he took several photos of her on Monday morning at Ella Brooke's, because one of those images appeared in that first batch of texts from Tuesday, and multiple others that must have been taken at the same time were used in today's game trailer.'

'Even if Thorne didn't make the film himself,' the DCS said, 'and didn't name Esmeralda at the press conference, he still helped The Actaeon Club by supplying her identity and photographs. That second batch of texts from yesterday seems to be referring explicitly to the trailer.'

As the DCS spoke, the ugly words of those messages flashed through her head again and she saw he was right. **Tomorrow your punishment begins.** The texts had also mentioned exposure and a starring role. 'Any guesses about who else Actaeon are targeting?' she asked.

'We'd considered Ella Brooke,' the DCS said, 'but Adam Holderness's death is too recent for her to be on their radar. Plus, Holderness didn't die at Ella's hands.'

Mary shook her head. 'That's a technicality. Ella only beat the holy shit out of him, blinded him in one eye, and got him put away forever. The coverage of Holderness's trial is in the public domain so the details are all out there. The way The Actaeon Club think, they'd hold Witness X – Ella – responsible for taking one of their precious serial killing rapists out of action. Now that he's dead, they'll say she's behind his murder.'

'But that's why Jason Thorne's involvement in The Actaeon Club doesn't make sense,' said Esmeralda. 'There's no way he'd let them target Ella. He'd kill anyone who hurt her.'

'Yes. As Adam Holderness demonstrates.' Mary was clicking and typing as she spoke, a series of moves so automatic she barely needed to think about them. 'The trailer must have been ready to go. Putting your face into

173

it was a relatively late adaptation — I think if they'd discovered the identity of a different target on their *Diana List* before yours, then they'd have gone with that.'

'Do you think the full game exists, ready to be played?' DCS Vane asked.

'Unlikely,' Mary said. 'The trailer on its own does the damage they want to achieve in terms of revealing the woman's identity and trying to humiliate her. Building the actual game is a completely different level of investment, in terms of time, skill, and money.'

DCS Vane put his notebook away in his jacket pocket. 'Take a rest day tomorrow, Esmeralda.'

'No, thank you. I want to be working like everyone else while Thorne's out there.'

'We need to make sure you're not exposed any further,' he said.

'It's hard to imagine any more exposure than I've already had,' she said. 'I told my daughter about what happened when I was fifteen, so there's no risk of her stumbling on that if we don't manage to contain the trailer.'

'Good. But I want you on site, and I don't want to see you before mid-morning tomorrow. Desk work for the time being. Duty of care. We need to shield you.'

'What do you think you're actually shielding me from?' When he didn't answer, she went on. 'The worst has already happened to me. It happened twenty-six years ago.'

But the DCS trumped her point with a more powerful one of his own. 'We can never rule out something even more terrible around the corner,' he said.

FRIDAY, 15 SEPTEMBER 2017

Compliance

Esmeralda woke later than usual on Friday morning, after a night of bad dreams and broken sleep. She sat at her kitchen table sipping coffee, but struggled to concentrate on the case notes that had arrived from Scarlett a few minutes earlier.

The game trailer was horrifying enough, but the worry she really couldn't shake was that she'd arrived home too late the night before to warn her dad and Líria about the altercation with Whistler. She'd also missed any chance that morning, with Líria rushing to school and her dad to the driving range.

Esmeralda tried to tell herself that the press wouldn't be interested in her and Whistler. Surely, she reasoned, there were far more dramatic things happening with the hunt for Thorne. Nonetheless, she couldn't quell her sense of disquiet about the possibility of a photograph ending up in the public domain before she could speak to her little family.

Reminding herself that the best thing she could do

was to contribute to the search for Thorne, she forced her attention back to the case notes. Her interest in what she read helped to clear her head.

The man who'd been caught on CCTV at Florence Close was called Thomas Lederer. He'd received a six-month suspended sentence for burglary after climbing into an open window and stealing a woman's underwear. He'd also been given a restraining order against the victim and ordered to pay her £250 of compensation.

Mr Lederer was a twenty-three-year-old freelancer who did something mysterious in IT. Whatever the investigators had discovered about his business activities had been only what he allowed them to find. This included his work as a bug bounty hunter who hacked into the systems of multi-national companies and government bodies, and was then paid large sums for identifying their vulnerabilities.

These circumstances answered Esmeralda's question as to why Mr Lederer was quick to recognise two detectives and averse to any contact with them, but there was a long list of topics she still wanted to discuss with him. Among these – and Scarlett had highlighted the point – was his likely proficiency in creating bespoke encrypted channels. And in making video game trailers.

When Esmeralda arrived at work at eleven, she went straight to the reception area outside DCS Vane's office. Sylvie was at her desk as usual. Sylvie always made Esmeralda think of the word silvery, and not just because it echoed the sound of Sylvie's name. More than that, it was the cool delicacy of Sylvie's voice and manner, and the exact rightness with which she did everything. Even her hair shimmered in its perfect blonde knot at the nape of her neck, and her eyelids sparkled with faintly lavender powder.

On Sylvie's desk was an arrangement of tabloid newspapers that made Esmeralda realise her disquiet had been warranted. One had a photograph of Esmeralda in action, her ponytail swinging as she slapped Whistler's wrist. The headline said, *DC ESMERALDA AVELAR, MORE VIOLENT THAN JASON THORNE?* Another article zeroed in on Esmeralda's face. *BEAUTY AND THE BEAST – JASON THORNE'S NEW LOVE.* 'Slow news day,' Esmeralda said softly, but she saw how impossible it would be to protect her father and daughter from this.

Sylvie reached out to touch Esmeralda's hand, then put a finger to her lips and signalled to the waiting area with a tilt of her head. Sitting in an armchair in the corner with her eyes closed was Scarlett. Why did she look even more heavily pregnant than when Esmeralda had seen her two days ago, in the Central Image Investigation Unit? Was it because her hands were resting on her increasingly prominent belly? Esmeralda guessed that Sylvie had insisted that Scarlett rest a little, and had also made her the cup of tea that was sitting on a low table to the side of the chair, scenting the air with peppermint.

Esmeralda peered into the DCS's glass-walled office. The interior blinds were open to the reception area, so she could see that he was talking to a furious-looking Ben, who must have felt her eyes on him, because he suddenly noticed her and tilted slightly sideways in his chair before correcting himself and seeming to wipe his face into blankness.

Almost immediately, the DCS's door flew open and Whistler stalked out as if he'd been hiding in a blind spot ready to pounce. 'You,' he said to Esmeralda, as if she were the most awful thing he could have imagined encountering at that moment. 'Why are you here?'

'I need to ask the DCS a question.'

'Ask me.' When she took a step back and said nothing, he added, 'That's an order.'

She considered refusing, but it wasn't worth the trouble she'd bring on herself. 'I want to visit a property, to talk to the man who occupies it. I want to check if DCS Vane is happy for me to do that.' Remembering the DCS's command that she arrive late to work and stay on site, she had been certain he would say no, but still felt impelled to try.

'And you think a routine visit to a property by a DC warrants a personal talk with the DCS? You really think you're special, don't you? Don't waste my time or his, Esme. Just go.' He turned on his heel and slammed out of the building.

She shot a quick glance at Sylvie, who appeared to be occupied with multiple important tasks. This was usually the case, though Esmeralda thought Sylvie was trying to spare her the embarrassment. She pressed her palms against her eyes for a few seconds, to clear her head and calm herself.

'I'll come with you,' said a voice, 'seeing as DI Flub says you can go.' Scarlett's eyes were open and she was watching Esmeralda with her usual interest.

'Flub?' Esmeralda asked.

'Fucking Lazy Useless Bastard,' said Scarlett, in a theatrical whisper. 'Don't take any notice of him, Esmeralda. Anyway, I've had enough of sitting around here.' She muttered what sounded like 'Bloody risk assessments' and shot the words 'Leave it' at Sylvie, though in a tone that was as much affectionate tease as warning. Then, Scarlett took a final sip of peppermint tea and heaved herself to her feet.

A Routine Visit

As she drove, Esmeralda reflected on Scarlett's relegation to desk work, and was anxious about whether this was because of a medical complication that Scarlett hadn't mentioned to her. But Scarlett was adamant about coming along, and had been exceedingly irritated with Esmeralda for even suggesting that she remain on the constabulary site.

Nonetheless, when Esmeralda pulled the car into Adelaide Road and Thomas Lederer's tall but strangely narrow house loomed into view, Scarlett widened her eyes and covered her mouth with a hand in mock horror. The property was near-derelict, the windows so badly smeared with dirt any inhabitants would struggle to see through them.

'So creepy,' Scarlett said. 'Do you think I can protect the baby from contamination if I just – I don't know – maybe not breathe while we're in there?' Scarlett was struggling to unfasten her seatbelt, and Esmeralda had to stop herself from reaching over to help.

'There may be a flaw in that plan,' Esmeralda said. 'Are you sure about this, Scarlett?'

'Old woman,' Scarlett muttered yet again, shooting Esmeralda a dirty look that made her decide she had no choice but to give up on the argument. 'Fuss-pot,' Scarlett added.

'All right,' Esmeralda said, opening the car door. 'I get it. Anyway, I'm glad you're here.'

Paying for excellent legal representation and compensating the victim whose underwear he'd stolen had posed no problem for Mr Lederer. Taking care of the visibly squalid building, however, clearly did, and Esmeralda didn't need a PhD in psychology to ask herself if the decay was a reflection of his mental state rather than his bank balance.

More weed than lawn, the grass was strewn with discarded tins and drug paraphernalia. There were plastic bags, and a syringe, all of which had been pelted by the night's rain. A vomit-green sofa was upside down, leaking stuffing onto the soaked earth.

The two of them sidestepped an overturned black bin that was half-blocking the footpath and surrounded by rotting, sodden rubbish. When they reached the front door, Scarlett said, 'You really are having a week, aren't you?'

'Which horror do you have in mind?'

'Maybe your wrestling match with DI Flub?' Scarlett wrinkled her nose as she considered. 'Actually, Thorne trumps Flub.' Then she shook her head. 'But no again. The winner has to be the video game trailer. By the way, everyone knows about that, despite the DCS's dark warnings.' She made a face of exaggerated foreboding with the last two words. 'Only fair that you know that we know.'

'I got that from your annotations of Thomas Lederer's case notes, but thanks.'

Scarlett added another of her theatrical whispers, 'We all talk.'

Esmeralda was concentrating more than necessary on pushing the button for Flat 1.

'That trailer's not very good, you know,' Scarlett said. 'It may not look that way to you when it's your face they used and your history they revealed, but it's an obvious deep fake.'

Esmeralda wasn't sure she believed this, although when she thought of Ben watching that film she wanted to. Even so, she couldn't forget Mary saying that the video looked very professional. Deep down, she knew Scarlett was just being kind.

'Oh, hello,' said Scarlett. 'He's kicking. Did Líria do that a lot?' she asked.

'I suppose.' Esmeralda was studiously looking at the front door, but she felt Scarlett's eyes on her. She tried the bell again. 'I wonder where Mr Lederer could be,' she said.

'If he invites us in, there's a real chance the smell will make me throw up. They said the sickness would go after the first trimester. That's a big lie. Were you still puking at seven months?'

'It's hard to remember.' Esmeralda added, 'You can wait in the car, Scarlett, if this is making you too queasy.'

'No way I'm doing that. I've told you a million times.

I've had enough of their bloody well-being crap.' Scarlett rolled her eyes. '*Stay on site, Scarlett. Desk work only, Scarlett. Can we pass you the smelling salts, Scarlett?*'

Esmeralda couldn't stifle a grim laugh. 'Let's see if one of Mr Lederer's tenants knows where we might find him.' She pushed the buttons for each of the three flats above his.

'Easy, tiger,' Scarlett said. 'Maybe one bell at a time next time?'

It was a full minute before they heard footsteps coming down the stairs, and the door was opened by a young woman of about twenty. She had wavy brown hair that fell below her shoulders, and she wore a dark green velvet dress covered in bright emerald flowers. The dress peeked out from a lilac and brown leopard-print coat made of fake fur.

'We're hoping to have a chat with Thomas Lederer,' Esmeralda said, 'but he doesn't appear to be home.' They showed their warrant cards.

The woman glanced behind her. 'Oh, he is in. I know this.'

'I see,' Esmeralda said. She noted the woman's name, Adelina Ortega Garcia, and her phone number. 'Maybe you could tell us a little bit about Mr Lederer?'

'He is my landlord, and he is – how do you say – a creep.' A split second later, the hallway went dark. 'And also he is very cheap.' Adelina punched a button that made a bare bulb come back on, casting its low wattage over a threadbare carpet and peeling paint. 'He has the lights with a timer of only sixty seconds.' She was staring at Scarlett. 'I am sorry that there is no chair in this hall for you to rest.' Esmeralda could see Adelina thinking through her words and grammar before she spoke in her perfect but heavily accented English.

'I'm fine standing, but thank you,' said Scarlett.

Adelina did not appear to be convinced, but she went on. 'At times I feel a bit of pity for him. I am a waitress, and brought him some leftovers from the restaurant last month – he is so thin – and now he stares at me all the time.'

'Would you be more comfortable speaking Spanish, Adelina?' Scarlett asked. 'DC Avelar is fluent.'

'Do you speak it too?' Adelina asked Scarlett. When Scarlett shook her head, Adelina said, 'Then no thank you. It would be rude to have a conversation if you cannot understand too.'

'Your English is wonderful, anyway,' Scarlett said, and Esmeralda agreed.

'I like to practise.' Adelina punched the button for the lights again. 'He keeps his door open waiting for me to come or go.' She pointed, and Esmeralda could see a crack of light at the end of the hallway. 'I am the only other person who lives here.'

'Do you feel at all threatened by Mr Lederer's behaviour?' Esmeralda asked.

'He is not dangerous. Only disgusting.' Adelina appeared puzzled. 'I think maybe when I am not in my flat he has a glance at my things. They move a little. Sometimes they are missing, but then I find them again.'

Esmeralda handed Adelina her card. 'You don't have to put up with that. If you feel worried by anything Mr Lederer does you can phone me on this number.'

'Thank you, but I don't have the certainty nor the proofs.'

'Adelina,' Scarlett said. 'We can put you in touch with an organisation that will help you find a better place to live.'

'You are nice,' Adelina said. 'But it is not always so bad. And the flat is all I can afford. Last night also his door was open when I returned late from work. Usually he sticks his head out to watch me, but I didn't see him. Although I heard him.'

'What did you hear?' Scarlett asked.

'Only his voice. But often he talks to himself when he is alone.'

'And what time exactly was this?' Scarlett asked.

'Soon after midnight, I think,' Adelina said.

'And is the door in the same position now as it was then?' Esmeralda asked.

'Perhaps the gap is a little less,' Adelina said. 'But I do not have the certainty.'

'And he made no appearance today either?' said Esmeralda, deciding enough time had lapsed to punch the bell for Flat 1 again. The noise was louder with the door to the building open.

'No,' Adelina said.

'And you didn't hear him this morning?' asked Scarlett.

'No.' Adelina glanced at the bright orange face of her wristwatch. 'Sorry, but I have to leave for work now. I will let you go in first.'

Adelina stepped outside, allowing Esmeralda and Scarlett to pass her and enter the building. 'Enchanted to meet you,' she said. Then she hurried away along the rubbish-strewn path and disappeared from their sight.

The Lair of the Blue Man

Esmeralda knocked firmly on Thomas Lederer's door, using her shoe to stop it from opening beyond the existing gap. 'Mr Lederer?' she called out. 'My name is Detective Constable Avelar. I'm here with my colleague, Detective Constable Woodfield, and we would really like to talk to you.' She knocked again, still louder. 'Mr Lederer?'

Esmeralda turned to Scarlett, grateful to have someone more experienced along to make sure she was doing everything right. 'Do you think a welfare check is justified? We have the continued lack of response since last night and now the open door.'

'I think it is,' said Scarlett.

'Right.' Esmeralda had come prepared with two pairs of blue gloves in her jacket pocket, because she liked to protect herself with double layers. She pulled them out and offered a pair to Scarlett, who took it with thanks.

'Mr Lederer? This is the police. We're about to enter

your property to check that you're okay, but we'll stop if you call out.'

There was still nothing. Scarlett gave her a nod and Esmeralda stepped in, noting two unbolted Chubb locks and a dangling chain on the doorframe. The stench of baked-in tobacco smoke and stale sweat made her want to cover her nose with a hand. 'Stay at the door if the smell's too much,' she said in a low voice, but Scarlett hissed her name in irritation and followed close.

Although the grubby curtains were drawn, a bare and apparently low-watt bulb cast a feeble light from the centre of the cracked ceiling, though this was boosted by the additional glow of multiple laptop screens, all left on.

Esmeralda began to cross the room. As she moved, she passed a single counter with a sink that contained several centimetres of putrid water, an open tin of congealed baked beans, and a half-eaten pot of instant noodles. Beside the sink was a grease-smeared hotplate, plugged in and no doubt an electrical hazard, as well as a toothbrush with the bristles bent and dark dots caught between them.

A full-length looking glass had been turned to reflect the wall. Everything in this place was crazy, a kind of mad version of Wonderland, but Esmeralda was saddened by the thought that Thomas Lederer found his own appearance too painful to contemplate.

She turned the knob of a door, and was hit by the reek of urine and the sight of a mould-covered shower. 'I've visited petrol station loos that are infinitely less disgusting,' she said, closing the door quickly.

Scarlett was gagging and covering her mouth. Though still retching, she managed to say, 'Come have a look at this.'

Esmeralda went to join Scarlett at what she designated in her own head as Laptop Number 1. The machine rested on a mildewed chest of drawers and displayed a screensaver that must have been Thomas Lederer's bespoke creation. At the centre of a pulsing image was the simple illustration of a blue man, the kind you would find on the door to a public loo, though this one had his mouth arranged in a frown. The man was encircled by strands of what Esmeralda first thought to be jewellery but then realised was barbed wire. Outside these strands were a dozen bright pink women, all smiling.

The message, clearly, was that the man was in isolation and couldn't touch a single one of the cheerful female figures. Esmeralda knew this was a variation of an image that incels sometimes used. All at once, the chains evaporated, a crown materialised on top of the man's head, the corners of his lips turned from down in a frown to up in a smile, and the women vanished briefly before popping back, each with a noose around her neck and a tongue falling grotesquely out of her mouth. The sequence then replayed.

'Good to see a young man using his IT skills so creatively,' Scarlett said.

Esmeralda thought she might be feeling as nauseated as Scarlett. She pictured George Rossiter and the Men's Rights symbol engraved on his torso. This incel iconography also came from the manosphere, though a different faction.

'Let's have a look at the other machines,' Scarlett said. 'We'll need to get Mary Armstrong's team on this. Be good to take a quick survey so we can brief her.'

The second and third laptops sat side by side on two rickety wooden chairs that had been pushed together in the corner of the room.

'Even with the gloves don't touch anything,' Scarlett reminded her. 'We don't want to mess with how the machines have been left.'

'I thought incels were supposed to be ultra security conscious,' Esmeralda said. 'As in . . . super-duper secretive.'

'They often are.'

'Then why haven't these machines powered off through inactivity?' Esmeralda asked. 'The sleep mode function must have been disabled. Surely someone as tech-savvy as Thomas Lederer wouldn't leave his machines vulnerable like that if he stepped away?'

'Nope,' Scarlett said. 'He wouldn't. No way.'

They were scanning the Instagram page left open on Laptop 2, for an actress whose affair with a married director had recently been exposed. Using a fake name, Thomas Lederer had commented on a photograph of the actress posing in a dinner jacket that she wore over her underwear and bra. u r a hor riding a cock carasel, u no u cant close your legs u cum-dumpster, kepe um open cuss were cumming for u, gonna stuff all your holes then were b-heding u.

'Nice chap,' Scarlett said.

'I don't suppose Mr Lederer's written anything like that to the man she had the affair with,' Esmeralda said, but her real attention was on Scarlett, who was beginning to appear clammy and pale. She accepted that Scarlett didn't want to be treated any differently because of her pregnancy, and she had been trying to refrain from further comment, but Esmeralda's anxiety was growing. 'Please go wait outside,' she said. 'I can have a quick look at the other laptops while you call Mary.'

'I said no. You're worse than Sylvie.' Scarlett was studying Laptop Number 3, which had been left open on a Facebook post from a barristers' chambers that highlighted their successful prosecution of a rapist by one of their female barristers. Thomas Lederer had added his own comment from what must have been another anonymous social media account. drink bleach bich im gonna find u an kil u an fuk u up the ass

Scarlett moved to the opposite corner of the room, to take a look at Laptop Number 4. She was gripping the edge of the rickety table which held the machine. Esmeralda pulled out the chair, expecting Scarlett to be angry. Instead, she gave Esmeralda's wrist a weak but grateful squeeze and sat down, taking care to avoid any accidental contact with a saucer that was overflowing with cigarette butts.

Another live screen had been split into two windows. The first of these displayed a Tweet from a feminist politician who was angry that a man had been sentenced to a mere two years of wearing an electronic tag for stalking a female journalist. Using yet another fake account, Thomas Lederer had written, She is lucky to be admired considering her troll-like face. Females are such hypocrites, always saying the opposite of what they feel.

Bet she loved the attention. The phrasing made Esmeralda think of Mrs Thorne, who also referred to women as females. And of DI Whistler too. **Attention seeking. Press whore.**

The second window contained a newspaper article by an academic on the subject of male violence against women. To the unmoderated comments, Mr Lederer had added his own. **YOU ARE NEXT YOU TREACHEROUS WORTHLESS FUCKiNG DEAD SLAG.**

'He could market that skill of his writing love letters,' Scarlett said. 'We should name this investigation Operation Cyrano de Bergerac. And you have to hand it to him – I mean, the way he keeps changing his register is kind of impressive. In a horrible way, but still . . . Don't you love that he can spell treacherous but not bitch?'

Esmeralda took a short, sharp breath, though she kept her voice light when she said, 'I'm not sure love is quite the word I'd use, but I see your point.' The imperfect renditions of bad English made her think of the texts she'd been sent. Thomas Lederer's multiple personae had much in common with those poisonous messages. And the bug-bounty-hunting Mr Lederer was a genius at navigating the online world illegally and anonymously. Esmeralda was sure he had made his malicious communications untraceable.

'Go check that one.' Scarlett pointed to Laptop Number 5, which was on the floor beneath the horrifically filthy curtains. 'Then we can leave. There's no way I'll be able to bend that far and I am not sitting on the floor. I swear I just saw something crawling on it.'

The machine had been placed on the carpet beside an

overturned games console that appeared to have been tossed there. Esmeralda crouched to take a closer look. 'Oh,' she said, nearly losing her balance.

'What?' said Scarlett. 'What is it? Tell me.'

Esmeralda's voice was flat, as if in inverse proportion to what she was feeling. 'Top and centre, in a Gothic script, it says "Shrine to The Fallen". Below this are photos of three men. They're labelled "Hugo Green", "Rhys Morgan", and "Adam Holderness".'

'Three absolute gentlemen,' said Scarlett, her voice dripping sarcasm.

'Who is Rhys Morgan?' Esmeralda asked. 'It feels like I've heard that name before.'

'He was a stalker,' Scarlett said. 'His victim killed him in self-defence. It's a miracle she's alive at all.' Scarlett was looking at Esmeralda. 'But sometimes miracles happen.'

'I suppose they do.'

'She was given anonymity, like you and Ella. Morgan had clearly date-raped her, which was when the obsessive behaviour started, but she hadn't reported it because she thought we wouldn't take her seriously.' Scarlett shook her head. 'She wasn't wrong.'

Esmeralda had lost count of the number of female detectives who'd told her they wouldn't report a rape if it happened to them. 'What would be the point?' Dinah had said. 'It would end up as another NFA.' Esmeralda had forgotten what the acronym stood for and secretly looked it up. No Further Action.

'Tell me more about what you're seeing on the screen, Esmeralda,' Scarlett said.

'Each of the men has a remembrance wreath suspended

over his head, like a halo.' Despite the fact that this only confirmed the growing suspicions that she and Scarlett shared about Thomas Lederer's skillset and likely involvement, Esmeralda was feeling too sick to scorn the absurdity of those wreaths. 'There's a strip of rolling subtitles, below the photos.'

'Read it,' Scarlett said. 'Exact words. From the beginning so I can hear all of it.'

Esmeralda read. '*The Actaeon Club honours its great heroes. We seek. We expose. We avenge. Diana List Status Update 1: Hugo Green, identified and in progress. Diana List Status Update 2: Rhys Morgan, searching. Diana List Status Update 3: Adam Holderness, likely hit, awaiting confirmation.*' Esmeralda returned to Scarlett's side. 'The more we see, the more certain I am that somebody wanted us to find the screens like this.'

Scarlett touched Esmeralda's arm, a gesture meant to comfort. 'We know what "identified and in progress" means with respect to Hugo Green after yesterday's video game trailer. The texts you were sent show that too. I'm assuming "likely hit, awaiting confirmation" for Adam Holderness means they may have identified Ella Brooke but aren't yet certain.'

Esmeralda was marvelling that Scarlett could listen so attentively and recall so perfectly. 'If Jason Thorne has anything to do with The Actaeon Club,' Esmeralda said, 'and we're already pretty certain that he does, then he's not going to allow them anywhere near Ella.'

'I agree.' Scarlett was still paler than Esmeralda liked, but perhaps she had regained a bit of colour while sitting down.

'Actaeon haven't worked out the identity of Rhys Morgan's victim,' Esmeralda said. 'We need to make sure they don't.'

'And that they don't get any further with Ella Brooke,' Scarlett said.

'Are you happy to get hold of High Tech so they can come and look at these machines?' Scarlett was already taking out her phone as Esmeralda crossed the room. 'I'm going to have a quick look in the wardrobe, in case there's another one in there.'

Her gloved hand was on the handle of one of the slatted double doors, and she pulled it open. But it wasn't the built-in wardrobe it appeared to be from outside. It was, in fact, a box room, and it was being used as a small bedroom.

Stick with the training, Esmeralda told herself. Follow the actions you've been taught. But she was muddled, and the more she stared at the body on the single bed, trying to process what she was seeing, and what she needed to do, the more muddled she became.

The Game Maker

Standing in the doorway of what looked like a grisly theatre set, Esmeralda was viewing the dead man from the side. A blanket had been arranged over his lower half, but he was exposed from the waist up. The bedding was stained red beneath his torso, though his skin was clean. She realised that whoever did this had washed away the mess from the victim's chest as they worked. There'd been no visible traces of blood anywhere else in the flat.

There was a noose around the man's neck, which was attached to the headboard of the metal bedframe. Each wrist or ankle was bound to one of the bed's four posts. A gag covered his mouth, though enough of the face was visible for Esmeralda to recognise Thomas Lederer from his custody photo. Engraved on the bare torso was an exact duplicate of one of the frowning men from the incel screensaver, but in this case the man was the one hanging from the scaffold with a tongue falling out of his mouth. In the lower-right corner of this carving were the initials *JT*, the artist's signature.

Esmeralda knew she couldn't enter the room and risk contaminating the evidence. Having stumbled onto a murder scene with no proper barrier clothing, wearing nothing of use beyond her blue gloves, she continued to look in from the doorway. Her throat was tight with pity and horror for this lost man who'd been so filled with hate.

During training, Esmeralda had been shown photographs of dead people where they'd been found. She always noticed the signs of how they were connected to the living, to the people who loved them and would miss them. Two cups of tea, discarded on a coffee table. Family photographs on a chimney-piece in the background. A child's toybox. But nowhere in Thomas Lederer's flat was there a sign that he was loved by anybody. Finding this man in his sad world was much worse than looking at George Rossiter in a setting so remote from his own life.

There was a bedside table on the far side. On it was a framed and doctored photograph of Thomas with his arm around Adelina. The faked image was done with heartbreaking clumsiness for someone as tech-savvy as Thomas Lederer, as if a child had cut Adelina out of a magazine and pasted her in. Esmeralda wondered why he had chosen to do it this way. Had he thought it was somehow more real? Adelina had the appearance of a film star who'd been unknowingly snapped, so Esmeralda would need to mention to High Tech that there were likely to be hidden cameras in the building.

She replayed Adelina's point about hearing Thomas's voice just after midnight. It was likely that he'd been talking to his murderer then. Maybe he'd even invited him in. The killer had come prepared and been in control. If he'd left any traces, it was because he wanted them found. These were Esmeralda's thoughts when something else caught her eye.

On the floor, half a metre away, was a note on blood-stained A4 paper. The writing was large and clear, so she needed to lean forward only a little to read it.

Mr Lederer and I have had an entertaining visit. You will see that he kindly gave me a lesson in Advanced IT. There is a cliché that imitation is the highest form of flattery, but I explained to Mr Lederer that his attempts to implicate me in the texts and rhymes he sent to Esmeralda were neither convincing nor well-received.

Tell Esmeralda that this is to avenge her, and I am filled with admiration. Tell Ella I did this to protect her, and that she should be proud of her nephew for his skills as a photographer and spy – I'm not often taken by surprise, but he managed it. Finally, tell them both that I have changed. Now, I only kill bad people. A man must have his fun, but it is important to be useful and just. Our world is certainly improved by Little Thomas's removal.

JT.

The *JT* with which Thorne signed the note was as beautiful as calligraphy. It was the same *JT* he'd engraved on Thomas Lederer's torso. The same *JT* Esmeralda had seen in crime scene photographs of the women he'd murdered, who he decorated with tendrils and daisies. The same

JT he added to the exquisite toys and furniture he carved from wood. The same *JT* that only partly remained on George Rossiter's decomposing chest. The same *JT* with which he'd ended the letter he left for her in the Pleasure Gardens beside the water lily. And the same *JT* he'd ordered his friend to carve so crudely into Adam Holderness's skin.

At last, Esmeralda found her voice. 'Thomas Lederer is dead, Scarlett. It's looking like Thorne's work, and he wants us to know it. Can you call it in, please? We'll need the coroner, and pathologist, and . . .'

She threw in anything she could think of, jumbling the order, not able to work out the logical sequence of priorities, trying to recall who'd been present on that motorway access road only two days earlier. Uniform, the police surgeon, cordon officers, forensics, a Senior Investigating Officer and a Crime Scene Manager, an exhibits officer, videographers and photographers. When her eye fell on the wall to her right, she stopped speaking.

How had she not noticed? Was it because she'd been so absorbed in studying the body and reading JT's note she hadn't looked? Hanging there, directly opposite Thomas's bed, was a home-made poster, pieced together from four A4-pages that he must have produced on the home printer she'd seen on a small table. It was a still image from the game trailer, with the woman viewed from behind as she ran through the jungle, the man's shadow looming behind her.

'It's looking like we were right to wonder if Thomas Lederer made the game trailer,' she said, before resuming her list. 'So we'll need your friends in the Central Image

Investigation Unit, and maybe Digital Forensics.' She shook her head as if trying to clear the screen of an Etch A Sketch where she'd muddled the design and needed to start over. 'I doubt we'll find Thomas's phone, but maybe Thorne has it – he's left a note on the floor and he mentions his outrage that Thomas tried to frame him for the bad rhymes in those texts.'

There was a groan. Esmeralda spun round to see Scarlett, still sitting in the chair.

'I – I'm not feeling very . . .' Scarlett said, but she wasn't able to finish the sentence. Her head wobbled like a heavy flower on too thin a stalk, her eyes fluttered closed, and she began to topple over.

Before Scarlett hit the floor, Esmeralda sped across the room and managed to catch her. As she kicked the chair out of the way and lowered Scarlett onto her left side, her only thought was that she had to somehow protect Scarlett's head as well as her baby.

Fumbling in her utility belt, Esmeralda managed to hit the red Code Zero button of her police radio and say that a pregnant officer was down. Following the directions of a voice that was so calm it seemed to be generated by artificial intelligence, Esmeralda checked for an airway, made sure nothing was blocking Scarlett's nose or mouth, confirmed that her chest was rising and falling, noted that there didn't seem to be any liquid or blood coming from between her legs. She felt Scarlett's wrist for a pulse and after a fumble that nearly made Esmeralda's own heart stop, found it, throbbing faintly. Finally, she pulled Scarlett's left knee up towards her chest.

It was essential that the paramedics be able to get in. There was no alternative but to leave Scarlett briefly to run to the door of the building and open it, moving as fast as she could. She was away for less than a minute, pausing to insert a fat stack of junk mail in the crack of the door to stop it from closing.

It was only after she'd done everything she could for Scarlett that Esmeralda explained into her radio that they'd stumbled on a murder scene, understanding in her own bones what it meant to triage. Despite having been drilled in the principle of the golden hour and the need to secure significant material before it was lost, all that mattered was the unconscious woman.

Esmeralda lowered herself back onto the floor beside Scarlett. Lightly, fearfully, she touched Scarlett, pulled her hand away, hovered it, then lowered it once more. A sob caught in her throat when she felt a kind of wave of movement below the fabric of Scarlett's maternity top, as if a sea creature were turning just below the surface of murky water.

She smoothed Scarlett's hair from her face, forgetting that somebody was listening at the other end of the radio as she whispered, 'It's okay, Scarlett. You're okay. You're going to be fine. Your little one is too. He just said hi to me.'

She repeated the words again and again, as if in prayer, trying to believe that if she said them enough times they would have to come true. Finally, after what seemed like hours but was really only minutes, Esmeralda heard the beautiful noise of sirens and saw the dim blue of flashing lights on the other side of the filthy curtains.

Late Evening

As soon as the ambulance sped away with Scarlett, Esmeralda helped the first responders to set up an emergency cordon. Other officers arrived quickly, trailing into Thomas Lederer's house single file. They were as anonymous and inhuman in their hooded white jumpsuits and shoe covers and gloves as Esmeralda herself had been when she visited the deposition site for George Rossiter's body two days earlier.

The Senior Investigating Officer was DS Hannah Beresford. The surprising sum of her disparate features – short baby hair, lanky build, and elfin chin, nose, and ears – was a kind of refined authority that made everyone rush to do her bidding. Esmeralda stood with DS Beresford and the Crime Scene Manager, explaining the moves she and Scarlett had made and what they had observed.

When Esmeralda was walking to her car to leave Adelaide Road, she crossed paths with Dinah, who said, 'You did well – don't let anyone tell you otherwise.' Dinah was looking in Whistler's direction as she spoke. Whistler was huddled with DCS Vane and Ben, and all three men looked as grim as Esmeralda felt.

She thought she'd hit saturation point when that second batch of texts had induced a panic attack in front of Ben two days ago, but she hadn't properly imagined then what saturation really was. Her fear for Scarlett and her baby was whirring at such a high pitch in her head and chest and heart she thought she just might scream.

Esmeralda was in a half-trance as she sat on the hospital's vinyl-padded chair, alone in the maternity unit's reception area. This was where her father had waited in shock as she gave birth to Líria nearly eleven years ago. It was so quiet, so blessedly peaceful here, after the whirlwind of Adelaide Road, though the buzzing in her ears continued, and she felt the beat of her own heart, pulsing in her temples.

According to the hospital clock, it was nearly eleven when the double doors next swung open and she looked up to see a midwife walk through them, leaving the delivery suites and postnatal wards behind. Esmeralda knew from the badge the midwife wore on her blue smock that her name was Nina Murray.

Earlier, Nina had met Esmeralda's anxious questions with kind patience, and promised to return to talk to her as soon as she was able. Although Esmeralda had feared that Nina would forget, here she was. 'They did an emergency caesarean,' Nina said, taking the chair beside Esmeralda's. 'Scarlett is still in the theatre recovery area under observation but baby's gone to Neonatal Intensive Care – his other mum is with him.'

Esmeralda gulped, imagining Rosie's shock and terror. 'But he's two months early.'

Nina gave Esmeralda's arm a gentle squeeze just as a man entered, headed towards them, and stood close. There was no hovering or hesitation, no sign that he had any awareness of the possibility that he was interrupting, or intruding where he wasn't wanted.

'Detective Chief Superintendent Dominic Vane,' he said to Nina, putting out a hand that the midwife hesitated to take, then touched only briefly. 'I was hoping you could fill me in on how Scarlett Woodfield's doing.'

'I'm not able to discuss my patients with you.' Nina's voice had changed. There was a stiffness in her tone that hadn't been there when she spoke to Esmeralda, and Esmeralda had a faraway thought that perhaps it was his smooth authority in the context of work that made people appear to like the DCS. Without that armour, not everyone did.

Nina turned from DCS Vane, to dismiss him, which wasn't a response he was used to or appeared to enjoy, and Esmeralda admired this lack of awe. 'Why don't you go home now, love?' Nina said, pressing Esmeralda's hand a final time before standing.

'Sounds like good advice,' said DCS Vane.

As Nina began to walk towards the security doors, DCS Vane called out, 'Nina, I'd be grateful for a word.'

Nina turned, frowning, but agreed with a curt nod and waited near the doors.

The man standing before Esmeralda now was nothing like the solicitous mentor of the previous days. 'I told you to remain on site today,' he said, when he was sure

Nina was out of earshot. 'You ignored my order.' His icy blue eyes were impenetrable, without depth. It made her cold to look at them.

'I didn't ignore your order. I tried to see you late this morning to explain about the need to visit Thomas Lederer, but you were busy with DS Sachs. DI Whistler came out of your office and when I said I was waiting to ask you a question he insisted that I ask him instead. So I did, and DI Whistler told me to go.'

'Look,' the DCS said, seeming to consider whether this could be true, and why Whistler hadn't admitted it. 'You've had a run of hellish shifts. Take this weekend off and get some proper rest. There's a lot of interviewing and intelligence gathering to do now, so leave that in other people's hands.'

Her dismay must have been visible, because his expression softened and he added, 'We'll catch you up at Monday morning's briefing – you've earned the right to be looped in. But after that you will turn around and go home and work there flexibly for the rest of the week. I'll get Well-Being Support to contact you.'

'Sir,' she began to say.

'No stigma. You've been through it the past few days.' He looked over his shoulder. 'I need to go. That midwife clearly isn't happy waiting for me.' Moving out of Esmeralda's realm already, he strode briskly away towards Nina.

She had missed film night with Líria, sending sorry texts as she waited in the hospital foyer. At first, Líria had replied furiously, then she had gone quiet.

Filled with guilt and self-recrimination, Esmeralda fumbled with the machine to pay for her parking. At last, she stepped outside. When she felt a shadow behind her, she spun around, ready to smash her car keys into the face of any threat.

A familiar-looking man she was too exhausted to place staggered backwards, looking terrified and holding up his hands to defend himself. 'Sorry, DC Avelar,' the man said. 'I know it's late, but I'd be grateful for five minutes of your time . . .' He was short and stocky, with a head she thought he deliberately shaved as a fashion choice.

She continued to maintain her fight-ready stance. 'Who are you?'

'Larry Fawcett.' He put out a hand that Esmeralda didn't take. It hung there, embarrassingly, for several seconds before he let it drop back to his side. 'I was at the police press conference yesterday. I'm the journalist Jason Thorne phoned.'

'How did you find me here?'

'Things are busy in Adelaide Road.' He tapped the top of his head three times with an index finger, as if to call attention to his exceptional brain. 'I was waiting outside the police cordon in my car. I saw you speed away in yours and followed you here.'

'Why?' She was cursing herself for her subpar anti-surveillance measures.

'I want to know what happened at Adelaide Road. So how about you tell me something interesting, and in exchange I tell you something?'

After a few seconds she said, 'How about I tell you there are lives at stake and this isn't a game where we take turns? If you have something relevant to say, you say it.'

Fawcett appeared to consider this. 'How about I interview you? Breakfast television. You'd be perfect, a total star. Your little squabble with DI Whistler's already made the tabloids. How about you tell your side of the story?'

She blew out air in disgust. 'Not happening.'

'But you're a natural. They'd love you. You look right – you sound right – you have the right.'

'You have got to be joking. I bet you trot out that seduction line about triple rights on a daily basis.'

'Look. We both know there's a lifetime anonymity order here from when you were a child, so identifying you as the teenager who escaped Hugo Green is a criminal offence.'

She felt as if a stone had landed in her stomach. 'You figured that out from the game trailer. You saw it, somehow.' Her voice sounded dead. She thought her heart was too.

'Thorne's text with the game trailer link went to an iPad I neglected to mention to DI Whistler. The real problem for you is that the anonymity order isn't going to hold up in the internet age. Pretty much anybody who digs can discover your whole family tree.'

'I don't need you to explain the law to me.' She blinked hard.

'Look.' He shrugged, as if helplessly. 'Jason Thorne's mother's been in touch, wanting to tell me her sob story about the way you treated her when you visited her house.'

'Mrs Thorne can say what she likes. I don't discuss cases. Anyway, why don't you go on television and talk about it all yourself? Increase your following. Maybe get yourself a promotion. You can tell them all about Hugo Green too. Make up whatever you like about Thorne's mother. Throw in my former name and you may even get your own show.' She bit her lip, then said, 'Show them the game trailer. I bet you made a copy.'

His face went redder. 'I wouldn't expose you.'

That's when it came to her. 'Thorne threatened you, didn't he? Before you handed your phone to DCS Vane, Thorne told you not to talk. He told you not to dare share anything that came to your number, didn't he? That's why you sat on the game trailer.'

'No it isn't. It's because I have a code. Because I have integrity.' His lips and hands were trembling.

'But you're frightened,' she said softly.

'Of course I'm fucking frightened,' he said. 'We're talking about Jason bloody Thorne, not a fluffy kitten.'

'You should get back in touch with DI Whistler and tell him Thorne threatened you.'

'I share Jason Thorne's preference for talking to you. Have you spoken privately to him, DC Avelar? One to one? There seems to be a special connection there . . .'

Esmeralda rolled her eyes and began to move away. When she felt the journalist's hand on her wrist she whirled round, throwing him off her. 'You've no right to touch me.'

'I'm sorry,' he said, steadying himself. 'And my comment about the connection between you and Thorne was uncalled for. He's clearly got a thing for you, but that's solely from his deranged point of view. Say you accept my apology, DC Avelar. I mean it sincerely.'

'I accept,' she said quietly.

'Thank you.' He stretched out a hand, which she saw was shaking, to offer her a card with his contact details. 'In case you change your mind about an interview.'

She knew she wouldn't, but a small spark of pity that he probably didn't deserve prompted her to take the card and slip it into her bag. 'Goodnight, Mr Fawcett,' she said. 'Be careful out there.'

Part III: Nemesis

At last he came to the room where Talia was lying, as if enchanted; and when the king saw her, he called to her, thinking that she was asleep, but in vain, for she still slept on, however loud he called. So, after admiring her beauty awhile, the king returned home to his kingdom, where for a long time he forgot all that had happened.

Meanwhile Talia gave birth to little twins, one a boy and the other a girl, who looked like two little jewels . . .

Giambattista Basile, 'Sun, Moon and Talia', from *The Pentamerone, Or, The Story of Stories, Fun for the Little Ones*

SUNDAY, 17 SEPTEMBER 2017

The Doctor

Ben was growing increasingly disturbed by the idea that Dominic Vane was using Esmeralda as bait in Operation Leopard, and that this was why he'd wanted her in Major Crime in the first place. The note Thorne left at the scene of Thomas Lederer's grimly staged murder had certainly reinforced the DCS's recent suspicion that Esmeralda might be hiding something. Every phase of her life was now being investigated, and Ben, lucky man that he was, had been told to examine the period around the birth of her baby.

As he drove into the near-deserted hospital car park that Esmeralda had left late on Friday night, Ben was wondering if she'd deliberately avoided him at Adelaide Road. If she were to learn that he was snooping into her past, she might close him out completely. But for now, Ben didn't see what choice he had.

It wasn't yet seven on a Sunday morning, so all was quiet as Ben headed towards the maternity unit entrance. He walked by what he guessed to be a new father, sitting on a low wall and smoking despite the clearly displayed sign saying it was forbidden on hospital grounds.

Sylvie had been working overtime since Thorne's escape, and had spent a good part of the previous day performing her usual impossible magic to arrange this meeting. As she'd instructed, Ben followed the signs pointing him to the Antenatal Unit. It was shut for the weekend and the chairs in the centre of the large waiting area were empty, the doors of the examination rooms that lined the walls closed.

Ben cleared his throat, knocked on the door of Exam Room 7, and was greeted by Dr Catherine Tilly, the consultant obstetrician who had overseen Líria's birth nearly eleven years earlier. Dr Tilly aimed a tight, professional smile at him. 'Please,' she said, gesturing towards a visitor's chair at the side of a laminate desk. She smoothed her charcoal-grey pencil skirt and pushed the sleeves of her cashmere sweater up above her elbows.

As he sat, Ben had the impression that the imperious and elegantly slim Dr Tilly would be as comfortable having tea with the Queen as she was in her maternity unit kingdom. 'Thank you for agreeing to see me,' he said, taking note of the props on the other side of the room. There was an examination table, a sink with drawers and cupboards beneath it, and an ultrasound machine sitting on top of a metal cart with wheels.

A folder sat on the desk. It was labelled ESMERALDA AVELAR, DOB 29-02-1976. 'I went by the Medical Records building this morning,' Dr Tilly said. 'The good news is that I had no trouble locating the maternity notes your colleague requested. The bad news, I'm afraid, is that patient confidentiality means that there is nothing in the medical records we hold for this patient that is sharable. I'm sorry for your wasted journey, DS Sachs.' With these words, Dr Tilly rose to show Ben out.

He remained seated, pretending not to notice the doctor's almost-imperceptible frown. No doubt she was accustomed to a small posse of terrified junior doctors trailing behind her, jumping to obey her commands.

'DS Sachs?' she said, opening the door. 'I have a caesarean section to perform this morning on a high-risk patient. I really must be getting on.'

'Your duty of confidentiality can be set aside to prevent or detect serious crime,' he said, 'and that's the circumstance you and I find ourselves in.'

'You'll need a court order, then,' she said, 'or the patient's written consent.'

Ben knew when to back off and try a different approach. 'Does it help if I assure you that I'm not seeking this information to hurt or prosecute Esmeralda, but to protect her?' Despite his knowledge that she passionately wanted to be part of the hunt for Thorne, Ben wanted to punch Dominic Vane for keeping her in play.

Dr Tilly didn't move from the door. 'I can't take this conversation any further if you don't tell me what this is really about.'

He nodded slowly. 'I can say – and I ask you to keep this in confidence – that Esmeralda is on the radar of an extremely dangerous man. This is someone who has murdered several women, and it seems he's now become active again. We need to understand why she has come to his notice. Doing this may well help us to catch him and save lives, including Esmeralda's own.'

The doctor let go of the door and it slowly swung closed. 'You're talking about Jason Thorne,' she said, returning to her chair. 'I saw the police press conference on Thursday.'

The carefully edited version, Ben thought. 'We're looking at every period of Esmeralda's life,' he said. 'It may be that something occurred around the time she was pregnant. That's why I am *requesting* these disclosures.'

'We will need to proceed with great care,' she said.

'I agree,' Ben said. 'Is it okay if I begin by asking a few simple questions?' She nodded her consent. 'Did you re-read Esmeralda's medical notes before I arrived?'

'Of course.'

'Was that because you couldn't remember her? I realise it was over a decade ago.'

'I often think of Esmeralda,' Dr Tilly said. 'I didn't need the help of yesterday's tabloids for that. I didn't really need the notes, either, but I felt duty-bound to review them.'

'Is that unusual after so long?'

'I oversee so many patients they begin to blur together. Most are largely cared for by the midwives or delegated to junior doctors. I only remember a few.'

'You may not know that Esmeralda is a detective now,' he said.

'The newspapers made that clear.'

'When Esmeralda joined the force, she told us about

Hugo Green, so you wouldn't be breaking any confidence in relation to those events.' Ben sat back in his chair, startling himself with what he said next. 'You know, Dr Tilly, I don't need the actual maternity notes.'

Ben knew that if this were about anybody other than Esmeralda he wouldn't be hesitating. But he didn't want to be holding whatever material evidence was in that folder until he had some idea of its likely nature.

'All I need,' he said, feeling his way as he spoke, 'is to understand anything that might be relevant to someone with circumstances like Esmeralda's. In other words, what if you and I were to speak hypothetically? Would that make things easier for you?'

'It might.'

'So, hypothetically,' he said, 'if a patient has been a victim of kidnap and rape as a child, and experienced dissociative amnesia as a result of those events, then she's likely to be memorable to any doctor who looks after her, isn't she?'

'I'm sad to say that it isn't unique to see a patient who has been the victim of a violent crime in her past. That wouldn't necessarily be enough to make her memorable.'

'What would?'

'If the medical circumstances were especially unusual, on top of those previous traumatic events. Theoretically, anyway,' she added.

'So was there something unusual about this hypothetical woman's pregnancy?'

She gestured towards the file on her desk. 'Are you familiar with maternity notes, DS Sachs? I mean the old-fashioned, paper kind Esmeralda had, as opposed to the apps and electronic notes that we're increasingly going over to.'

'Not personally. I have no children.'

She nodded as if his inability to see what was in front of him finally made sense. 'If you haven't been closely involved as a birthing partner then you won't recognise that Esmeralda's notes are unusually slim.'

'Why might that be?' Once more, Ben pushed aside his certainty that Esmeralda would be enraged were she to learn that he was acquiring this deeply personal knowledge.

Dr Tilly looked hard at him. 'One possibility would be that the woman didn't have any antenatal care. In such circumstances, the notes would relate only to the delivery of the baby, and postnatal care in hospital after the baby was born.'

'And why might that happen?'

'Perhaps our hypothetical woman didn't realise she was pregnant until she went into labour, so the maternity unit had no record of her existence until she landed there.'

Ben felt his face crease with the difficulty he was having in taking this in. 'I've heard of that happening to young girls, but not to a thirty-year-old, highly educated school-teacher.'

Dr Tilly shook her head. 'That's a false idea, DS Sachs. Pregnancy denial – sometimes we call it cryptic pregnancy – it doesn't happen only to young girls. We are theorising the case of someone who experienced severe trauma as a teenager, and that's a significant psychiatric risk factor for pregnancy denial. It may be that this pregnancy triggered something in relation to those past events. The woman then suppressed any recognition of it in order to keep the memories of what happened to her buried.'

'So how did she end up in this hospital in labour when she had no idea she was pregnant?'

'Someone, perhaps a family member, may have seen she was in pain and distress, and brought her to A&E. Who then sent her straight to the delivery suite.'

Ben thought briefly. 'You used the term "high-risk" about the caesarean you'll be doing this morning. Was the case of our theoretical woman high-risk?'

'Potentially, given the lack of antenatal care and screening. Even more troubling is that such a woman would be unprepared for what was happening to her. She'd likely be quite fearful and confused. She might experience labour as a kind of violence, especially when she'd been the victim of such terrible violence in her past. I was bleeped because it was a cryptic pregnancy and there was no record of the woman's attendance in clinic.'

'So you were present when this baby was born?'

'Along with a midwife. There was also a paediatrician on standby to examine the baby immediately after birth – he found her to be healthy and developed to full term.'

'And how would such a patient feel towards her baby?'

'That's an excellent question. There's an increasing amount of research into pregnancy denial, but it's a difficult area. Any studies are necessarily retrospective – they can only focus on the aftermath. The hypothetical case we're discussing is unusual, though, in that the mother–child attachment scores were extremely high.'

'And you wouldn't expect that?' Ben was thinking about Esmeralda's visible love for Líria, and how happy and at ease the two of them seemed together, despite his glimpses of what he guessed was a normal edginess, perhaps even possessiveness, for a child Líria's age.

'We'd need to be prepared for the opposite, given the fact that the birth would have been a form of trauma and shock for the mother.' Dr Tilly's phone buzzed. 'Excuse me, please, DS Sachs.' She answered with her name. After a few seconds she said, 'I'll be there straight-away.' She looked up at Ben. 'I'm afraid I really do need to go now.'

Tributes

Ben was in the hospital canteen, drinking bad coffee at a table in the corner. A large screen, hung like an enormous painting, was showing a Sunday breakfast show, on silent but with rolling subtitles.

There was the usual montage of Thorne and the women found in his basement. Penelope Hastings, smiling proudly at her graduation from her physiotherapy degree. Claudia Bertrum, standing by a river in wellies, taking water samples as part of a project she'd been doing for an environmental agency. Julia Smithlin, who'd been a passionate runner, beaming as she caught her breath after finishing a 10k. Did Jason Thorne ever think about what he'd stolen from these women, and their families and friends, and the world?

The television switched to the newly released image of Lucy Reed, accompanied by the words, LATER THIS MORNING, THORNE'S FIRST AND LAST LOVES, FORENSIC PSYCHOLOGIST BRETT HART GIVES HIS EXPERT VIEW. Ben's mood wasn't improved when one of the tabloid photos of Esmeralda at the end of the police press conference was shown, with Whistler cropped out. There'd been no reference to Hugo Green or Harriet Sapphire, and Mary's team appeared to have contained the game trailer, but Ben still grimaced as he turned away from the screen.

He reflected on what it was that always struck him about Esmeralda. It was as if she shone, as if something light and miraculous was in her skin, and that it had gone there when she was underground to protect her and help her to see in the dark. He knew that others were affected by her in this way too. Come to think of it, Whistler probably was, which might partly explain his perversely inflamed hatred.

It occurred to Ben that Esmeralda never talked about Líria's father. But why would she? That was natural, wasn't it? Arthur Dalloway had been dead for over a decade, and Ben and Esmeralda were only just getting to know each other. But as he turned back to his tablet to scroll through articles about the accident that killed Arthur Dalloway, Ben realised he was frowning again. BOXING DAY BLOODBATH. FAMILY WIPED OUT. DEATH CRASH FOUR NAMED.

Beyond the depth of personal tragedy, there was nothing remarkable about the accident itself, or about the fact it had been caused by a drunk driver who'd veered onto the wrong side of a single carriageway, causing the family's car to swerve, smash into a tree, and roll down a slope before landing upside down. The drunk driver survived – they always somehow did – and was sentenced to the maximum fourteen years for causing death by dangerous driving. CCTV in the man's building showed him staggering down the stairwell, then stumbling through the car park before entering his vehicle. He'd ended up serving half his sentence and been free on licence for the last few years, while Arthur Dalloway and his parents and sister were in the earth forever.

Ben knew that Arthur Dalloway had died on the 26th of December 2005. Nine months later, on the 23rd of September 2006, Líria Avelar was born. Ben had learned from his morning's research that pregnancy wasn't about calendar months, but lunar. Pregnancy was all about the moon. Using an online due date calculator, he plugged in a range of different numbers for the first day of the last menstrual cycle. The 17th of December was the magic number that gave the due date matching Líria's birthday: the 23rd of September.

Ben thought this through, and didn't like where it was leading him. The due date calculator's parameters were for a textbook forty-week pregnancy. It worked on the principle that actual conception – close to ovulation – was fourteen days *after* the first day of the woman's last period. By this reckoning, Esmeralda wouldn't have actually conceived her daughter until the last day of 2005, on the 31st of December. By that time, Arthur Dalloway, the supposed father, was already dead.

Ben paused for a moment. What was he doing? He couldn't deny to himself what he would never admit aloud. The job left him no choice in driving this search forward. Now, he wouldn't stop even if he could.

The delivery of Esmeralda's baby had been normal, at least in obstetric terms, and the paediatrician had declared the infant to be healthy. One website explained that a typical pregnancy could be anywhere between thirty-seven and forty-two weeks; forty weeks was only an average. Another website said that sperm could survive for up to five days, and a woman could ovulate earlier or later than day fourteen. Given these additional facts, it was within the realm of possibility that Arthur Dalloway was Líria's father.

Why then, did Ben still feel uneasy? He let his mind relax, closed his eyes, and tried to put himself into a state of what his old English teacher called 'negative capability', which meant you should trust your imagination to find the way forward. That's when it came to him. What was bothering Ben was that there was nobody to corroborate anything about Esmeralda's relationship with Arthur Dalloway.

Arthur himself was dead. Arthur's sister, who he might have confided in, was also dead. Ditto Arthur's mother and father. What was more, there was nobody on the supposed paternal side of Líria Avelar's family to make any claim on her. You only had to look at the number of children in orphanages to know that such a situation wasn't unheard of. But the circumstance was very convenient – a word that Ben often found bothersome – for a mother who'd had a cryptic pregnancy and didn't want to be asked any questions.

Ben loathed DI Harold Whistler. He thought Whistler was like bad Wi-Fi, useless when you really needed it but sporadically tuned in when you didn't. As Ben replayed a meeting he'd attended late on Friday morning, he had to ask himself if he'd disregarded a rare instance when Whistler might just have been tuned in.

* * *

They had been in DCS Vane's office, with Ben and the DCS arguing against Whistler, who was adamant that they needed Esmeralda out with immediate effect, before she compromised the hunt for Jason Thorne even more than she already had.

'She's playing you. She's playing us all. Nothing about her sits right with me. Can we even be certain she isn't faking her memory loss?'

At this, Ben began to jump up, ready to punch Whistler, and only stopped himself when Vane said his name in warning and waved him back down.

'Her amnesia is medically documented,' Vane said. 'I don't want to hear that again.'

'Fine. But she's violent. You saw her attack me. I'll be launching misconduct and grievance proceedings.'

'You grabbed her,' Ben said. 'You touched her first – and she defended herself, which she had every right to do. I'll be advising her to launch those proceedings right back at you.'

'You're only saying that because you want to fuck her.'

The DCS actually chopped a hand sideways to cut Whistler off.

That led to Whistler storming out and Ben visibly startling when he turned and saw Esmeralda through the glass window of the DCS's office. When their eyes met, she flinched.

Ben believed Esmeralda's amnesia was real, more now than ever after talking to Dr Tilly, but had he been too quick to dismiss Whistler's general suspicion of

Esmeralda, blinded by his own enduring bitterness towards the man? And blinded also, Ben had to admit, by his feelings for her. Whistler had put it crudely, but he wasn't wrong – Ben had been drawn to Esmeralda from the moment he met her six months ago.

He was worrying that he'd come on too strong and too fast on Wednesday, inviting her to stop for ice cream. Sitting on that bench beside her the following day, watching the sunset, he'd struggled like a schoolboy to hide his disappointment when she'd politely refused his casual invitation for Friday night drinks and he'd tried to play it cool.

For now, Ben needed to let this exploration of Esmeralda's past take him where it would. He turned back to the articles about the car crash that killed Arthur Dalloway. One provided a link to a tribute page – now dormant – that had been set up the month after the family died. DONATIONS MADE IN MEMORY OF DAVID, MARGARET, ARTHUR AND RACHEL DALLOWAY, it said, top and centre.

The organiser was a man called Fred Potter, and Ben quickly ran an internet search for him. By far the most likely of the hits was a retired paramedic who'd worked in the same ambulance service as Arthur. But Fred Potter wasn't going to be of much help, given that he'd died of a heart attack two years earlier.

The comments themselves veered between trite and excessive, with the usual handful left by trolls. None captured anything near the enormity of the obliteration of four people. Ben had seen too many such expressions of grief in his time. He scrolled through, wanting to find leads he could follow up quickly, on his own, because he still had an instinct not to share or record any discoveries he made about Esmeralda.

Well-loved colleague . . . Deepest sympathy . . . Devastating loss . . . So sad and sorry to hear . . . Heaven has four new angels . . . Rest in eternal peace . . . Sincere condolences . . . May the drunken bastard who did this burn in hell for all eternity . . . Heartbreaking news . . . You helped so many . . . One of the most generous and kind couples you could ever hope to meet . . . You are in paradise . . . Precious and irreplaceable family . . . Lost for words . . . I will never get over this . . . You will be missed . . .

Most of the messages had been left over the first few months of 2006, then dwindled to almost nothing over the rest of the year. Ben kept hitting the 'Show More' button, continuing to scan for something useful, buried deeply in all of those mostly anodyne words.

He paused over a message written by someone who called himself Sebastian Grayling. **Honoured you chose me as your friend, mate.** Esmeralda had told the vetting officers that her relationship with Arthur had lasted three months, but Arthur may have talked to a friend about her. Ben did a quick search for Sebastian Grayling and found pages of stories about a fictional television character he'd never heard of. The username had probably been chosen to protect the person's privacy, or as a joke. In any case, the comment wasn't significant enough to follow up when what Ben needed was ready-made intel.

He was past the point of believing he'd find any. That was why, when his eyes first skimmed over the tribute from Emily Jane Waters, he didn't properly take it in. He scrolled back up to re-read it. **Arthur, our relationship was new, but I know I have lost the love of my life and you were 'the one'. You will always be in my heart and I will think of you every day.**

At the time Arthur Dalloway died, having just made his new girlfriend Esmeralda Avelar pregnant, a different woman thought *she* was the love of his life. It was possible that Emily Jane Waters was a fantasist. Or that Arthur was seeing more than one woman in late 2005, but something about the man Ben had been researching made him doubt that.

Ben did a quick search for Emily Jane Waters. She lived in a village on the outskirts of the city, where she ran a small dance school. He plugged in the address, and saw that her studio was the ground floor of a house that she appeared to live in. The surest thing, he decided, would be to go there and knock on her door. As he was thinking about this, a text from Esmeralda pinged through.

Join us for a walk in the botanic gardens this afternoon? Líria will be grumpy and my dad will be stealing seeds when he thinks nobody's looking – don't nick him.

There was only one answer he could give. **Tell me where to find you.**

The Father

The directions Esmeralda texted were detailed, because the section of the botanic gardens where she suggested they meet wasn't commonly known. As Ben walked, the sounds of the town faded and the rushing of a nearby stream grew louder. Before long, he found himself on a stone path whose entrance was hidden between upright shrubs of pale pink fuchsias.

A slight man who looked to be in his mid-seventies was bending over a bed of lemon-yellow and fire-red dahlias. Ben watched him gently tap a flower, extract several seed heads, then slide them into a small paper bag that he labelled before slipping it into a pocket of his grey golfing trousers.

'Mr Avelar?' Ben said. The man's hair was startlingly white and stuck up so dramatically Ben would have thought it a wig if he hadn't known better from Esmeralda's fond descriptions.

'Isaac,' he corrected, straightening up, then holding out a hand. 'Great to meet you, Ben.'

'You too.' Ben looked around but Isaac answered his unasked question. 'Esmeralda dropped me off. She and Líria went to your sister's new place to pick up some ice cream. How about we sit for a bit, before they come back?' As Isaac led Ben to a wooden bench, he pointed to some nearby bell-shaped blooms, pale lilac but creamy white at the centre. 'Those autumn-flowering crocuses are toxic. I had some in our garden. Tore them out when Líria was born.'

Ben imagined the shocked urgency with which Isaac would have done that, given the unexpectedness of Líria's appearance, but said only, 'It's a good thing you knew that.'

When Isaac looked Ben straight in the eye and said, 'Esmeralda trusts you,' Ben saw the man he had been in the television interviews he gave when the fifteen-year-old Esmeralda was missing. When Isaac added, 'I'd like your professional opinion about something,' Ben saw the strength he'd had to show ever since she was found.

But Ben felt a kind of dread. 'I'll try. If it's a police matter – there are things we can't really talk about. Esmeralda has probably explained about all that . . .'

Isaac gave a dismissive grunt. 'Why did Esmeralda tell Líria about Hugo Green when she came home late on Tuesday night? She said someone discovered who she was. From when she was fifteen and before we changed her name. Can you tell me who that someone was, please?'

'Have you asked her yourself, Isaac?'

'Do you think I don't know the game you're playing, pinging back my questions? Do you think I didn't spend more time speaking to the police than I'd wish on anyone? Of course I didn't ask her when she was already overwrought. If I had, I wouldn't be asking *you*.'

How could an encounter that started so well have gone so very wrong so very quickly? Ben was startled to hear himself saying, 'That someone was Jason Thorne.'

Isaac gripped the arm of the bench so tightly that his knuckles went white and the hairs on the back of his fingers appeared darker. He seemed incapable of speech, and though Ben was left in no doubt about the man's shock and horror at hearing Thorne's name, surely he had seen the speculation about his daughter and Thorne in the press?

Ben considered further. Perhaps Esmeralda would not have told her father how powerfully she'd captured Thorne's attention in recent days. Was this carefulness the result of her devotion to the job or her wish to shield those she loved? Probably both, he decided.

And there was another possibility, too, voiced by Dominic Vane, who suspected that Esmeralda had a connection to Thorne that she was deliberately hiding. The tabloids had suggested that Esmeralda and Thorne were lovers. Could they have actually got that right?

Ben didn't like where this was leading him. He tried to reason that even if Esmeralda had been involved with Thorne, she'd done nothing wrong. Thorne had clearly been effective at persuading women to go with him, and nobody knew what he was storing in his basement freezers, then. But that little voice came back, whispering in Ben's ear again. Why, then, would she have kept it a secret? And how did she survive when nobody else did?

Ben's tone was as neutral as he could make it. 'We think it's possible that at some point in the past, Thorne and Esmeralda crossed paths.'

Isaac slapped the top of his head several times with the palm of a hand, and that extraordinary hair of his kept springing back up. He rose from the bench and began to pace along the side of the stream. He was mumbling, talking to himself more than to Ben. 'It can't be.' He stopped to study the water, swaying a little, forward and backwards. 'Not him. It can't be him.'

Ben came to Isaac's side, ready to grab him if he lost his balance, but his own heart was racing as he replayed his recent research about the timing of Líria's conception in light of Isaac's words. 'What can't be him, Isaac? What do you mean?'

The older man only shook his head and said again, 'Not him. It just can't be.'

Ben's detective's instinct activated, and he said, 'If Thorne and Esmeralda met, the likely window was December of 2005.' He was closely observing Isaac. Staring down but seeming to see nothing, the man doubled over, gripping his knees. Ben took Isaac's arm. 'How long until Esmeralda and Líria arrive?' he asked.

Isaac swallowed several times, then said, 'Depends how busy your sister is. Half an hour, maybe.'

Ben steered the older man away from the water's edge and back to the bench. He didn't know exactly what he was going to say until the words were out of his mouth, but he did know he needed to continue to push Isaac. 'I went by the hospital this morning,' he said, 'to meet Dr Tilly.'

Isaac's hands were on his lap. He was studying them as if the answer to something impossible would be found there. 'Why would you do that?'

'I was sent there by my boss.' Ben hesitated, then said, 'I'm going to ask you something that will definitely come up. I'd rather it falls to me to find this out than someone else, so I can try to work out what, if anything, needs to be done with the information.'

Isaac was blinking fiercely. He opened his mouth but no words came out.

And then Ben voiced the question that had been on his mind since his visit to the hospital that morning. 'Did Esmeralda lie about the identity of Líria's father?'

TWELVE YEARS EARLIER –
FRIDAY, 23 DECEMBER 2005

The Pick-Up Artist

The absence of CCTV was Jason's first requirement. He had visited this pub several times over the past few months, studying the layout during these reconnaissance missions.

The place had been around since the early eighteenth century, starting its life as a coaching inn. As the town grew around it, the pub's location became more central. Most people arrived on foot or by taxi, entering and exiting through the main door at the front of the building. There was a second door at the back, which opened onto the small car park where Jason had used gloved hands to feed spotlessly clean pound coins into the simple pay and display machine. Preparation was everything.

The pub was full. Jason knew from experience how much easier it was to be overlooked in a crowd, especially when that crowd was tipsy with festive cheer. He arranged himself on a green velvet chair in the corner, obscured by a pillar that was garlanded with tinsel. There was a small table to the side for his drink. He was wearing his favourite jeans and a navy wool jumper he'd had for years, enjoying the smell of his own aftershave and hoping somebody else would soon enjoy it too.

Jason was amused by the pub's pseudo country-house decoration, which struck him as a poor imitation of his grandmother's place. A bunch of already-drunk Hooray Henrys laughed at their own wit as they hung baubles on a pair of antlers that had been mounted in the centre of a wood-panelled wall, then resumed their places on the button-back leather sofas nearby. Jason kept his face placid and fantasised about breaking their noses.

A group of sixth-form girls who must have been carrying fake IDs were giggling and gossiping and bopping to the usual Christmas songs. They were too young, and their skirts too short, and the lacy corsets they wore were more like lingerie than clothing. A big part of Jason wanted to tell them to go home where they would be safe.

Each time the front door opened, Jason was filled with new hope. With the *potential* of the night. He needed a woman who was drinking alone. He had a vision of what she would look like, what she would be like, when he brought her home.

It had been six months since the last one, who Jason had taken during her morning run. It had been easy to disappear Julia Smithlin onto the back floor of his parked car and throw a blanket over her – because, yes, planning and preparedness really were everything. What hadn't been easy, though, was how bothered he'd been to see Julia's mother weeping during a televised police conference about her missing daughter.

Jason had a remarkable degree of self-insight. He knew he had a soft spot for mothers who genuinely loved their children. That was why witnessing Mrs Smithlin's distress had disturbed him more than usual. Nonetheless, Jason's response to Mrs Smithlin's tears had been like the emotional release that watching a sad film gave. He could cry, but the remorse didn't stick. The need to hunt again, to make another woman his, was stronger than any fleeting desolation. In the end, Julia Smithlin and her mother were no more real to Jason than fictional characters. The credits rolled, and on he went.

A group of businessmen in expensive suits spilled in, loosened their ties and ordered champagne. A mildly arresting woman in her mid-thirties tripped when her heel caught on the edge of a sisal rug. She looked around and seemed to reassure herself – wrongly – that nobody saw. She was a bit glossy for his taste, and trying too hard, shivering and goose-bumpy in her barely-there gold sequinned dress.

He took another sip of his beer, and when the main door opened he swallowed so hard and fast he nearly choked. But there she was at last. After fourteen years of waiting and hoping, his Holy Grail, the woman of his dreams, had walked directly into his life.

Harriet Sapphire was Jason's obsession. Lesser beings worshipped rock singers or film stars, but to Jason, nobody was more deserving of fame and adoration than Harriet. As a teenager, against all odds, she had escaped a serial killer who was nearly as cunning as Jason himself. She had lived, while the man, probably thanks to her, had not.

Harriet was extraordinary. In those months after Lucy, she had become the deserving focus of Jason's fascination. And although his efforts to find her over the last decade and a half had failed – likely because of the heavy protection of the police and courts – Jason had been unswerving in his belief that he would someday come across her.

He had kept every newspaper story, and drawn her face each year not just to celebrate and commemorate her escape, but also to learn her very bones. Deep down, he knew he'd recognise her anyway, but there was a pleasure in the act of drawing her. He'd imagined the subtle changes over time, knowing she would grow into herself, her beauty deepening until she ceased to be a child and became a woman who could love him back.

Now, he saw he had been right in every detail. His gift for faces left no doubt. Seeing her in person, finally, he knew absolutely that she was his destiny. He worshipped everything about her. The long, dark red hair that she'd caught up in Christmas ribbons. The charcoal-grey Fair Isle cardigan with a subtle parade of reindeer worn over a burgundy-coloured dress. The chunky black boots. The heart-shaped silver locket on a chain-link necklace.

The terrible complication was that she was not alone. There were no tables left so her little group bought their drinks at the bar, then clustered together near the log-burning stove. A man whose skull Jason wanted to smash handed her a glass of mulled wine. After a while, the stove's heat made her shrug off the cardigan, and Jason caught his breath. The dress was silky, flowing over her breasts and waist and legs.

Lip reading was a talent Jason had always cultivated.

Before long, he'd worked out that Harriet and her companions were teachers, and he was even more impressed. She had devoted herself to children.

He could see that Harriet and the others were all in their late twenties or early thirties, and that the lucky bastard standing next to her was clearly infatuated. She, on the other hand, was oblivious to her admirer, and this observation made Jason's heart squeeze with relief and excitement. As he watched, it struck him that she seemed to glow. Jason seldom fumbled for the right words, but that was what was happening when he tried to describe her.

He had entered this place searching for a woman to take, to bundle out of there. Jason was, after all, a man who walked around with a syringe full of tranquilliser in his pocket. But he wanted so much more with Harriet. With her, he wanted everything. She would be his first real relationship since Lucy. In fact, she would be his last. With Harriet, there was a proper connection. He could feel it, and she would too. She must. There would be conversation, and there would be love, and the rest would follow. Such a sequence of events departed entirely from Jason's usual order of service.

But what could he do when she was surrounded by people? Nothing but wait and watch.

What happened half an hour later confirmed Jason's certainty that this could only be fate. There was talk among the teachers of trying somewhere else for dinner, because the pub's restaurant was fully booked. Jason watched Harriet smile and say she couldn't, another time perhaps. Someone said, 'Bye, Esmeralda,' loud enough for Jason to hear. *Esmeralda.* So that was her name now, changed, no doubt, for the sake of her privacy. He repeated it softly, his mouth tasting the syllables, and decided that it was good.

There were kisses and hugs and wishes of 'Happy Christmas, see you next year.' Esmeralda lifted an open hand, then shut it in a final goodbye as her colleagues left through the front door. Then she walked over to the bar and abandoned her almost full glass.

Where would this shining creature go next? The answer thrilled him. She skirted the pillar he was hiding behind, then slowed. She was less than two metres from his velvet chair, clearly searching for something. Her eyes slid over him, and they were the most startling emerald green he had ever seen. With those witchy eyes, and that dark red hair and pale skin, and yes, that glow, he was startled to find himself not just dazzled, but also a little frightened. This woman was enchanting and powerful and dangerous. Maybe it was what he knew of her past, intensified by that extravagantly romantic bent he'd inherited from his father, but Jason couldn't shake the idea that she was a near-mythical being.

Although at the moment she was being reassuringly mortal. From the way she'd been scanning the room it was obvious that she had lost herself in this maze of a place. He didn't doubt what she was seeking. Women always were. He realised he was literally holding his breath, but he cleared his throat and somehow managed to say, 'I think it's over there,' pointing over her shoulder and towards the right.

'Ah,' she said. 'Thank you.' She gave him a near-smile

without really looking at him. Then she turned and walked in the direction he'd indicated, towards that quiet corridor with three doors, one of which was little-used and led to the small car park.

He couldn't remember his pulse racing like this. Nothing made Jason's pulse race. Ever. But he knew he couldn't just sit there. He must run into her again, as if by accident. He must talk to her. He must ask if he could buy her a drink. He could not let her leave.

It was a gamble, Jason knew, but such opportunities were never risk-free.

He counted to ten, rose, traced the steps that his heart-stopper had taken, then waited beside a closed door with a 1950s-style silhouette of a woman beneath the word 'LADIES'. What would he do next? It was all so new, this way of proceeding with a woman who would remain conscious when they left together.

But nothing worked as he'd planned. He was considering his possible moves when she emerged and the door blocked him from her view. How had he not foreseen that when normally he foresaw everything? And now she was about to walk away without realising he was there, without their even speaking. He couldn't let that happen, couldn't let her just leave, couldn't let himself vanish from her brain and heart like an incidental stranger in a crowd.

TWELVE YEARS LATER – SUNDAY,
17 SEPTEMBER 2017

The Lie

Isaac was hunched over, with his elbows against his waist, and Ben could feel the pulse in his own forehead as he waited for the man to answer him. When at last Isaac got control of himself, he raised his head and met Ben's eye. 'You don't understand. You can't begin to fathom what it is for your child to be hurt in the worst way imaginable short of death, and you didn't protect them. You didn't save them.'

'You're right,' Ben said. 'I can't imagine what that must have been like.'

'Then let me spell it out. My daughter leaves for school. She's fifteen years old, still my little girl, and she comes back four months later after being imprisoned in a god-forsaken burial crypt and – well – I don't need to be explicit. Whatever that evil bastard did to her was so horrifying she blocked out all memories of it.' Isaac stopped, covered his face briefly, then dragged his hands downwards before saying, 'She must have cried for me every day, alone in the dark, not understanding why I didn't burst in to save her.'

'You must have felt like you were in hell,' Ben said.

'Hell could not be worse.' Isaac smacked a hand against the centre of his chest. 'Do you understand what Esmeralda is? How superhumanly strong she had to be to survive what she has, but also how incredibly fragile?' He smacked twice more. 'From the day she was born, even when my wife was pregnant with her, we called her Hummingbird. We didn't fully imagine how perfect that name was. Do you comprehend what I'm telling you?'

'I think so.'

'Esmeralda genuinely believes that Líria's father is Arthur Dalloway, but I put that in her head. The story of what happened to that family was everywhere. It caught my attention because I vaguely knew Arthur's father from a horticultural society I used to belong to. Nobody else knows the truth. Just me, and now you know too. You said they'll be asking questions about Líria's birth soon. Tell me I was right to trust you.'

'You were right to trust me,' Ben said. 'But why did you lie? How could you think it wouldn't matter – that it wouldn't come out somewhere down the line? Don't you worry about what Esmeralda and Líria will feel – what they'll *do* – if they discover this?'

Isaac shook his head so fiercely Ben thought he might hurt himself. 'They won't.'

You can't know that, Ben thought, but he didn't press the point because Isaac had the look of a man who'd just opened his front door to a police death knock.

Isaac went on. 'The doctors explained that Esmeralda had experienced pregnancy denial, and that the situation she found herself in had triggered another episode of traumatic amnesia. You can't imagine how terrified I was that her mind wouldn't come back from that again.' Isaac's brown eyes were so unlike his daughter's green, but the intensity of his gaze moved Ben. 'When they asked her, Esmeralda said she had no idea who Líria's father was.'

'And you had no idea either?'

'Until now, none whatsoever.'

They both sat for a few seconds, replaying those two words. *Until now.*

Isaac went on. 'I couldn't let her suffer through the kind of interrogations she'd had when she was fifteen. She was vulnerable enough with this unexpected new baby in her arms.' Isaac seemed to consider, then said, 'I knew there'd be no one to question Arthur Dalloway's name on the birth certificate, least of all Esmeralda, because she'd blanked out the last few months of 2005. She came to believe she was so distressed by Arthur's death it wiped away her memories of him. I led her to believe that.'

Ben found himself taking a deep breath. Then he asked another question he knew Isaac would not like. 'Did something happen to Esmeralda in December of 2005, Isaac? You were upset when I mentioned that time frame a few minutes ago, and you say she blanked out the last few months of that year, so that makes me wonder.'

With a gesture that was slight but definite, Isaac turned his body a little away from Ben, defensively. 'Wonder what?' Isaac licked his lips and swallowed hard after he said this.

'Wonder if there was anything unusual in her movements? An event that stands out?' Ben was trying not to lead, trying not to be too explicit, trying . . . What was he trying? Never before had he felt so powerfully that he was groping in the dark. And never before had he allowed the job to be so clouded by his own emotions. 'Can you recall if somebody or something upset her?'

Isaac opened his mouth, then shut it. Ben was in no doubt that there was something there, something that Isaac was refusing to speak. 'Nothing. There was nothing.'

Ben needed a different approach. 'What was Esmeralda like when she was pregnant?'

'She actually grew thinner. She'd never properly got her appetite back since being in those crypts.' Isaac slumped at the weight of the memory. 'The aftermath of all that, the way she was turned into a specimen, she hated having anything medical, so she avoided seeing her GP. With hindsight, I can see that towards the end she was wearing looser dresses, and that whatever was happening wasn't simply a matter of her being run-down.'

'And Líria? Can you tell me about when you first saw her?'

Isaac looked at Ben without seeing him, as if he were watching a film of himself all those years ago. 'Dr Tilly brought me to a side room in the maternity ward, where Esmeralda was in a bed holding Líria.' His face softened. 'This little human person who'd materialised from out of nowhere, so entirely innocent and pure. I can't explain the mixture of love and terror and shock I felt. She looked so like Esmeralda.' He tapped his chin with an index finger and almost smiled. 'And so like my beautiful wife. Except for . . .' Isaac stopped.

'Except?' Ben asked, holding his breath for Isaac to continue.

'Except for that dark gold hair. And for those eyes. Esmeralda put the baby in my arms and Líria gripped my finger in her little fist. She opened her eyes and looked up at me with such trust and wonder. Nobody in our family has eyes like those, that strange, beautiful amber that was there immediately, that didn't wait to emerge like it does in most babies, that never changed.' Isaac seemed to focus on Ben again. 'You will have noticed that Esmeralda's eyes are green.'

Ben kept his face impassive, but thought, Yes, of course I noticed. How could I not?

Isaac brushed a tear from his cheek, roughly, seemingly angry to find it there.

'What are you thinking, Isaac?' Ben said.

Isaac folded his arms across his chest, leaned back, and answered Ben's question. 'I'm thinking that my granddaughter is completely perfect, but the very fact that she exists at all is likely down to the fact that her father is an evil monster.'

To identify that monster aloud was not possible. The two men knew this, just as a child knows they cannot chant the name Bloody Mary into a mirror, though the temptation to look at that mirror and say that name pulsed away, making it almost impossible to think of anything else.

Infatuation

Isaac was looking intently at Ben's face, his eyes narrowed, as if Ben were a small font he was struggling to read. 'So let me ask you this, Ben. Would you want one of the people you love most in the world to know that about herself, that she came from that? Are you going to tell her?'

'Of course not,' Ben said. 'She's only a child.'

'And are you going to tell Esmeralda the truth about Arthur Dalloway?'

'I don't know,' Ben said at last, and this was true. He ran through what material evidence there was about the circumstances of Esmeralda's pregnancy and Líria's birth, and fully admitted to himself that he had deliberately refrained from laying his hands on any of it or recording anything he had learned in his notebook. Nothing material was in his possession, and his tablet had been in stealth mode as he conducted his researches in the hospital café, ostensibly because he'd been in a public place.

'You *don't know*? I trust you with all of this, and that is all you have to say to me?'

'You can trust me to do the best I can for Esmeralda.'

'Cryptic pregnancy is a form of denial, but it's not the only package denial comes in.' Isaac was looking at Ben with an unnerving mix of contempt and pity.

'What are you trying to say?' Ben asked.

'I'm trying to ask if you're being honest about your feelings for Esmeralda. About the depth of your fascination with her. Telling yourself this investigation into her pregnancy and the identity of Líria's father is all in the line of duty.'

Isaac had voiced exactly the thought Ben himself had had multiple times that day. When Ben didn't answer, Isaac shrugged, making it clear he was sorry for him. 'I've seen it before, but Esmeralda is always oblivious to the besotted sods who trail after her.'

Ben couldn't help himself. 'She invited me here today, knowing I would meet you.'

'You're the first she's introduced to me,' Isaac said slowly. 'But far from the first to become infatuated with her.'

Before Ben could formulate a response, Isaac went on. 'If you have any brain and heart you will do *nothing* that forces the knowledge of what we've been discussing on Esmeralda and Líria. Will correcting a birth certificate resurrect the dead? Will it give you vital new information? No and no.' He shook his head. 'But know this. Esmeralda didn't lie about anything. That was all me.'

Isaac stopped to glance at his phone. 'Líria just texted. They'll be here in around fifteen minutes. You'll probably find them near the children's play area – that's where Esmeralda always parks. I'd appreciate it if you made your excuses to them and left.'

Ben took out a card and scribbled hastily on it. 'If you ever want to reach me directly, this number goes straight to my desk. I wrote my personal number on the back.'

Isaac's fingers closed around the card. Without looking at it, he slid it into the inside pocket of his fleece, against his chest.

Ben stood on the grass bank, watching Esmeralda guide her little grey hatchback into a tight space.

Líria got out of the car first, approaching him carefully, seeming to weigh each step. 'We got strawberry for you,' she said. 'Mum and Amy both said it's your favourite.'

Ben managed a smile. 'I bet Amy wasn't that polite. She said I was boring, didn't she?'

'Maybe,' Líria said. 'Here's Mum. I'll go ahead with the ice creams to Grandad.' She took a few steps, then turned and looked behind her, and Ben saw an anxiousness in her face that he'd glimpsed before. 'Don't take too long, Mum, or it'll melt and I'll be mad.'

Everything but Esmeralda disappeared from Ben's vision as she walked towards him wearing faded jeans, white trainers, and a black sweatshirt with a small red hourglass placed above her heart. Her hair was loose, a strand lifted by the slight breeze, looking like dark fire in the sunshine. Whatever had happened to this woman in the past, Ben trusted her, though he noticed her glancing nervously at Líria's retreating back.

At the same time, he smoothed his face into as much

neutrality as he could, thinking about the fact that he was her boss, and she was vulnerable given her history and what was happening to her now. 'Does the hourglass on your sweatshirt mean something?' he asked.

She smiled. 'It's a present from Líria. You might know that a black widow spider has the red hourglass mark on her abdomen. There's this superhero called Black Widow who Líria says I remind her of – I think it's really just the hair colour.'

'That is weirdly sweet and scary at once.'

She laughed. 'Sweet and scary at once perfectly sums up Líria.'

And you, Ben thought, though he didn't say this. What he said instead was, 'How's the weekend been?' Making his excuses and leaving would not be easy when there was nowhere he'd rather be. Despite the messy circumstances, standing in this park beneath these trees talking to this woman was the happiest he'd felt since he could remember. Again, he reminded himself he needed to be professional, he mustn't overstep. The last thing she deserved was for someone like him to misuse his power over her.

'A little tricky, to be honest.' Esmeralda looked up at the bright sky. 'I thought a bit of fresh air would do my dad and Líria some good. And me too.'

She was standing close to him, much closer than the space bubble colleagues normally maintained. The scent of her shampoo made him think of orange blossom, and he knew he should move away, but couldn't bring himself to do it. The resolutions he was trying to make about her were not easy to keep.

'Everything okay, Ben? You look . . . worried.'

'All good, but something's come up so I'm going to have to shoot off.' He could hear how casual he sounded, how offhand, and see the confusion in her face. 'I've already made my apologies to your dad.'

'It's the video trailer, isn't it?' Her voice was soft. 'I understand. I've been thinking about it since Thursday. I invited you this afternoon as a kind of dare to myself, to force the issue because I couldn't stand not knowing. But now I do. You can't unsee those images.' She shook her head. 'I know I can't.'

He couldn't maintain the façade of hardness that was usually so easy for him to wear. 'You can't believe that of me, Esmeralda. You can't believe that's how I think.'

She hesitated. 'I thought you were horrified every time you saw me, since viewing that game trailer. You've hardly looked at me.'

'Horrified by what was happening to you.' He wanted so badly to comfort her. 'Horrified for you. Never horrified with you or by you or at you.' He imagined touching her cheek, lifting a strand of her hair, but he didn't do either of those things. 'That trailer is nothing to do with you. It's the pathetic creation of a pitiful troll.'

And I've permanently erased it from my brain, he silently added. I only see you. Just you. As you are. Everything he'd just imagined saying to her was true, but when he next spoke, he told a lie. 'Amy needs help with Toby – to keep the shop open for the next few hours – Liam – her husband – has been called away unexpectedly. That's all it is.'

She looked crushed. He could see she didn't believe

him, but she said only, 'Then you must go.' She rose on her tiptoes and brushed her lips over his cheek so quickly and lightly he thought of a butterfly's wings, and he feared she saw it as a final goodbye. He couldn't shake the thought that she was giving him a first and last kiss, and it wasn't even a proper one. Then she was gone.

MONDAY, 18 SEPTEMBER 2017

Early Morning

There had been moments of happiness over the weekend. On Saturday morning, Líria had run upstairs with the newly delivered Black Widow sweatshirt, shining with pride and excitement at the gift she had wrought. On Sunday afternoon, Esmeralda had seen Ben, and her mix of nervousness and joy at being near him was replaced by heartache when he left so abruptly.

Her emotions were volatile. How, she wondered furiously, could Whistler be allowed to reveal her identity and manhandle her without even a slap on the wrist? Over those two supposedly restful days she'd often found herself silently raging at the horror show of headlines that had been forced on her father and daughter.

Líria was uncharacteristically distracted, beginning a homework task only to forget what she was doing, or slipping a shoe onto a foot and then freezing for several seconds before remembering to tie the lace.

Her father, especially, seemed disheartened, particularly on Sunday evening after they'd returned from the botanic gardens. He'd said he liked Ben, but Esmeralda sensed there was something he wasn't telling her. At dinner he was pinched and pale, and kept repeating that old-fashioned phrase about 'today's news being tomorrow's chip paper'. He would pick up his fork only to leave it there, hanging in the air.

Unbroken sleep was impossible. There were the images of the three murdered men she couldn't get out of her head, with the gruesome iconography engraved on their torsos. Adam Holderness with the Pinocchio emoji symbolising the lies he'd told about Ella Brooke. George Rossiter with the Men's Rights symbol he would have worn with pride in life but never imagined carved into his skin in death. Thomas Lederer with the horrifying hanged man that was a perversion of his own incel imagery.

There was Scarlett, lying unconscious on the filthy carpet in that sad flat, now in hospital with her premature baby. There was Esmeralda's anxiety about the briefing that would soon be upon her. There was Whistler, tormenting her whenever he could. And there was Jason Thorne, whose hand was everywhere and in everything.

She woke at four on Monday morning, sat up in bed, and pushed the quilt away. A funny groove in her brain kept replaying Larry Fawcett's comment about how anybody could find her family tree, once they knew the name she'd been born with. With her police access to multiple databases, Esmeralda could play that game too.

She switched on her laptop and started with the General Register Office, where she could bring up any birth or marriage or death certificate instantly, not needing to wait weeks for a brown envelope in the post. As she made the searches, she knew that multiple detectives would already have taken these steps, but she still wanted to see for herself.

It was a daisy chain of linked evidence, following one birth certificate backwards in time to another, tracking Jason Thorne's maternal ancestral line. Thorne's birth certificate showed that his mother, Elizabeth Thorne, had been born Elizabeth Cavendish on December 3rd 1942. Elizabeth Cavendish's birth certificate showed that her mother, Jason's grandmother, was Charlotte Cavendish, and she had been born Charlotte Montague on January 26th 1917.

Esmeralda paused over the fact that Thorne's mother and grandmother shared the same place of birth. 'Folly View Cottage' was written on both of their birth certificates, and it was in a parish just three kilometres west of the city.

She brought up a satellite view and was struck by how far the definition of cottage could stretch. This looked more like a small-scale Georgian manor house with several outbuildings, surrounded by high stone walls and backing onto fields and woodland.

Esmeralda's next step was to access the Land Registry website to check for the current owner, only to discover the property was unregistered. She rested her elbows on the little dressing table she used as a desk, propped her cheeks on her fists, and stared at the screen.

Only a small minority of properties in the country were unregistered, maybe ten or fifteen per cent at most.

If Folly View Cottage had never been registered, that meant it had never been sold, so it had been passed down through many generations, probably staying in a rich upper-class family for centuries.

The police knew that Thorne's paternal line was old and monied. Surely they hadn't overlooked the fact that this was true of his maternal line, too? Nobody would deny that mistakes sometimes happened, but the difference for the police was that the consequences could be much more serious than was the case for most professions. Esmeralda knew that all too well, given the horrendous oversight she'd made a week earlier when she'd failed to notice Thorne sitting in his car on Ella Brooke's street.

Was she right to compare herself to police officers who'd neglected to detect killers under their noses, or shared images of murder victims? The first scenario, yes, but definitely not the second. She thought about how the police had failed to catch the Yorkshire Ripper, even after interviewing him nine times – *nine!* – during a manhunt that lasted half a decade.

How many unexplained deaths, she couldn't help wondering, hadn't been properly investigated? How many serial killers were running around out there, frolicking with Jason Thorne? She knew all too well that the different elements of an investigation were not always joined up. Even if something was noted it might not go anywhere useful. She herself had been saved by an accident. By a woman putting her foot through a floor. Not by police work.

Whistler had assured Esmeralda that the Financial

Crimes Team were looking for any properties the Thornes might want to hide. She imagined him sneering at her that she was an arrogant know-it-all, but she still couldn't shut down her thoughts. If a property was unregistered, it was ultra private. Nobody would know of Jason Thorne's connection to it, and that would suit him perfectly. Even if someone had logged the property, it wasn't beyond possibility that the information had been whirring through the system ever since and never followed up. Not to mention the fact that people like the Thornes knew how to hide. That kind of privilege made it easier for them to cover their tracks than it was for most.

The Pit and the Rim

Esmeralda was at her desk before eight, rehearsing the questions she needed to ask during the briefing. She wanted to confirm that Folly View Cottage had been looked at.

Once again she imagined how Whistler would scorn her for raising this. A big part of her was dangerously close to shrinking away from the inevitable public humiliation, but she kept picturing Thomas Lederer's face, frozen in pain and fear. Her mother's voice was in her head too, telling her to do what was right, so Esmeralda knew she would have to brace herself for the insults and press on with her questions, regardless.

The huge shared workspace, which they all referred to as the pit, was open-plan, and always made her feel as if she were sitting in the bottom of a bowl. In her current mood, it struck Esmeralda as an amphitheatre where she would soon be thrown to the lions.

She took a quick look around. Mary Armstrong was busy with Mike Dinsdale. The two of them were in a corner playing with a large display screen. The Senior Investigating Officer for Thomas Lederer's murder, DS Hannah Beresford, was standing above them all on the rim, a balcony that completely encircled the pit, talking into her phone. The good news was that DI Whistler seemed to be absent.

The bad news was that Ben was nowhere to be seen either. Esmeralda guessed that the DCS had sent him on a Thorne-related quest. Since she'd joined Major Crime, just knowing Ben was in the room had always given her a sense of safety. She felt a pang at the idea of not being able to meet his eye and see the hint of a smile on his face, then reminded herself that those fleeting exchanges were a thing of the past now, anyway.

Dinah wandered in, sipping coffee, and aimed herself straight at Esmeralda. 'Friday,' she said, shaking her head in amazement. 'You are my One True Queen!'

'I'm not sure the DCS sees it that way.'

'You spotted a person of interest nobody else noticed. You tracked them down.'

'Thanks to Scarlett,' Esmeralda said softly.

'Thanks to you both.' Dinah pressed on. 'You found a victim when the scene was fresh. You got us a huge amount of intel on Jason Thorne.'

Esmeralda touched Dinah's arm lightly in gratitude. She knew no one else viewed it from this perspective but she was moved that Dinah did. 'Intel on myself, too,' she said wryly. 'As if there weren't enough of that already. It may actually be my fault that Thomas Lederer is dead. You know about the note Thorne left on the floor near the body?'

'Don't mind-fuck yourself like that,' Dinah said. 'You

aren't responsible for the unhinged way Thorne thinks.' DS Beresford was descending the stairs from the rim into the pit, aiming herself at Mary and Mike, who everyone called M&M when things were less grim. 'Something's about to kick off,' Dinah said, as she and Esmeralda gathered with the others.

DS Beresford stuffed her hands into the pockets of her burgundy jacket. 'I want to bring you all up to speed. But before I begin, I can tell you that I spoke to Rosie this morning, and it's looking like Scarlett and baby Teddy are doing as well as we can hope.'

Esmeralda couldn't shake away the idea that it was her fault Scarlett was in hospital with her premature baby. Should she have foreseen the danger and fought harder to stop Scarlett from going with her? Had the stress of that visit to Thomas Lederer's sad flat been too much, and precipitated the medical emergency? She felt a new wave of rage at Jason Thorne. What he did to Thomas Lederer had caused harm to Scarlett and her baby too. They may not have been his intended victims, but he had hurt them, nonetheless.

'Right,' said DS Beresford. 'We need to get on, catch that bastard, and make Scarlett proud. So here's where we are.'

It didn't surprise Esmeralda to learn that Jason Thorne's fingerprints were all over Thomas Lederer's flat. The DNA results wouldn't be back until the next day, but there were multiple pieces of evidence that Thorne had been there. There was the note Thorne left at the scene. There were his signature engravings and artist's initials on the body.

There was the fact – and this was new to Esmeralda – that Thorne had been spotted on CCTV driving into Adelaide Road at 11.47 p.m. on Thursday the 14th of September and driving out of it at 4.12 a.m. on Friday the 15th. The extraordinary thing was that after ten months of scrupulous hiding, he was now splashing evidence all over the place.

A uniformed police constable hurried into the room and drew DS Beresford aside, speaking in a low voice. 'We have the vehicle,' DS Beresford said, rejoining them. 'Another dark SUV. This one's 2007 registration year. Like new with almost no mileage despite its age. It was abandoned on a country lane just north of the city.' She shook her head. 'He has to be storing these cars some-where, and it's quite a stash.'

It was the preliminary opinion of the forensic patholo-gist who attended the scene, DS Beresford reported, that Thomas Lederer died from ligature strangulation, though this couldn't be confirmed until after the post-mortem.

'Thomas's voice was heard by a neighbour just after midnight, so we believe he died sometime between then and four that morning.' DS Beresford looked straight at Esmeralda. 'I believe you spoke with this neighbour, DC Avelar. She is currently in Visitors' Reception and she's understandably distressed. I'd like you to take her state-ment after we finish here.'

Esmeralda was imagining how traumatised Adelina must be, away from her family, the horrible building she'd tried to make a home in crawling with police and a man she'd shrunk from horrifyingly murdered.

As DS Beresford went on, it didn't surprise Esmeralda to learn that the ligatures had cut into Thomas Lederer's wrists and ankles, suggesting he had strained against the ropes. But she was relieved to learn that he was probably dead by the time Thorne added the carvings. She suspected Thorne had no wish to spare his victim pain, but rather, that he was on a time crunch. Or maybe he didn't want his canvas to be moving and his artwork spoiled by a heart still pumping blood.

Esmeralda had never really allowed herself to consider Thorne's methods for engraving skin. She saw that he would have had to improvise in less than ideal conditions with Thomas Lederer and George Rossiter. But perhaps Thorne didn't care about having an extended period alone with his male victims. Unlike the women he'd kept in his basement.

DS Beresford ran her fingers through her hair, which was silky straight and cut to only a few centimetres. 'There's no sign of forced entry, so we're taking seriously the possibility that Thomas was expecting a visitor late on Thursday night.' Esmeralda was struck by the way that victims were referred to by their first names, to humanise them, but suspected perpetrators by their surnames, to keep them at a distance.

'We don't yet know what pretext Thorne used to persuade Thomas to invite him over,' said DS Beresford, 'but we have reason to believe that Thomas didn't know Thorne's real identity until it was too late. Thomas appeared to be quite a fearful person, given the multiple locks he'd installed.'

'Fearful of dealing with real people,' said Mary, 'but not of tormenting them anonymously online.'

'Preliminary toxicology suggests Thorne injected Thomas with a mild sedative soon after gaining entry. This would be to gain control of him, but we're not talking about a long-lasting drug and not a high dose given the evidence of interaction between them. We have some intel on how the two men came into contact – I'll hand you over to Mary to explain.'

Mary stepped forward and adjusted her glasses as DS Beresford withdrew. 'There were five laptops in Thomas's flat,' Mary said. 'All of these had their password protections and sleep modes disabled. It's likely that as the sedative wore off, and with Thomas restrained, Thorne tortured him into giving him access to the machines. Thorne's prints are all over the keys. We believe he selected what the displays were showing, as well as the windows that had been left open behind them. Mike?'

Mike cleared his throat. 'So as Mary was saying, it appears that Thorne wanted us to discover what Thomas was up to. You all know about The Actaeon Club, as well as the note Thorne left in Thomas Lederer's bedroom.'

Esmeralda felt her skin prickle as eyes turned towards her.

'Thomas researched Adam Holderness's trial, which took place three months ago, in July,' said Mike. 'Last weekend, Thomas accessed the daily reports in the national tabloids and broadsheets, the detailed coverage on the BBC, and the sketches by the court artist. Especially significant is the local coverage by our good friend Larry Fawcett.'

'That's likely why Thorne targeted Fawcett during the press conference,' Mary said. 'Holderness's trial involved Ella Brooke, so Thorne would have been following it.'

Mike nodded. 'Fawcett's pieces were nearly as good as a court transcript, and Thomas filed all the stories in a folder that he named "Witness X: Ella Brooke?" Note the question mark after Ella's name, suggesting Thomas had worked out this was her with some degree of confidence, but not complete certainty. And this is where Jason Thorne comes in.'

Avatars

Mary pressed a clicker and the large screen blazed to life. 'What you're seeing here,' she said, 'are the avatars used by the members of The Actaeon Club. Ugly Duckling, Nemesis, and Bluebeard. These images were shown in the background during an online meeting of the club that Thomas Lederer recorded, almost certainly without the others knowing. We believe that Thomas created and operated the conferencing software they used, and that the meeting took place two months ago. Mike, you explain the next bit.'

'You'll see that the visuals of the avatars remain static through the whole meeting,' Mike said. 'In other words, the meeting was audio only – they were hiding their identities, even from each other, so they used voice-disguising software. Nemesis kicked off the proceedings, almost certainly using text-to-speech software spoken by an AI voice generator. Right. Have a listen to him inciting the troops.'

Mike clicked again and a bombastic voice filled the room.

'*In order to save the entire terrific and well-respected male race that everything is rigged against, the brave and noble and wonderful and incredible and highly regarded members of the greatest gathering of the most important club in the history of the whole world are going to avenge our fallen heroes by identifying and destroying the evil and vile lowlife bitches who murdered three of the bravest men who ever lived—*'

Mike stopped the sound, cutting Nemesis off and mimicking him with an accuracy that took Esmeralda by surprise. 'Perfectly expressed! Spirit like never before! Amazing!'

'I'm exhausted just listening,' Mary said. 'But let me tell you a bit more about the avatars. Thomas Lederer's was this vintage illustration of a rather sad-looking and bedraggled Ugly Duckling.' She highlighted it with the electronic pointer's red dot.

'So if Thomas Lederer is the Ugly Duckling, am I right in guessing that Nemesis is Jason Thorne?' Dinah asked.

'The overblown voice he chose is a bit of a giveaway.' Mary moved the pointer to Thorne's avatar. 'But Thorne either doesn't know, or doesn't care, that Nemesis is usually female.'

He knows, thought Esmeralda. She was familiar with the figure Thorne had chosen to represent himself. A thick-necked, broad-faced, purple-skinned giant of a villain who appeared at the end of one of the superhero films Líria loved. It occurred to her then that the pompous recording they'd just heard sounded rather like that villain too.

'We're working on the theory that Thorne was keeping

an eye out for any credible threats to Ella Brooke,' Mary said. 'He then drew those individuals in by founding The Actaeon Club, pretending to be an important collaborator. Thorne knows how to talk to these people. He spent years surrounded by them while he was in the secure psychiatric hospital. Poor old Thomas never guessed that his online buddy Nemesis wanted vengeance against the club's members rather than the women it was trying to destroy.'

'We're working on the theory that Thomas identified Ella,' said Mike, his usual calm neutrality reinstated, 'and that he was going to use her face in the game trailer by means of the deep-fake technology we saw in the film. That's likely why he was on Ella's street at the start of last week. Maybe he even went there to gloat. When Thorne got wind of Thomas's plan, he somehow convinced him to hold off. Probably persuaded him they couldn't yet be certain that Ella was Holderness's victim. But Thomas had put a target on his own head.'

'Still,' said Mary, 'there's one way in which Thomas got the better of Jason Thorne. It appears that Thomas managed a small-scale data breach. He accessed Thorne's recent photographs of Hugo Green's only surviving victim, along with her name and telephone number. In other words, Thorne unwittingly supplied Thomas with an alternative to Ella Brooke for the game trailer.'

Mike ruffled his hair, a nervous habit Esmeralda had seen in him before. 'Thorne said in his note that Thomas's murder was both *to protect* Ella and *to avenge* Esmeralda.' Several people turned to study Esmeralda with undisguised curiosity. Mike couldn't keep her name from the conversation – that horse had bolted some time ago. 'My point here is that Thorne never wanted to out Esmeralda. In his own warped view, he was acting as her protector.' Mike was rubbing his chin as he thought. 'But one of the things I really want to understand is how the hell Thorne got Esmeralda's phone number in the first place.'

'So do I,' Esmeralda said, feeling a bit like a pet who'd heard the humans repeatedly mentioning its name and shocked them by actually speaking.

'We can be pretty sure how Thomas got the number,' Mary said. 'He must have stolen it when he breached Thorne's data, and that's how he was able to send you the texts. But we still haven't located the phone Thomas used – my bet is that he destroyed it, though there's a slim chance Thorne took it. Not that it matters much, because if we do manage to lay our hands on it, I expect the device is going to purge itself.'

'Have you identified the person behind the Bluebeard avatar?' Dinah was frowning at the colour illustration of the fairy tale serial killer brandishing a sword in his right hand. With the left, he was dragging his disobedient wife by the hair to the murder room.

'Our strongest theory is that Bluebeard was the body Thorne left for us on the motorway, George Rossiter,' Mary said. 'Thomas was clearly teaching his friends a few tricks, because Rossiter's devices all wiped themselves into oblivion. But Rossiter definitely fits Thorne's new victim profile. Woman hater. Wife murderer. Manosphere hero. It seems that Jason Thorne is annihilating The Actaeon Club's members, closing them down and making sure any intelligence they've gathered disappears.'

'So Thorne selected Rossiter not just because he was an evil bastard – we all know there are plenty of those – but because he was part of Actaeon,' Mike said.

'I have a couple of questions,' Esmeralda said, ready at last to ask about Folly View Cottage. But she broke off, unnerved to sense a presence close by, and realised that DCS Vane had somehow approached without her noticing, and was at her side.

'I need a private word, Esmeralda,' the DCS said quietly. 'Now, please.' There were dark circles beneath his blue eyes. He led her away, up the stairs to the rim, then sat heavily on a sofa as she lowered herself beside him.

'This isn't a proper interview, but can you tell me where you were, please, all of yesterday and until you arrived at work today?'

'What's going on, sir?'

'I'd appreciate it if you'd answer my question.'

'Over yesterday morning I was in my bedroom writing my report on Adelaide Road. I filed it around noon – you can check the time stamp. Líria and my dad and I had lunch. I dropped my dad off in the botanic gardens around two, then Líria and I went off to buy ice creams at this new shop Ben's sister just opened. The plan was that Ben was going to join the three of us for an afternoon walk, and Líria thought we should bring treats.'

'Did you interact with Ben?'

Her chest was starting to tighten. 'Briefly. He met my father in a little hidden place by the stream, but he was called away. Líria and I ran into him as he was leaving.'

'So you encountered Ben in this hidden place?'

'No. Near the children's play area. It's where I parked.'

'And why was Ben called away?'

The alarm was spreading, moving upwards, so that the words were tight in her throat. 'He said he needed to look after his nephew so his sister could work.'

'According to the conversation I had with Ben's sister early this morning, she hasn't seen Ben since Wednesday night at her ice cream shop, when he was there with you, and she had no plans to see him yesterday. What do you say to that?'

'I don't know what to say. I'm telling you what Ben told me.'

The DCS's face was impassive. 'What happened after you and Ben parted?'

'Líria and my dad and I ate our ice creams by the stream. We had a little wander through the botanic gardens as we'd planned, then we returned home. I helped Líria with her homework. We ordered in pizza for dinner and watched a film.'

'What film?'

'*The Parent Trap*,' she said, knowing he'd asked not out of interest but to try to catch her out. 'I said goodbye to them at seven this morning and came straight into work.' She paused, then said, 'Presumably you can see where my phone went?'

'The tracking is in line with the account you just gave. Assuming you were with it.'

She looked coolly at him, making clear her anger at this insult. 'Of course I was with it.' Did she only imagine that he visibly shrank as she met his eye? 'Has Ben been hurt?'

'What little I know I'm not able to share.'

Esmeralda felt as if she'd fallen suddenly, and her stomach had slammed into concrete a fraction of a second before the rest of her body.

'For now,' the DCS continued, 'I need you to go on restricted duty. I can't have you in an evidential, intelligence, or crime management environment.'

'That's not restricted duty. That's no duty at all. If Ben is in trouble I want to help.'

'I'm sorry, Esmeralda, but I can't see any alternative. You'll be on full pay. Would you like me to escort you off the premises? I'd be happy to ask someone else, if you prefer.'

She didn't need to think about it. 'Dinah,' she said.

He frowned at her answer, but said, 'Fine. I need you to surrender your warrant card, your pocket notebook, and any access keys. Leave them on your desk. Also, your police radio and your phone, laptop, and tablet.'

She wondered if she was actually having a heart attack, because her chest was squeezing so much it seemed to be burning a hole beneath her breast.

'I can see you're upset,' he said.

Of course I'm fucking upset. But she stayed silent. She had no more words to give this man. There was no room for anything beyond her desperation to know what had happened to Ben, to know he was okay.

'You're a good detective. These measures are unavoidable in the circumstances, but I hope to see you back here soon. In the meantime, talk to Well-Being Support later today. I've already arranged for them to call you.'

She watched him rise, hurry down the steps, draw

Dinah away from the group to speak briefly to her, then head out the door.

Esmeralda opened the small desk drawer where she kept a few personal items. She stared down at its contents, too dazed to work out what move she should make next.

'Let me,' Dinah said quietly, and then, 'Did the DCS tell you what's going on?'

Esmeralda shook her head. 'He didn't trust me with the details. It's to do with Ben.' She lifted her hands, at a loss. 'I think he's missing.'

Sylvie appeared, doing her usual trick of seeming to materialise from out of nowhere. She put a carrier bag into Dinah's hand, then glided across the room to Mary, who was still studying The Actaeon Club's avatars on her giant display screen, as if searching for a vital detail she had somehow overlooked. Sylvie turned her attention to the screen too, companionably, while speaking softly to Mary.

Dinah carefully placed Esmeralda's things in the bag. A packet of teabags. A box of tampons. Some paracetamol. Then she draped the bag over Esmeralda's shoulder as if she were a child.

'Will you check on Adelina Ortega Garcia?' Esmeralda asked. 'Take her statement? She's in Visitors' Reception.'

'Of course,' Dinah said. 'Ready?'

Esmeralda nodded. She pulled her lanyard over her head and dropped her warrant card on the desk beside the other items the DCS had said she needed to leave behind. Vaguely, she thought she'd missed something, perhaps more than one something.

She glanced behind her for a final time. Her eyes lifted to the rim, and that was when she saw DI Whistler was there, probably having been in the building all along, working in one of the small side rooms. He stared down at her but she didn't see the usual smug triumph in his face. For once, there was nothing there that she could read, except that his usual ruddiness was diminished, and he was unnaturally pale.

She averted her gaze, not wanting Whistler to be the last thing she saw before leaving. It was when she noticed that Sylvie and Mary were watching her from across the room, and each of them touched a hand to her heart to show their support, that Esmeralda blinked hard to stop any tears. She wasn't a crier and she was not about to become one now.

'Make him pay for what he's done,' Dinah said, squeezing Esmeralda's hand so that she turned away from Sylvie and Mary and saw that Dinah was glaring behind her and up at Whistler. And when Dinah added, 'Make them all pay,' Esmeralda knew that Dinah shared her view that Jason Thorne was far from alone in deserving her wrath.

The Intruder

When Esmeralda stepped into her house, there was a wrongness in the air, a scent with notes of lemon and geranium and sandalwood and lavender. It didn't belong to her or her dad or Líria, and though she couldn't place where she'd smelled it before, she was sure that she had. She paused in the hallway.

Point One. Her dad had said he'd be going for a round of golf after dropping Líria at school, so the house ought to be empty. Point Two. There had definitely been no sign of forced entry at the front where she'd entered. Point Three. If an intruder was inside, they would have heard her come in. Point Four. She had tools she could use, because Dinah had deliberately omitted to confiscate her utility belt, and she knew this wouldn't have been the case if the DCS had been the one to escort her off the constabulary site.

The question that kept pounding away at her was Ben. Was the disturbance in her house connected to whatever had happened to him? The fact that his phone wasn't available to receive calls and her texts were going unde-livered seemed ominous – he'd never not answered her before.

Esmeralda slipped the utility belt around her waist and fastened it. Multiple pouches were empty, including the one for her police radio, but she was glad to have the handcuffs and incapacitant spray. Once more, she silently thanked Dinah.

She held the spray in readiness as she entered the sitting room. It was empty, but her attention was imme-diately drawn to an absence at the centre of the chimney-piece, as well as a trace of the scent that had hit her when she walked into the house.

A framed photograph of her and Líria was missing, the two of them sitting together on the high side of a seesaw, taken when Líria was two. Both of them were laughing and joyous, Líria with her arms high in the air as if on a roller coaster, Esmeralda with her toes only just touching the ground, her arms around her daughter's waist to make a perfect seatbelt for her. Isaac Avelar had snapped the photo from his side of the seesaw. Why had it been taken? Had the thief been interested in her, in Líria, or in both of them?

Nothing in the kitchen had been disturbed, but the sliding doors to the garden weren't properly closed. Whoever had been in the house – or was still in it – had entered this way, and done so with skill, breaking nothing.

She made her way outside. At the end of the garden was a stone wall with a locked door that opened into an alley that ran behind the house. That alley was seldom used, so the intruder must have felt secure there when they lockpicked the door.

Her heart was beating fast as she returned to the house, but she reminded herself that she'd been trained to do this. The DCS had excommunicated her that morning, but he hadn't magically excised all of her skills.

She searched upstairs. Nobody popped out and said boo when she drew the shower curtain, but the aftershave lingered in her bedroom. A man's fragrance, she decided. Something about it made her queasy.

Líria's room was last. The red pyjamas she'd worn the night before were at the top of her laundry basket. The bed was beautifully made, without a single wrinkle in the dusty-pink quilt. That scrupulous neatness was Líria all over. But what wasn't Líria at all was that the photograph of her dad that she kept on her bedside table was missing. The frame, decorated with the word 'DADDY' at the top, and hearts along its other edges, was empty. This final discovery was so upsetting Esmeralda felt dizzy.

Having established that the intruder was now gone, she quickly left Líria's bedroom and went into her own. She tied her hair into a ponytail, then changed into black jeans, dark trainers, and a long-sleeved, fitted black T-shirt. As an afterthought, she threw on an oversized black jumper to cover up the utility belt.

Sitting on her dressing table was her police laptop. One of the things she'd omitted to return to DCS Vane, she realised. Thinking she'd be working from home the rest of the week, she'd left it there after making the Land Registry searches. That had only been a few hours ago, but already it seemed an age.

She replayed the DCS's comment about how they couldn't necessarily know that she was with her phone. Powering it down or putting it on silent might alert them to the fact that she was done with being followed and spied on. Instead, she turned the ringer to the lowest level, then buried the device beneath her quilt and muffled it further with pillows to make it difficult for anybody to hear it. They couldn't have it both ways, banning her from accessing all police intelligence while continuing to collect intelligence from her. Using her. Taking from her. She was done with that and with them. The break-up went both ways.

She was furious, and that fury was good and right. In a shoebox at the top of her wardrobe were two things that she needed. The first thing was a slim case, made of black leather. She picked it up to examine it, feeling as if she were greeting an old friend. Bifold in design, it opened like a clamshell, with a pocket on each side. These were filled with lockpicks that Esmeralda had secretly bought and practised using in advance of their training on home break-ins. The others had teased her for being good at it, a natural-born criminal.

She'd never admitted that her talent for this was no fluke. She'd watched videos and read books. As soon as she'd learned that those training sessions were on the cards, Esmeralda had recalled the gate the police discovered, hidden and locked, that gave entry to the crypts where Hugo Green had kept her. They'd found chains down there, too, screwed into the cold stone walls, which connected to the iron bracelets she'd been wearing when they rescued her. Objectively, she knew that there was nothing she could have done to get herself free as a fifteen-year-old girl, but she'd still felt a panicked urgency about taking the opportunity to hone those lockpicking skills.

Slipping the case into an empty pouch on her utility belt, she pulled out that second thing from the shoebox. A burner phone that she kept charged for emergencies, which was another tip from the criminals. The first call she made on it was to a local guest house, where she booked two rooms for two nights. Whatever she did, she needed to know her father and Líria would be safe.

The second call was to her dad, and she winced at the uncertainty in his voice when he said hello to a withheld number.

She needed to keep him away without alarming him, and decided to draw on a crisis that Dinah had experienced a few weeks ago. 'I'm afraid a pipe has burst in the kitchen and we can't be in the house while they're sorting it.'

'Why not?'

'Health and safety, the electricity needing to be off, you know the drill. I've booked us into that guest house we always say looks so pretty, the one near the botanic gardens. We have it tonight and tomorrow night, but we can extend our stay if need be, but we'll get the money back from insurance.' The lies just kept coming.

'What aren't you telling me, Hummingbird? Why have you hidden your number?'

'I'm using a friend's phone. Mine's out of battery.' This was not very convincing, given that she never let this happen, but it was the best she could think of under pressure.

'It's my job to take care of you,' he said, 'not the other way around.'

Her love for him made her heart hurt. 'No father could care more for his child than you. Now listen. I'm going to swing by the guest house in a few minutes to drop off some clothes and things that we'll need, so they'll be waiting for us there. Take Líria to the cinema and dinner after school – the two of you deserve some treats. I'll see you late tonight.'

He started to say her name, but before he could raise any further objections, she cut him off mid-word and ended the call. She did this out of necessity, despite knowing full well how averse he was to any parting that didn't end with a proper goodbye.

TWELVE YEARS EARLIER – FRIDAY,
23 DECEMBER 2005

Improvising

The sedative was in a syringe in one of Jason's pockets, his car keys in another, and he'd taken the precaution of leaving the boot unlocked in the event that he got lucky that night. But to bring all of this into play for Harriet – or rather, Esmeralda?

With Esmeralda, Jason wanted to be in the light. Everything that was life. To go on country walks, to eat together in restaurants, to wander through art galleries holding hands, to have a child together – this last, above all. There would be lots of sex, of course, but always because she wanted to and had a choice.

It was muscle memory that must have propelled him to do what he did next.

For an extremely tall man, Jason could move silently and with speed. He stepped out from behind the door she'd just opened and plunged the needle into the side of her thigh, right through the fabric of her dress so that the injection would be intramuscular. Slapping a hand over her mouth before any sound could escape, he pulled her backwards against him.

Almost instantly, she'd gone limp and he was holding her up, then carrying her out of the pub through that little-used rear exit, so conveniently near. Nobody came. Nobody saw. The gods really were on his side. The fact that he was so well-prepared, that he'd thought it all through, helped quite a bit too.

Less than a minute later, she was in the boot of his car, surrounded by quilts and blankets to keep her warm and protected. Then he was driving away and he was panicking. Panicking for the first time ever. Panicking because he had blown it with the love of his life, his idol, who would never forgive him. How on earth could he possibly have a normal conversation with her now? How could a relationship start like this?

Esmeralda's small handbag was at his feet, and he pulled the car over, realising he needed to get the SIM card out of her phone. He had never made mistakes like this before. Then again, he'd prepared to capture yet another stranger, but encountered instead the woman he'd been dreaming of for years. Two minutes later he had to stop again, this time on a deserted lane, so he could boost the sedative with an injection of a hypnotic that would keep her safely unconscious until he got her home. He didn't want her waking up in the boot and kicking out a light from inside to potentially draw attention to them, but he also didn't want her to be frightened.

He told himself there was no choice, now that he had done what he had done. Somehow, he would need to show her how much he loved her, and make sure she loved him back. Even if it became a deliberate case of Stockholm syndrome, one that he cultivated, well, that wasn't his first choice for how this would play out, but it would get them to where they needed to be in the end.

He loved her already. He'd loved her for fourteen years, before they even met. And she would love him back. Somehow, he would make it right. He would make her his. If she didn't kill him first.

But he didn't make it right. He made it worse. What was he to do? Jason studied her, asleep on the bed where he'd laid her, in his basement, and knew if she woke she wouldn't talk to him. She would scream. She would hate him. She would be terrified and enraged and she would fight. Would she see him as she'd seen Hugo Green? It wasn't lost on Jason that Green too had taken her underground.

The sheets were clean, of course, and he'd sterilised the waterproof mattress cover in readiness for his next guest, but that didn't change what he had done to the others who'd visited this room and been in that bed, whose frozen bodies were on the other side of the wall. This wasn't the place he'd ever imagined bringing Harriet – *Esmeralda* – to.

And she was so profoundly unconscious. Had her doses been too high? She was slighter than the others, who had woken by this time. Although her eyelids fluttered as she slept, and she stretched and sighed a little, he could tell from her breathing that she was in an entirely different world.

She would never know, he thought, if he touched her. Just her hair. That was all. It was so silky, when he let it fall through his fingers. It was safest to do this now, when her lack of awareness meant the action posed no danger to either of them.

And she would never know if he were to lie beside her and take her in his arms. And that dress, showing the shape of her body beneath it, lying like a crimson puddle around her. She would never know if he ran his hands over that fabric to find out how slippery it was, how it clung, how accurate his perception was of what lay beneath it. Would she move, if he did that? Just that? Only that? That would be all.

And if his hand slid beneath the silk, accidentally, to touch her skin, just to test if it was as smooth as it appeared, if it was warm under the fabric, she would never know, and he would stop there. That would be enough. Just her leg. Just her stomach. Just a single hip.

And if he turned her, just to see what she looked like at that angle, or another, and touched a breast as he arranged her, she would never know that either, and would never know as she slept on, that soon the dress was on the floor, and then the rest of her things.

And she would never know that his own clothes were off too, just to see what she felt like against him, entirely beneath him, with his weight pressing down on her, and she would never know, and that would be enough.

Except that of course it wasn't. Nothing he did would ever be enough. And each new barrier he broke, each new silent promise he made to her and to himself, each new threshold that dissolved almost as soon as he created it, led to the next.

Jason knew from the driving licence and credit cards he'd found in her handbag that her surname was now Avelar, and he far preferred that to Sapphire. He tested it aloud, though softly. 'Esmeralda Avelar.' Those two names together were so much more her. Then he tried again, with the necessary modification. '*My* Esmeralda Avelar.' Yes. That was better, though Esmeralda Thorne would be the most perfect.

Esmeralda he especially loved. It was original. A witch's name, he thought. He knew that he was romanticising her, but couldn't resist the idea that she was somehow mythical, with one foot in the world of the dead and the other in the land of the living. Only someone magical could survive Hugo Green. And only someone entirely out of the ordinary could earn Jason's own undying love, and his vow to do whatever it took to keep her safe.

But how the hell was he to get her out of the mess he'd made? How could they both move beyond this without harm? Forcing himself into brutal honesty, he examined all the possibilities, his brain working like a computer, sorting through contingencies, examining each way forward and its different branches. There was only one answer, and he didn't like it at all, because it meant her not knowing him, not loving him, and not remembering him. It meant no future for them. But he couldn't bear to lose her.

He lay down beside her again and took her in his arms. There was something wet on his cheeks, and he was astonished to realise he was crying at the thought of what his father would say. His father would say that Jason must do what he had not done for many years: the right thing. His father would say that despite the specialness of this woman he'd waited so long for, he must stop repeating the mistakes he'd made with the others. His father would say that the only way to break that pattern was to let her go.

She had been the girl who lived when she was fifteen. She would be the girl who lived once more. Jason heard these two sentences in his father's long-vanished voice.

Despite his worry that she wasn't waking up, Jason now needed her not to. That was her only chance. Praying the effects wouldn't damage her permanently, he reached for the syringe and shot more drugs into her arm, telling himself that forgetfulness was far better than death.

Jason had noted her address from the driving licence in her bag. The sun was coming up as he drove over icy roads to the deserted alleyway behind her house, as confident as he could be that it was too soon for anyone to have reported her missing, or at least for such a report to be acted on, especially in the busy run-up to Christmas. He leaned over to kiss her goodbye, telling her how sorry he was, vowing that he would never bother her again.

He popped the SIM back in her phone, turned it on, and quickly memorised her number. He might need it someday, but only if it were for her sake, absolutely and positively and only for that reason, because he would otherwise keep his promises. Then he put the phone back in her elegant little handbag.

Gently, he took her from the car and arranged her near the door that led from the alleyway into her back garden. He adjusted her position so that she was curled on her right side, her ear and temple resting on her bent arm to protect her head as far as possible from the frozen ground. Her bag was next to her. She, and whoever found her, would simply assume she'd returned home the morning after a drunken night before.

The only thing Jason kept was the heart-shaped locket, which he'd removed while she slept. It was heavy and large, and he'd worried that it was pulling too tightly around her neck. The locket contained one photograph, which was of Esmeralda as a toddler, smiling at the camera. She was in the arms of the beautiful, long-dead woman Jason knew was her mother. Just their shoulders and heads were visible, and the photo was taken from the side view, but it was obvious they were snuggled close. The mother's chin rested on top of her child's silky hair, and she looked so like Esmeralda did now.

He drove around the corner, stepped out of the car once more, and peered round, hidden by a stone wall. It was dangerous for her to be out in this cold for long. Already he could hear her phone ringing in the distance, muffled by her bag. A minute later, and to his great relief, the door between her back garden and the alley burst open and a slight man Jason recognised from the old news footage rushed out. The father had eyes for nothing but his daughter, and fell to his knees beside her, looking aghast, examining her, lifting her upper body into his arms, cupping her hands with his own to warm her, bending over her as she began, at last, to stir a little, and he began to try to get her to her feet.

All at once, Jason saw how she appeared to others, wearing the same clothes from the night before. He projected ahead, and saw that she would burn those clothes, and she would wash and wash. And all of this was on him. And there would be no forensic examination, because she'd been there and done that fourteen years ago, and the experience of being treated like a living crime scene wasn't one she would want to repeat. It wasn't one her father would have her repeat.

As Jason forced himself to tear his eyes from Esmeralda and slip away, he felt something unusual, something he wasn't used to. This strange emotion, he realised in a rush of horrified understanding that made his stomach clench, was fear. And it came with a disturbing new recognition that he did not deserve the reward that he'd always considered his due, of being given his heart's desire. He pictured Esmeralda, not as she was now, but as if imagining a drawing he was about to make. She was standing over him, a goddess of divine justice and retribution, pitiless and beautiful, and she was armed with a sword and scales.

Part IV: Hummingbird

The humming-bird is of an extremely pugnacious disposition, and will not hesitate to attack birds considerably larger than itself.

Lewis Spence, *The Mythologies of Ancient Mexico and Peru*

TWELVE YEARS LATER – MONDAY,
18 SEPTEMBER 2017

Folly View

What nobody understood, but Esmeralda knew about herself, was that she lived with a conviction that her life was borrowed and she would soon be snatched back to the land of the dead, where she belonged. That she'd ever escaped those crypts had been a fluke, a mistake that she always felt would someday be corrected. She wasn't Princess Persephone or Lady Lazarus, as she'd been called so long ago by the press. The footholds of those mythical creatures on earth, however shaky, had been more secure than hers, because Persephone could count on her six months in the sun, and Lazarus on resurrection.

Given the fragility of her existence, Esmeralda considered herself more akin to Eurydice, about to be dragged back into a forever darkness just before she could step into the light, and all at the whim of somebody else, because he couldn't bloody control himself. But that didn't mean she was going down without a fight. If her stolen time was about to run out, then she would spend those last miraculous minutes protecting Líria and searching for Ben.

A surprisingly large number of roads led in and out of the small village where Folly View Cottage was located, and numerous footpaths snaked through the surrounding countryside. How perfectly such an arrangement would suit Jason Thorne, Esmeralda thought, as she parked the car in a muddy layby and began to walk.

Soon after rounding a bend, she saw the long, cobbled driveway that led into Folly View's grounds, and was struck even more by how ideal a hideaway this place was. Thorne was not a man who would have spent the last ten months shivering and feverish in some disused and forgotten hovel. No long-abandoned tunnel beneath a river or disused war bunker for him. No, no, and no. Thorne would not be stepping through pools of stagnant water or shrinking from slimy walls, alone in the dank and dark with no plumbing and heat.

Ten metres along the driveway was a cantilevered sliding gate made of solid metal. Esmeralda guessed it was operated electronically. The gate was set into the high stone wall that skirted the boundaries of the property, with a visitors' bell to one side but no obvious place for leaving post. Over the wall, she could see the tops of trees, as well as the house's slate roof with stone chimney stacks rising above it and paned dormer windows below it.

She looked for cameras, trying to work out if anybody could be watching her, but saw nothing obvious. Keeping close to the wall, Esmeralda moved around the property's boundary. Soon, she came upon an oak door that was set into the stone. It was locked. Of course it was. A few metres away was an old beech tree with multiple thick branches stemming from its massive trunk. All of them curved upwards, so that the whole structure resembled a giant wooden tulip. Seeking a vantage point, Esmeralda began to climb.

She arranged herself at the midpoint of several branches, and felt as if she were being held in a cup. Looking over the wall, she saw that the gardens of Folly View Cottage were neglected but romantically beautiful. They made her think once more of the brambles that surrounded Sleeping Beauty's castle. The curtains were all drawn in the large sash windows on the lower floors, like the smaller ones she'd seen in the attic's dormers. No lights were visible, but telephone and electricity wires connected the house to the main grids.

When she landed again on the earth, she was sad to leave the beech tree, but she forced herself forward. Once more, she approached the door in the wall. This time she reached into her utility belt for the lockpicks. This man, this Jason Thorne, was trying to unravel her entire world. Most unforgivably, he was messing with her child, because Esmeralda didn't doubt who had broken into her house, and she planned to mess with him right back. A part of her wondered if something chemical or molecular had altered her brain that morning at work, leaving her maddened, stopping all caution, venting her pent-up rage.

Make him pay, Dinah had said. Make them all pay. Too many men had treated Esmeralda as if she were a plastic piece in a board game. And now she was evolving into something more, into something new and fierce.

The lockpicks were excellent, the perfect selection of instruments. Esmeralda had been a top student, practising and practising when they'd staged fake break-ins during training. She studied the door's 5-lever mortice lock, frowning a little at the prospect of how challenging it would be. Then she got to work, channelling patience and a sure hand.

Detective training had turned her into an excellent delinquent. After seven minutes and quite a bit of sweat, the lock clicked and she slipped into the walled grounds of Folly View Cottage, leaving the heavy door ajar and inserting a fallen branch in the crack to stop it from shutting her in.

On the west side of the property was what must have once been the coach house, now converted into a large garage. The door was locked, but it had a long slit of a horizontal window. Behind it, she saw a workbench covered with tools and small machines.

More important were the two SUVs, which seemed to be Jason Thorne's vehicle of choice. Esmeralda remembered Hannah Beresford saying he had to be storing cars somewhere. There was the shape of a third, smaller vehicle, but this had a huge black tarpaulin thrown over it. Was it Ben's? Had he followed the trail to this house as she had, and come to harm here? A slideshow of Adam Holderness, George Rossiter, and Thomas Lederer was playing inside her head, and she needed to turn off those constantly unspooling images of the men Thorne had tortured and killed. What good would she be to Ben if she allowed dread to overwhelm her?

Another outbuilding, on the east side of the grounds, surprised her by being unlocked. This one was filled with gardening equipment which, given the evidence all around her, was clearly underused. But the most hunted man in the country could hardly drive around on his ride-on lawn mower while waving to the neighbours.

A third outbuilding was made of golden stone and in the style of the giant playhouse that Thorne had built at his mother's. Esmeralda would bet money that both were in imitation of the chalet in the Georgian Pleasure Gardens. The door was secured with a padlock and the tiny windows were blackened from inside. She returned to the store of gardening equipment and grabbed a pair of heavy-duty bolt cutters she'd spotted there. Mere minutes later, dropping the broken padlock onto the ground, she pushed the door open as wide it would go and stepped inside.

She didn't expect to find Jason Thorne in the little hut, but she drew in her breath lest she see Ben, because to her mind this would be a place for stashing a dead body rather than a living victim. Dust floated in a streak of sunlight, and there was a sinister chemical smell that made her feel as if she were being poisoned. But except for a set of beautifully made shelves containing neat rows of sealed glass jars filled with a variety of powders and liquids and dried plants, the little building was empty.

In the pouch where her confiscated police radio normally lived was the burner phone. She grabbed it, switched on the torch, and aimed the beam to look more carefully. A handwritten label had been stuck onto each jar to designate its contents. Although Esmeralda had little understanding of the words and letters, she recognised that some were complex chemical symbols while others were in the language of botany.

She knew that the writing on those labels was not Jason Thorne's, whose creepily beautiful penmanship was all too familiar to her. What was more, the labels were desiccated, the glue losing its hold, giving her the impression that they'd been there for some time. She would think about what all this meant later. For now, she needed to stop messing around with these outbuildings and find a way to get herself into that house.

The Enemy

Detective Inspector Harold Whistler would be turning fifty in two months, and he had been dreading it. Now, he was praying that he would still be alive to celebrate.

Whistler had missed the briefing early that morning, but he'd watched Dinah escort Esmeralda from the building, bringing the gathering to an abrupt end. He was certain Esmeralda had clocked him, looking down at her from the rim after he finally emerged from the side room where Dominic Vane had left him to recover after their extremely difficult conversation.

If Esmeralda had thought the expression on Whistler's face was one of triumph as he watched her leave, then she'd been mistaken. What Whistler had been feeling at that moment was deep and brutal fear, as well as a determination not to show it.

Whistler opened the three scanned documents that Vane had shared with him. *At last.* The originals had arrived on Saturday by first-class post, but that bastard had kept the news from Whistler for two full days. *Two full fucking days* of Whistler's guard being down when it should have been as high as it could possibly be.

Maybe Vane actually wanted him to die a horrible death. Whistler wasn't convinced the man's offer of protection had been prompted by genuine concern. In any case, Whistler had waved it away as absurd, insisting that he would work normally like everyone else, resources were strained as it was, and every hand was needed in the hunt for Thorne, who was just showing off and playing games as usual.

But as Whistler re-read Thorne's letter, it was hard to view anything that psychopathic bastard said or did as merely a game.

Dominic my friend. Despite your efforts to keep it from the internet, I managed to locate a stray video of Mr Whistler's assault on DC Esmeralda Avelar at the end of your little performance for the press on Thursday. (I note that you made no attempt to stop the publication of the still images. Why might that be, Dominic?) While I am sure that you have lip readers of your own, I have, nonetheless, taken it upon myself to transcribe the extremely ugly things that Mr Whistler said to DC Avelar. A copy is enclosed. For the avoidance of doubt, Mr Whistler provoked DC Avelar deliberately and exposed her identity with ill intention. Bullies like Mr Whistler have no place in the police, Dominic, and since you will not eradicate them, I have no alternative but to do your dirty work for you. Mr Whistler must address his bad manners and make a filmed apology to DC Avelar, after which, justice will be served and his sentence carried out.

I have enclosed a copy of the design I have created especially for Mr Whistler, although I imagine he is already familiar with the Men Going Their Own Way symbol. Deep reflection seldom goes amiss, so I will assist the condemned man in the acquisition of whatever crumbs of self-insight and enlightenment he is capable of reaching in his last moments, and allow him to share any final words he may have. All of this will be captured for your viewing pleasure. Mr Whistler may wish to begin his preparations. What a spectacle it will be.

JT.

Whistler was goggle-eyed as he studied the second document, which looked to be a photograph of a page from a sketchbook: the Men Going Their Own Way symbol Thorne had referred to in his letter. Inside a circle was a straight vertical line. In the middle of that line, branching off to the right and upwards, was a short arrow. It was like an ugly traffic sign, with the road pointing to Whistler's own gruesome torture and death.

Whistler was also riled by the way Thorne referred to him as *Mr* but used Esmeralda's title. Perspective, Harold, he said to himself, noticing that the phone was quaking in his hand as he scrolled to the third document: Thorne's transcription of what he and Esmeralda said to each other on film after the press conference. Whistler had wanted to punch Dominic Vane when he asked if Thorne's lip reading had been accurate. Whistler said only that he would not dignify that question with an answer. In truth, Whistler knew that Thorne hadn't missed a single syllable. It was glaringly obvious that Thorne was sufficiently obsessed with Esmeralda to search for and actually find that damn video. And Thorne's question was niggling Whistler too – had Vane actually wanted the tabloids to publish those photos to draw Thorne in, not caring about how exposed this left Whistler?

He had to face facts. First, three woman haters had ended up dead in the past month. Second, they had all been killed, directly or indirectly, by Jason Thorne. Third and fourth, at least in Thorne's view, Whistler had behaved like a woman hater too, and to Thorne's bloody precious Esmeralda of all people. Fifth and sixth and seventh, Thorne meant to capture him before engraving that bespoke image on his torso and murdering him.

Whistler's predominant emotion was terror, but it was coloured by shame, because the idea that he had anything in common with Men Going Their Own Way humiliated him even more. How would his behaviour look to Jason Thorne? For one thing, Whistler knew very well what Esmeralda's name was, and had deliberately and repeatedly got it wrong. Although Whistler didn't really understand *why* he had treated her like this, he knew he had gone too far. Before Thorne had put a target on his chest, Whistler had gained some pleasure in replaying the things he had said and done to Esmeralda. Now, that film looked unshakeably different. What Whistler liked to think of as much-needed professional discipline and straight talking, Thorne would regard as bullying.

If Whistler pretended to recognise that his treatment

of Esmeralda was wrong, if he feigned regret, would that be enough to save his life in the grisly court of Thorne? Whistler swallowed, and tasted bile, because he couldn't kid himself that it would. Acting wouldn't work, he knew – Thorne would be a severe critic and Whistler had never been good at faking things. Real feeling and sincere remorse might just begin to cover it. But the best thing Whistler could do was to make sure he never ended up in that particular theatre.

Seeing in the Dark

Skirting along the house's external walls, Esmeralda saw more tall sash windows with their curtains drawn, and a six-panel front door of heavy dark wood set into an enclosed porch. To enter that way would risk drawing the attention of anyone inside. She was concentrating so hard on finding a safer way in, she almost missed the flash of deep orange and crimson.

But there they were, miraculously alive in this sunny haven, despite the lack of care. The Queen's Enchantment Rose. It might have been easily overlooked because of the mess of loose branches, a thicket that obscured the flowers. But it was there, and it was growing on a lumpen bed of earth the size and shape of a grave.

She forced herself to set aside any thoughts about what might be under her feet. *Keep moving*, she told herself, yet again. Some metres along, at the furthest edge of the house's back wall, a section of the building projected out, forming a sort of lean-to with a sloping roof. It had a door and a small sash window, which was curtained like the others.

She studied the lock, then selected the right tools and got to work, periodically wiping sweat from her hands onto her jeans. Practice was already making her quicker. After five minutes she pushed the door open, bracing for an alarm.

All was quiet. There was a counter within reach, stacked with dusty old recipe books. Esmeralda wedged them beside the doorframe, then stepped silently over the threshold, holding the canister of incapacitant spray for the second time that day.

The light was dim. One wall was lined with deep, beautifully made shelves, and Esmeralda didn't think she deserved extra points for guessing who had made them. She crept closer and saw baked beans, powdered milk, tomato soup, teabags, peaches, and digestive biscuits. All had expired several years ago, which told her that the food had been stored in this place about a decade earlier, before Thorne's arrest.

At the far end of the lean-to was an interior door. Hearing no noise on the other side, Esmeralda pushed it open, revealing an enormous kitchen. There was a huge range cooker, unlit and unused. She paused to inspect the contents of a sideboard, and discovered quilted fabric cylinders filled with varying sizes of old crockery that she guessed was valuable, with each plate or bowl protected and separated by felt. It all looked abandoned.

When she left the kitchen behind, Esmeralda paused for a few seconds to give her eyes time to adjust. She was in a large hallway, but there were no windows so it lacked even the weak light that had penetrated the curtains in the kitchen. There was a musty scent in the air as she felt her way along, squinting as her vision progressively improved and she began to acclimatise. She realised those four months in the land of the dead had given her a quickness at navigating the dark, and it was a skill she hadn't lost.

Off the hall was a drawing room, a dining room, a study, and a snug. Dust covers had been draped over furniture-shaped lumps. She lifted a few but found nothing beyond a confirmation of her guess that the objects beneath them were old and expensive. What did she expect? A map with an arrow pointing to a stick figure drawing of Thorne in his exact location? *He is here.*

She returned to the hall. At the far end was the enclosed porch she'd seen from outside. At the other, towards the rear of the house, was the main staircase. Noiselessly, Esmeralda climbed to the first floor. The bedrooms showed no signs of recent use. The chests of drawers were empty, the wardrobes without hangers, and the bedside tables bare. The bathrooms were old-fashioned. There wasn't a tube of toothpaste in a cupboard, the bathtubs and basins were bone dry, and she couldn't see even a single loo roll.

Certain that nobody was hiding on this level, she flicked a light switch on and off. The flash told her that the unregistered owner of the house was either paying for energy use or managing to connect to it illegally. The latter possibility was within Thorne's skillset. She took the next flight of stairs, narrower and more ordinary, up to the second floor, then a still-narrower flight to the attic. It was the same story of haunted-house desertion.

She descended the three flights of stairs, back to the ground floor's main hall, convinced the house was unoccupied and she'd learned nothing. She bent her knees, resting her elbows on her thighs and her head in her hands, squeezing her eyes closed as her anxiety about Ben seemed to block out everything else.

When she opened her eyes again, and looked slightly to the right, her ability to see had sharpened still further, and she noticed a closed door she'd missed before, behind the main staircase. She straightened up, realising that the Queen's Enchantment Roses were only a few metres away, on the other side of the house's back wall. Carefully, she approached the door and listened, but there was only silence.

The door was fitted with a basic Yale night latch. At best, it would merely slow an intruder. She knew this would be her easiest challenge so far, and it took only a minute of vibrating the tension wrench above the rake pick before all the pins were lined up, the wrench rotated clockwise, and the lock clicked. Although she flinched when the hinge creaked, she saw no light, so she pulled the door open the rest of the way.

A stairwell led down to a windowless underground that made Esmeralda think of the airless place she still sometimes visited in her nightmares. Rationally, she knew the latch could be turned from inside so it was not possible for her to be locked in. Nonetheless, she returned briefly to the sitting room, grabbed a bulky dust cloth, and arranged it at the bottom of the doorframe to stop the door from closing completely. Then she descended the stairs.

When she reached the bottom, there was another door. In the fine crack that went around it, she could see light. She paused, her heart beginning to pound fiercely. Her terror for Ben was growing, despite her relief at stumbling upon another part of the house where she could search for him at the very moment when she'd been in despair that there were no moves left to make.

She shook her head, forcing herself to behave like the detective she had been trained to be. They might not want her, but they couldn't take away what she was in her core. She grabbed the burner phone and started recording, then placed it in her utility belt to improvise a body-worn video camera. Hard evidence of any discoveries she made would be crucial. Plus, she knew there was a risk of something happening to her, so she needed to do what she could to give any intelligence she collected a chance of making it back to others.

This last door was unlocked, and opened onto an anteroom with three closed doors. Although she had been right about the lack of windows, everything she could see was slick and bright and modern. The overhead lights were cleverly positioned, and there had to be vents somewhere in the ceilings because the air was breathable and less dank than upstairs. She walked, silently as she could, across the flagstone floor.

The anteroom might have previously been the wine cellar. She put her ear to the door on her left, heard only silence, and carefully opened it, not relaxing in the least when she discovered a bathroom. There were drops of water in the shower and sink, stacks of loo roll piled on the side, a damp towel hanging on an electric radiator, and toothpaste and a toothbrush in a cup.

She felt a chill when she spotted a red splodge near the rim of the pristine white basin. At last, she made herself follow through with one of the thoughts she had been trying to push aside since she'd learned Ben was missing. There was no doubt that Thorne was fixated on her. If he'd seen her and Ben together – and it seemed likely he had – then that would make Ben a target.

She opened a free-standing cabinet. Along with shampoo and deodorant, she found a razor and shaving foam, boxes of hair dye, and heavy-duty surgical scissors that made her double-check her grip on the canister of incapacitant spray.

She left the bathroom, wincing when her trainers squeaked. After again listening for noise, she turned the handle of the door on the right.

It opened onto a kitchen. The cabinets were beautifully made, the shelves inside them stacked with items that appeared to have been taken from the larder she'd encountered when she first entered the house. There was a small fridge, containing only a carton of UHT milk, and an electric oven without a spot of dirt or smear of grease.

She re-emerged into the anteroom. If this were a terror film, she would be startled by whatever horror lay behind the third and final door, but Esmeralda thought she knew what she would face. Quickly, as if pulling a plaster from a wound, she pulled the handle.

Standing just outside the doorframe, her adrenaline

spiking and her heart beating fast, she took in everything, all at once. Her senses were heightened. She could feel the blood pumping into her muscles, and sweat between her shoulder blades.

The room was empty. It was also enormous, at least eight square metres. At the far end was a king-sized bed, neatly made and startlingly white, alongside a chest of drawers topped by four framed images. One appeared to have been cut from a newspaper clipping of Ella Brooke, sleek in black and deadly as Catwoman. A second was a snapshot of Lucy Reed that Esmeralda had never seen, wearing faded denim shorts and a soft pink sweatshirt, standing in a field of wildflowers with her hair loose and blowing, squinting in spring sunshine and smiling widely at whoever was behind the camera. A third was a drawing of Esmeralda's own face. She recognised it as part of Thorne's project of sketching her each year. The fourth was the stolen picture of her and Líria on the seesaw.

She took a few steps in, to check behind the open door. There was nothing there, so she continued to take stock. Against the right wall was a squishy-looking sofa, covered in burnt-orange velvet, but no other objects or furniture on that side of the room.

Along the left wall was a gym bench that doubled as a storage container for a set of exercise tools and weights. On the floor beside this was a brown-leather duffel bag that she somehow knew was a kill kit. There was also a desk. Resting on it was a closed laptop, a stack of nineteenth-century novels, and the watch strung with the brightly coloured beetles that she had seen on Thorne's wrist in Luke's iPhone footage.

The otherwise pure white walls were covered in images that made Esmeralda want to groan and roll her eyes at once. There was a series of early-twentieth-century black and white photographs of naked female mannequins. Of course there was. Because Jason Thorne wanted women to be like dolls he could manipulate and control and pose. The postmortems on the three women in his freezers made it clear that he'd shot them full of drugs to ensure they couldn't fight back. Apollo's pursuit of a terrified Daphne had been arranged as a companion piece to Hades carrying away the distraught Persephone.

Lovely, Esmeralda said to herself. A real mix of ancient and modern art. How eclectic. And not the least bit predictable. Nothing more to see here, she said to herself.

Except that there was. And it was dangling from a hook on the wall, catching the light. She'd almost forgotten how her skin warmed the precious metal, and what it was like to cup her palm over the white gold, pressing it against her own heart. Her father had given her the locket as a sixteenth birthday present, and placed a rare snapshot of her and her mum inside. She'd worn that locket every day until she lost it – she wasn't sure exactly when, but it must have vanished around the time she conceived Líria.

This last thought, coupled with the photographs that Thorne had stolen from her house that morning, made the dreadful truth about who had taken the locket, and why, and the great lie, rush at her so that the room seemed to spin. But despite the enormity of the realisation, she couldn't react. To contemplate this now would derail her completely and leave her incapacitated. There wasn't time to let herself feel anything when there were such urgent things to consider and do, and such terrible consequences if she were to fail.

Nonetheless, there was a basic fact that she could afford to deal with, since it could be addressed in a matter of seconds. *That locket was hers, and she wanted it back.* As if in a dream, hardly acting out of her own volition, she took a single, faltering step forward, reaching out a hand to reclaim it. That was when the lights went out.

Observations

Harold Whistler really was having an extremely bad day, but trying to pretend that all was normal as he leaned against his car and studied Esmeralda's house while waiting on hold for Sylvie. Despite his pounding on Esmeralda's door and shouting her name through the letter slot, she wasn't responding. Nor was she picking up his multiple calls to her phone. Why the hell had she chosen now of all moments to go out of contact? Present or absent, the woman was nothing but trouble. The curtains were open but he saw no sign of movement inside.

Whistler was involved in a long-running custody battle for his twelve-year-old son, but even his vindictive ex-wife couldn't deny that he had spent the previous afternoon and evening with his boy. Without this alibi, Whistler knew they'd have been looking at him, too, for Sachs's disappearance. Anybody could see the two men hated each other.

Whistler had been watching Esmeralda closely over

the six months since she joined Major Crime. It didn't take Sherlock Holmes' levels of observation to notice that she lit up whenever Sachs entered a room. Whatever had happened to him, and as much as Whistler would have enjoyed blaming her, he had an annoying instinct that she wasn't behind it.

Nobody had seen Sachs since he drove away from the botanic gardens the previous afternoon, where he was picked up by an ANPR camera as he exited. After that, Sachs vanished from any of the visual recordings they'd been able to find. Wherever he had gone, it was likely there was no surveillance, so Whistler guessed country-side or a remote village. Sachs's phone and tablet had been disconnected, with their last ping on the outskirts of the city's west side. That narrowed the location to a circle with a five-mile radius, which helped about as much as knowing which thousand haystacks might contain the needle.

Whistler looked over his shoulder, then up and down Esmeralda's street, as if expecting Jason Thorne to pop out from behind a bush to drag him off. At last, Sylvie came back. Whistler had discerned a hint of warmth beneath her glassy voice when she spoke to other people – Esmeralda and Sachs, to name but two – but there was only pure chill when she spoke to him, the Queen main-taining civility towards someone who had displeased her.

'High Tech have confirmed that Esmeralda's phone is inside the property and switched on.' Sylvie spoke with clinical precision, but beneath it was a musical grace that Whistler didn't normally let himself hear. 'I am also able to tell you in confidence that Well-Being Support have been trying unsuccessfully to contact her, as per a prior arrangement.'

Sylvie's disclosures left Whistler in no doubt that Esmeralda was not in that house. So why had she left her phone behind? One obvious answer was that she didn't want to be tracked. Another was that she'd had no choice, and that she was in serious trouble.

'Anything else I can help you with?' Sylvie asked.

'No. I'm on my way back.' He would be safer there, he thought, behind the secure walls of the constabulary. This show of being brave was fucking dangerous. In any case, it was normal for him to be on site, so nobody would think he was frightened and hiding. As an after-thought, imagining that Thorne himself was listening and making his judgements, Whistler uttered two words to Sylvie that he seldom used. Although his voice was a grumpy and grudging mumble, those words were thank you.

Muscle Memory

It was pitch black, even for Esmeralda's highly tuned eyes. She needed to control her breathing. If her fear overcame her she would lose before she even began. She'd fought before to survive, when she was fifteen, and though nobody was certain, a big part of her thought she really had smashed that viscount's thigh bone into Hugo Green's skull. She knew she could do it again if she had to.

There was the click of a door. At first, she thought it came from the right, but that couldn't be the case, because she'd seen no door there. Every instinct she had told her to dive away from where she was standing. But where? She hurled herself forward.

Almost immediately, she slammed into what could only be an extremely tall human being and heard a male grunt of surprise. The incapacitant can flew from her hand. A pair of arms went tightly around her, pulling her into an obscene mockery of a lover's embrace. Body to body, lips fumbled for her own and she bit hard, so the man groaned, his arms loosening in shock. She heard the clack of what sounded like glass hitting the floor.

When she kicked hard at what she thought was an ankle, they both smashed down. He was impossibly strong, forcing her onto her back, with the lower half of his body between her legs. She fought to keep her feet flat on the ground in case that purchase could help. Her arms were pinned to the floor, bent at the elbows into wings.

Her hair had come loose, and was plastered against her forehead and neck, in her mouth. Her breath was coming too fast. He was grinding himself against her, between her legs, and that woke her up, filling her with so much hate she wanted to tear his eyes out. He froze, and Esmeralda realised in a clarifying jolt that the man on top of her was trying to decide if he could consolidate her two wrists into one of his hands, so he would have the other free. She couldn't let that happen. She couldn't allow herself to panic at what he might do with that hand. Hit her. Strangle her. Cut off her clothes. Drug her. All the things that had happened before.

When he spoke, the voice was familiar, but lower, less controlled than she'd ever heard it. Was it Thorne? Of course it was Thorne. It could only be Thorne. 'You smell wonderful,' he said. And she heard him inhale deeply, stealing the very air she breathed, yet another of his countless invasions and encroachments.

She felt him raise his lower body so that he was on all fours. This was it. Esmeralda exploded her hips straight upwards, so fast and forceful he grunted in surprise. Inhale that, she thought. The motion knocked him off balance, so that he tipped forward headfirst. He had no choice but to release her wrists to break his fall. The instant her hands were free, she twisted away and aimed a final kick at what she thought was his bad knee, satisfied to hear him scream and hoping this last blow would incapacitate him.

This man, this cowardly bastard. Let him see what it was like to deal with a woman who was awake, who he hadn't drugged into oblivion. Yes, she was hurt, but her eyes were open and she could strategise and react and cause him all sorts of trouble.

Esmeralda half-crawled, half-dragged herself away from him, in what direction she wasn't sure, until she was stopped by a wall. All she could think was that she had to get up, had to be on her feet and not on the floor, but she was too winded. The best she could do for the moment was to heave herself into a sitting position. Groping in her utility belt, she found the burner phone. Shaking, she somehow managed to activate the torch.

A Certain Lack of Respect

Whistler was back at the constabulary, safe behind its walls as he rifled through Ben Sachs's desk. Whatever he'd been up to, Sachs had left no trail of it, and if Dominic Vane knew, he wasn't telling. Or at least not telling Whistler. The bastard. Whistler propped his feet on the top of Sachs's desk, crossing them at the ankles just as Dinah walked by.

'Get your filthy shoes off,' Dinah said.

Whistler's response was to lean back into Sachs's chair more deeply, stretch his legs out further, and grind his heels into the shiny fake wood. Was he losing everyone's respect, so that even a relative underling like Dinah didn't hesitate to scold him? He felt strangely hollow as Dinah walked away, shaking her head as if pursuing the argument was beneath her. A part of Whistler knew he'd been childish about Sachs's desk, and that such actions were why Dinah and others viewed him as they did.

'Fuck off,' Whistler said, but nobody was close enough to hear. He tried to recover his train of thought about

Sachs. It was bothering him that the man had left no evidence of anything he had done over the past few days. His force-issued tablet was offline – presumably with Sachs himself – so their attempts to track him that way had so far failed.

Whistler was pondering all this when Sachs's desk phone rang, startling him as if a ghost had grabbed him by the shoulder. He groped for the receiver.

'Ben?' It was a man's voice, and he sounded breathless.

Whistler didn't correct the caller. 'Yeah.'

'I couldn't get through on your personal phone. This is Isaac Avelar. Esmeralda's father.'

Clumsily, Whistler heaved his legs and feet off the desk, banging them noisily on the floor. 'Yeah,' he managed to say again.

'I can't reach Esmeralda and Líria's school just phoned.' The man sounded as if he'd been crying. 'The headmaster's telling me they don't know where Líria is. She left the school grounds and they only just discovered she's gone.'

Whenever Whistler considered Esmeralda's history, the feelings it evoked were never for her, but rather, for what her father must have gone through while she was missing. Whistler had seen the interviews Isaac Avelar gave all those years ago, and been moved by them. It didn't take a professional empath – and Whistler certainly was not that – to recognise that the voice at the other end of the phone had room for only one emotion: the pure terror of a man who already knew what it was for a child he loved to disappear.

Whistler closed his eyes. 'This isn't DS Sachs, Mr Avelar. It's DI Harold Whistler.'

'Do you know what you've done to my family? What my granddaughter went through over the weekend? Trying to be brave after you dragged her mother in front of those cameras? She's probably run off because of what you did. You're likely the reason we can't find her. You're why she's missing and in danger.'

Whistler couldn't find words. All he could think was that Jason Thorne would learn of Esmeralda's missing child and be even more determined to capture and punish him for it. If anything actually happened to Líria Avelar, it would be much worse for him. Thorne the protector of children. Thorne the avenger. Whistler's back was sweating.

In the face of Whistler's silence, Isaac Avelar continued. 'What has my daughter ever done to you?'

Whistler inhaled. Being asked this question by Esmeralda's father pierced him in a way that Thorne's death threats had not. Perhaps it was because Isaac Avelar, unlike Jason Thorne, had the right to a decent answer.

Whistler had hated Esmeralda for being beautiful but indifferent to him, and for being faultlessly polite and professional but nothing more. He had found it humiliating to see her looking hopefully at a man he envied and disliked, and to watch that man so obviously love her back. And it had been mortifying to admit that she had on many occasions figured things out that Whistler himself had missed. Above all, he had resented her for rising above an unimaginably horrifying past with grace, and without temper. Without carrying the ugliness of what life had done to her, but rather, overcoming it.

333

Again Whistler imagined Jason Thorne listening in to this conversation, and judging his conduct, awarding marks for honesty and perceptiveness and contrition.

He swallowed hard. To his own astonishment, he heard himself saying, 'Esmeralda did nothing to me.' He added, 'If you want to punch me later you can go right ahead.'

'I'm not a violent man,' Mr Avelar said, and Whistler admired his strength. 'But I may well make an exception for you.'

'Let me help you find your granddaughter, Mr Avelar.' Whistler was going to have to venture outside again, beyond the safety of the constabulary's security perimeter. A part of him thought: So be it. Another part thought: If I have Esmeralda's father with me that might keep me safe, might even dissuade Thorne from coming near.

'I want Ben. I don't want you. Get Ben now.'

'Unfortunately, for reasons outside either of our control, I'm all you've got,' Whistler said. 'Tell me where you are. I want you to stay on the phone while I drive so we can make a plan of action. We'll go from there.'

The Encounter

The first thing Esmeralda saw was Jason Thorne, eerie in the beam of the burner phone's torch. He was on the floor in front of the orange sofa, doubled over and clutching his left knee. When he looked up at her, he was grimacing in pain. Good, she thought.

She continued to take stock of her surroundings. The door to the anteroom was still open, only a metre away and set in the wall she was leaning against. She could bolt, she thought, feeling herself actually rise up a few centimetres, already in movement. She could be away so fast Thorne would have no hope of catching her.

But almost as soon as the idea of fleeing came to her, she pushed it away. Her fear for Ben reasserted itself, along with her instinct that he was nearby, and her certainty that the force wouldn't fight hard enough to save him. Time was running out, and she was all he had. If their positions were reversed, she knew Ben wouldn't give up on her. He would never leave her in a hellhole like this.

Terrifying as Thorne was, she had to confront him head on. In a silent conversation with herself, she tried to talk up her own confidence, reasoning that she was the best and only person to negotiate with him. Given Thorne's infatuation with her, and her unwelcome understanding of his warped defence of vulnerable women, he didn't present the same degree of lethal danger to her that he did to others. She wondered also if he shrank from the idea of hurting her to her face, in full light and with both of them awake and aware.

In any case, her brief chance of escape was now gone. Thorne was pulling himself into something resembling a sitting position, with his back against the sofa.

'There's a light switch,' he said. 'Above you.'

She felt for it, not taking her eyes from this man who had tortured and killed at least six people, and the room flooded with such brightness she winced. When Thorne hoisted himself up onto the sofa, then used his arms to heave up his left leg, as if he didn't want to put weight on it, she tried to say *Don't move, Stay where you are*, but couldn't form the words.

She glimpsed the can of incapacitant spray beneath the desk, uselessly far away. On the floor near the sofa was a syringe. He would have done to her what he did to those other women. He would still try. She knew it like she knew the taste of blood in her mouth, his mixed with her own, so she wanted to spit.

He saw her seeing the syringe, easily within his reach. 'I dropped it when we first started fighting.' He broke off, then said, 'That wasn't meant for you.'

Then why the fuck do you have it?

She made herself think logically, and sensed that her brain was beginning to sharpen again. What had made the clicking sound just before she moved forward and slammed into him? If there was another door, and Ben was behind it, she needed to know.

'I wasn't expecting that we'd meet at your instigation, rather than mine.' Thorne's voice was stronger than she liked. 'Clearly, the attraction isn't just on my side.'

She managed to speak at last. 'That's your interpretation of what just happened, when you tried to assault me, Mr Thorne?'

There were only three metres between them, and she wanted to place her heavy lockpick case on the floor against the doorjamb, so the door stayed open. Keeping her eyes on him, Esmeralda used her free hand to grope in her utility belt, and pulled up a piece of smooth metal tangled in what felt like a chain. She lifted it, felt the shock of recognition register in her face, and saw her understanding mirrored in Thorne's.

Her locket. She realised he must have slipped it into the toolbelt pouch while they fought, ensuring his possession of that gold heart was not seen or known by anyone but her. She calculated that it hadn't been in the frame of her improvised body-worn video, and that the lights had gone out almost as soon as she'd noticed it. The two of them could not discuss it. Probably not ever, but especially not now, with that video recording away.

'I allow it may be wishful thinking for me to imagine the attraction goes both ways.' His eyes were on her shaking hand as she dropped the locket back into the toolbelt pouch. 'I'm sorry,' he said, and she knew he was referring to all of the things he could not say explicitly. There were too many to list.

It struck her that Thorne had saved the locket all this time, and given it back as soon as he had the chance, protecting her – and Líria – from letting anyone else know. If the locket were discovered, and she was asked, she would say she'd brought it with her as a protective talisman – she'd seen other police officers hide good luck charms in their tactical vests. But she wasn't thinking straight. She realised she was over-complicating things. She could simply say Thorne had stolen it from her house that morning when he broke in, and she'd taken it back. But she didn't have time to think about this now.

'Sorry?' she said. 'Sorry that you would have raped me? That you would have tranquillised me? That you would have tortured and killed me?'

'Quite likely the first two. Certainly not the last. I'd hoped to do better, but when the opportunity came. Well . . .' He shrugged, as if he'd merely helped himself to a piece of cake despite having sworn off sugar. 'You're difficult to resist.'

She double-checked yet again that the phone was still recording, resisting her temptation to stop it. She needed justice to be done for Thorne's victims, so she had to ensure that whatever intelligence she gathered down here had a chance of making it out even if she didn't. Even if that intelligence put her at risk. He'd murdered four women, if she counted Lucy. He was also behind the recent killings of three men.

She couldn't bear to think that Ben might bring the count to four. She wouldn't. She tried to tell herself that while she had Thorne in her sight, at least he couldn't be hurting Ben. But that didn't change the fact that Ben might already be badly injured. She needed to find him, and quickly.

Follow the protocols, she told herself, stating her name and police rank.

'We've already established, quite intimately, that I know who you are.' He was looking pointedly at the pocket of the toolbelt where her locket rested. The significance of why he had it, how he must have obtained it, and when, rushed at her again, but she shook the thought away. She needed to keep moving and reasoning and acting according to her training.

Even with an injured knee that seemed, at least for now, to have immobilised him, and near-emaciated thinness, Thorne was a dreadful threat. He was wearing a short-sleeved orange T-shirt and loose-fitting black cargo trousers, and she could see the taut muscles and cords in his wiry arms. To be in a room alone with him made her feel like she was trapped with a leopard, despite the fact that he was wounded. But Esmeralda knew all too well that injured and threatened animals could be especially dangerous.

She explained that she was arresting him and taking him into custody on suspicion of the murders of Adam Holderness, George Rossiter, and Thomas Lederer, on the grounds that there was material evidence of his involvement in all three cases. Then she recited the police caution, hoping he didn't guess that she was trying to work out what to do next.

Intelligence

Harold Whistler's ex-wife wanted him to pay for every little thing she could squeeze from him. When it came to his son, Whistler actually liked it this way, but he enjoyed making her wonder with each new demand whether or not he would agree.

One of the many things Whistler paid for was a family plan that covered his personal phone as well as Max's. This meant he could see all the calls Max made. Although Whistler would have liked to respect his boy's privacy, he knew too much about the horrors that children could face, so he kept a close eye on Max's contacts and activities.

As Whistler drove to the golf course, he fired questions over the car phone. First, had Mr Avelar used Find My Phone to try to trace Líria? The answer was yes, but that it was off. Whistler tried to offer reassurance that Líria herself might have disabled Find My Phone because she didn't want to be caught doing something or going somewhere she shouldn't. He didn't voice the darker possibility that someone had taken Líria and removed the SIM from her phone, but he knew the grandfather would get there on his own.

Whistler's next question was whether Líria's phone was part of a family plan. The answer, thankfully, was yes, so he patiently and methodically talked Mr Avelar through the steps to access Líria's call log. It was a matter of minutes for them to learn that the last number she dialled belonged to a taxi firm.

'Call them now,' Whistler said. 'Find out if they picked her up. If yes, where from? Get them to tell you the location and time they dropped her. I'll be pulling into the golf course car park in less than five minutes. You can update me then.'

The Promise

Esmeralda had been through simulations, but those involved perfectly planned fake arrests with trainees swooping in a team. She had watched actual arrests caught on bodycam and been amazed by how calm those officers were, even friendly, as if they and the suspect were in these unfortunate circumstances together. When the subject was aggressive and resistant, there was always a swarm of officers to overpower them.

Nobody had ever produced a how-to guide for the situation she was in. Trying to appear calmer than she felt, she said, 'Please show me your hands, Mr Thorne.' To her surprise, he slowly stretched out his arms, flipped them so his palms were face-up, then flipped them again to ensure she was able to examine his hands front and back.

Once more, he was looking at the pocket of her tool-belt with the locket. 'I would never hurt you, you know, Esmeralda.'

'That's an interesting take on things.' She lifted the

bottom of her T-shirt to wipe the blood from her nose, silently telling him to fuck off when his eyes narrowed and his nostrils flared at the sight of her bare belly. 'Considering that you just did.'

'I'm sad that you doubt me.' That irony of his was back in his voice.

She slid herself upwards, against the wall, until she was on her feet again. 'Just before we fought and the lights went out, how did you turn them off?'

'Ah.' His eyes flicked slightly to the right. 'That would be telling. Surely you have more interesting questions for me?'

The truth was she had too many questions to count. *Where is Ben? What turned you into a murdering rapist psychopath? What happened to Lucy?* All she allowed herself to say was, 'I've cautioned you. I need to handcuff you now.' She was dreading having to get close to him again.

'Sounds fun. All my dreams are coming true.'

'I need you to understand,' she said, 'that the handcuffs are for my protection and yours, on the basis of the past instances of your violence. Including the violence you showed towards me only minutes ago.'

'To be fair, Esmeralda, I did think you were an intruder. You broke into my house.'

'To be fair,' she said back, 'you are an absconding murderer suspected of several new killings, and I believe there may be another victim somewhere in this property who is in danger. So perhaps think again before you try that one.'

'Let's call it even. How about I make it up to you?'

'I suspect you and I have very different ideas about how you can do that.'

'On the telephone, before the Pleasure Gardens, you asked what my mother and I argued about seventeen years ago, on Christmas Day. I told you it was Lucy, and I promised to explain when we were alone.' He looked delighted with himself. 'I see I have your attention. You wouldn't be a good poker player, you know. Your eyes give you away.'

She needed to say the right thing, so that the burner phone captured her adherence to form as well as any intelligence. 'Please remember you're being recorded. I've cautioned you. Any discussion ought to be during a formal interview with your solicitor present.'

'I appreciate the warning but I don't care about that.' He inhaled, then said, 'The first thing you need to know is that Lucy was pregnant when she disappeared.' Thorne had turned pale, and she wondered if he had ever spoken these words to anybody else. As if reading her mind he said, 'You're the first person I've told. You look . . . upset.'

Esmeralda thought of the Queen's Enchantment Roses, above them but so close, and her instinct that this was where Lucy was. If she was right, were the bones of an unborn baby there too, curled inside its mother? 'Did you kill Lucy, Mr Thorne?'

'I loved Lucy. I wanted to be a father more than I'd ever wanted anything. The things I did later – I always knew I had it in me to do them but I hadn't yet acted on those impulses. With animals, yes, and insects, but not with human beings. Like the police, I thought someone had taken Lucy. That was my assumption for the best part of a decade.'

'But you'd cut your mother out of your life when you turned eighteen,' Esmeralda said slowly. 'What made you go to her house that Christmas Day, all those years later?'

There was a near-smile on his face, though the sadness remained. 'You understand me, Esmeralda,' he said.

She thought, No I bloody well don't, but waited silently for him to continue.

'I went because my mother said she had information about Lucy.' Thorne swallowed, as if to speak this was still too hard. 'She told me the baby wasn't mine – I don't know how my mother even learned Lucy was pregnant. Probably from the private investigator she'd hired. He'd found evidence that Lucy was unfaithful to me at Durham, taken photographs of the two of them. My mother had known this all along.'

'Why did she wait nine years to tell you?'

'She claimed she hadn't wanted to hurt me with the truth, but that my continued rejection of her could no longer be tolerated. She also had some new news. Apparently, she'd had the investigator continue to look for Lucy. Nearly a decade later, he'd finally found her. She was alive, living with the man she'd left me for and their child. I know you'll ask, but my mother wouldn't tell me where Lucy actually was, just that it was a different country.'

'Lucy wouldn't have done that to her parents, leaving them all this time in anguish about her. She wouldn't have done that to you either, from what I know of her.'

'Thank you for saying that, but she did.'

'You were ready to believe she did because you wanted an explanation for what happened to her. Even more, you wanted an excuse to be angry, to do the things you soon began to do. You were converting your basement before your mother told you all this. You were already planning to start kidnapping and killing women and you wanted to tell yourself they deserved it. Lucy's supposed betrayal made you think you had an excuse.'

'That's all probably true, but there was proof, Esmeralda. You know my gift for faces.' The last sentence was spoken with extra slowness and emphasis. He paused, intently watching her for a reaction to this reminder of his special talent, but the reaction never came, and at last he went on. 'My mother showed me the investigator's photos. It was certainly Lucy.'

'You and I both know all too well about deep fakes.' She was thinking of Thomas Lederer and the game trailer. 'Your mother could have fabricated the evidence by using existing images of Lucy.'

'That's true, too, but the first batch of photos of Lucy and her lover at Durham was from two and a half decades ago, just before Lucy disappeared, when she was mine.' He blanched, and she realised something in her expression must have given away her distaste at that last word. 'The second batch, the ones of Lucy with her partner and child, were from a decade and a half ago, when my mother's investigator found her.'

'People have been doctoring photographs since the nineteenth century. Were the faces of the man and the child visible?'

'The man's back was to the camera in the Durham

photos, but they were – what is that coy word prudish people like to use? – *compromising*. In the later photos, the faces of the man and the child had been deliberately obscured – a coloured square over each.'

She doubted the truth of what his mother had told and shown him, but believed that Christmas Day had played out as he described. 'Do you have the photos, or the name of the man?'

He sank back a little. 'I wish I'd snatched them from my mother, but at the time I didn't want to touch them. My mother thought telling me all this would win me back. It only made me hate her more. She would never disclose the man's name.'

If he'd been anyone else, she would have touched his arm in comfort. She meant it when she said, 'I'm very sorry for you. And for Lucy.'

'I can see you are.' Thorne cleared his throat. 'I watched the interviews your father did while you were missing. Your parents loved each other. They loved you. That was what I wanted with Lucy and the baby. It's what I want with you.'

She'd been ambushed by pity for him, but to hear him talk about her parents, the insanity of the disclosure he'd just made, was so repugnant and frightening the pity blew away. She said, 'Why tell me all this now?'

'So you know I keep my promises to you. So you know you can always trust me.'

'I need to put these cuffs on you now, Mr Thorne.' Her voice was calm but she was struggling to remember what she had practised during training.

'Need is such an overused word these days.' Thorne's

usual ironic tone was back. It brought home to her how he had softened when he spoke of Lucy.

'I *need* to search this room for a hidden place where you may be holding someone. To ensure that I can do this safely, you *need* to be restrained.'

He sighed. 'Such difficult choices, you and I must make. Minor or major evil, Esmeralda? That's always the question for us, isn't it? Again and again.'

She said nothing as he continued.

'What is worse? Living with a buried secret that may never be discovered, as I have for so long, or facing the explosion of a devastating revelation? A chronic injury that eats away at you and diminishes your life a tiny bit each day, or sudden death?'

She could only stare as he said, 'Answers, please. I do so love to educate, you know, and you will not learn if you do not venture forth in debate and conversation.' He shrugged, then grimaced when the movement hurt. 'We are more alike than you think – I suspect you would choose the first of those options.' He lowered his voice to a whisper. 'Am I right?'

'I've learned to follow my instincts.' She'd surprised herself by telling him this.

'Hmm. Well, instincts can be useful. Your father's instinct that he saw something when you came home late on Tuesday night was right. What he saw was me.'

'I don't like being spied on, Mr Thorne.'

'What a well-chosen neighbourhood you live in. Such excellent public services.' His jaw stiffened. 'Hard-working delivery men. Beautiful parks for all the family to enjoy.'

The message behind his words was clear. As she'd

guessed and feared, Thorne had seen Ben. On Wednesday night bringing the ice cream and talking to her and Líria outside the house. On Sunday afternoon in the botanic gardens, the two of them standing as close as lovers, though not touching until she rose on her toes to kiss his cheek. Before he vanished.

An Uneasy Alliance

Whistler drove into the golf course car park. Standing in front of the clubhouse entrance, waiting for him, was Isaac Avelar. There was no mistaking the slight but straight-backed man Whistler had seen in old footage from twenty-six years earlier.

Although the older man shot Whistler a look of disgust, he climbed into the front passenger seat. With no preliminaries, he said, 'You're sure there's been no issue with a burst pipe and flooding at my house? No water services people there fixing it?'

'Like I said, no. Did you get through to the taxi firm?'

Mr Avelar was visibly trying to process the fact that Esmeralda had lied to him about why he shouldn't go back to the house, as well as his recognition that she must have discovered something wrong there that she'd wanted to protect him and Líria from. His eyes were red and puffy, but the contempt he continued to show for Whistler was clear. 'The company director refused to tell me anything. Kept going on about data protection.'

'Give me the address. We'll go straight there.' Whistler was feeling more like himself than he had since speaking to Dominic Vane in what had only been that morning but already felt like a lifetime ago. Bullying, Whistler thought, was sometimes necessary. Too bad that so few people appreciated that. 'We'll make him tell.'

The Hidden Door

Esmeralda kept her expression neutral. Right now, she had to figure out how to cuff Jason Thorne without getting herself killed. She was also worried about any weapons he might have hidden.

'Please roll onto your stomach and place your arms behind your back, fully extended. Tops of your hands facing each other. Keep them well away from your pockets and turn your head to the side so you're looking at the back of the sofa rather than at me.' If he did all those things, she could get over there fast and kick the syringe away before cuffing him. She realised she was going to have to touch him again. There was no avoiding it.

'Hmm.' He appeared to consider. 'I think not.'

She'd have to let it go for the moment. There were plenty of other battles to fight. She was looking around the room. 'Where did you come from, when the lights went out?'

'I do so wish to be helpful,' he said. 'So I will tell you that while your camera will work, your phone won't. I put signal blockers in, so only the devices I authorise get through – if I'd known you were coming I'd have authorised you. And baked a cake.'

'This room was empty when I first entered it. You were in front of me, but the door I used was behind me. I need to know how you got in here.'

'Ah,' he said. 'You could try to guess. If you guess right I will tell you.'

'I know you said at the press conference that you like games. I don't.'

'That's disappointing,' he said. 'You're fun to play with.' He turned slightly and briefly – involuntarily – to his right. He had done the same thing a few minutes ago, with his eyes.

She looked harder, and that was when she saw it. At the far end of the sofa, a metre beyond Thorne's head, was the faintest outline of a door, as if someone had drawn it with the lightest application of a pencil. Because there was no obvious handle or lock, the door blended into the white wall almost to the point of invisibility.

He must have been on the other side of that door when she first entered the room, and controlled the lights from there too. 'What's behind that door, Mr Thorne?'

'I'm sorry, Esmeralda,' he said.

'If you mean that, then tell me how the door opens.'

He shook his head. 'My apology is for the game trailer, for failing to stop its release. But Thomas Lederer will never hurt you again. What I did to him, I did for you.' Whatever he saw in her face made Thorne add, 'Adam Holderness, and George Rossiter, and Thomas Lederer. They all deserved to die. They all hurt innocents who weren't being defended by anyone. Only by me. Don't tell me you've shed tears for George Rossiter.'

She recalled the photograph of Rossiter's murdered wife from a newspaper photograph, holding her twin boys in her arms, and felt her usual sick rage.

'You're thinking of Monique, aren't you?' he said.

He'd got that right, but she wasn't about to start confiding in Jason Thorne. She told him a different true thing. 'I'm thinking that Thomas Lederer never actually killed anybody.'

'Morality and ethics are complex things, aren't they? I couldn't allow Little Thomas to get away with what he did to you. I've done more for you than you know, more than I have for anyone. You will come to see this, but right now you're hurting my feelings.'

There was a stiffness in his jaw that showed her he really was very angry, but she forced herself on. 'Please tell me what's behind that door, Mr Thorne.'

'Historically, I've worked in trilogies, but I'd been planning a quartet, with Mr Whistler as Number Four. Still, artists must sometimes improvise. Late yesterday afternoon, a new opportunity unexpectedly presented itself, so this will be a quintet and Mr Whistler will have to move back in the queue and wait a little longer for his turn.' His eyes flicked to a sketchpad, propped against the sofa cushion near his feet. 'Would you like to see?'

Her throat was so tight she could only nod. He raised himself, stretched an arm to grab the sketchpad, and held it out to her. She wasn't about to get close enough to take it. 'Put it on the floor, please,' she said, her voice shaking. 'Slide it over with your foot.'

He did as she asked, kicking the book several metres, so it stopped in front of her. Esmeralda picked it up, her eyes moving constantly between him and the pages as she turned them.

She recognised the first three designs from his victims' torsos. The Men's Rights activist symbol he'd carved on George Rossiter. The Pinocchio emoji for telling a lie he'd had his friend engrave on Adam Holderness. The hanging man he'd used to decorate Thomas Lederer. He'd added his signature JT to all of them. The mark of Thorne.

The next image was new. Inside a circle, Thorne had drawn a straight vertical line. From the line's middle, a short arrow pointed to the right and up. 'What is this?' She dreaded the answer.

'Are you familiar with the Men Going Their Own Way symbol? That design will be perfect for Mr Whistler, don't you think? I sent my good friend Dominic a preview. . .'

She shook her head. 'DI Whistler is not part of that group, Mr Thorne.'

'My dear Esmeralda.' He spoke with the loving but disappointed patience you'd use towards a deluded child. 'Never mind.' His eyes lit in excitement as he visibly switched into gameshow host mode. 'Turn the page if you want to see what awaits us right now behind curtain number four. I completed the blueprint just before you arrived.'

She did turn the page, and saw that Thorne had outlined the clichéd perfection of a warrior's profile, with a strong brow and jawline and chin, and a thick neck. Esmeralda knew that incels used such images to signify a Chad, an absurdly handsome man who was exceedingly successful with women.

Her heart was beating so hard and fast it seemed to be inside her head, drumming in her ears. 'Who is this supposed to be?' But she was in no doubt, and the horror that washed over her seemed a physical thing.

'A sudden, unplanned inspiration of the kind that true artists must always be ready for. In fact, I was about to get started, but then you came to visit. It's an unexpected pleasure, having you here with me, but the question is, what do I do with you while I work?'

'Who is behind that door, Mr Thorne, and is he alive?'

'My actions,' Thorne said, 'are for you, for us, despite your ingratitude. Which, by the way, I will enjoy helping you to correct. I am confident you will come to a better view, with my guidance.'

'I don't need your correction or guidance,' she said. 'I need you to tell me how to open that door.'

But Jason Thorne didn't tell her how to do this. He didn't make a sound. He was staring at something behind her with an expression of such profound shock Esmeralda couldn't help but take her eyes off him to look over her shoulder.

The Daughter

What she saw made her say her daughter's name, more breath than language, though Esmeralda didn't dare to look for more than a few stunned seconds before turning back to Thorne with a spearing fear in her gut that he would already be hurling himself at them. But he was perfectly still, his gaze riveted on Líria.

Esmeralda felt a squeeze of her heart that hurt so much she thought it might just stop. She risked another fleeting glance at her daughter, and though she saw that Líria appeared to be free and whole and unharmed, standing on her own two feet, Esmeralda still said, 'Are you hurt? In any way hurt?' The words came out as if she'd choked them.

'I'm fine.' Líria's voice sounded very small.

'Did this man take you, Líria?' She was pointing at Thorne. 'Did he bring you here?'

'No.' Thorne spoke quickly, before Líria could, then said in a voice that was so gentle Esmeralda hardly recognised it, 'How did you get here, Líria?'

Esmeralda's eyes were flicking between Thorne's face and the area immediately around him. 'If there's a danger to my daughter I need to know about you'd better tell me.'

'Not from me. Never from me.' He shook his head to emphasise the point, then said, 'Did you come here alone, Líria?' The way he addressed her was so careful, so soft.

As he spoke, Esmeralda was certain of four things. First, that her daughter had an instinct never to address this man. Second, that he relished saying Líria's name. Third, that his question was prompted by genuine concern for Líria rather than himself, and fourth, that despite this, the sick terror of having her daughter in his presence was overwhelming her.

'You need to leave, Líria,' Esmeralda said. 'Get out of this house *right now*. Phone 999 and wait *outside* until the police arrive.'

If Thorne moved even a millimetre Esmeralda would launch herself at him with everything she had and fight until Líria was out. She'd somehow, miraculously, grab that syringe before he did and plunge it into his soul. She pictured it happening to the last move. But Thorne remained motionless, as if Esmeralda had turned into Medusa and frozen him.

'I know who he is,' Líria said. 'His picture's everywhere.'

There was a buzzing in her ears, but every syllable Esmeralda spoke had the clarity of a bullet. 'Go. Right. This. Minute.' She couldn't have Líria breathing the same air as this man.

'You're bleeding, Mum.'

'It's only a bloody nose. It's stopped already. Go, Líria. Now.'

'Why has he got our photo?' Líria said, and Esmeralda realised she must be looking across the room, where it was displayed on the chest of drawers by Thorne's bed.

'I'm ashamed to say,' Thorne said, in that new gentle voice of his, without even a faint trace of the usual sardonic irony, 'that I broke into your house this morning and stole it. I shouldn't have done that and I'm sorry. Your house should be a safe place for you. It will be from now on, I promise. You don't have to worry.'

Did he really not imagine the worthlessness of any reassurance he ever gave, or more to the point, its inverse effect, because anything he ever said only increased fear?

'That drawing is of you, Mum.' The anxiety in Líria's voice was palpable. 'Why? Why would he do that?'

'Because I thought your mum was beautiful, Líria. That's why.'

Esmeralda wished he would just shut up, and wasn't sure how she would be able to bear hearing her daughter's name on his lips even one more time, though so much was whizzing through her brain she seemed, again, to have become incapable of speech.

'But how did he know where we live?' Líria said. 'How does he know you?'

Thorne seemed to consider for a few seconds, but not enough to stay quiet. 'I was spying on your mum. I knew she was one of the detectives trying to find me, so I followed her home from work on Tuesday night.'

Great, Esmeralda thought. I'm sure that makes Líria

feel a million times better. Nonetheless, his tenderness towards Líria, his protectiveness of her from so many other awful truths, shocked her. This was despite the fact that the terribleness of the ones he was actually telling couldn't be diminished.

Somehow, Esmeralda knew she had to shake herself out of the state she was in and control the emotions that were ambushing her. She had to work out how to manipulate the situation and exploit whatever benevolent impulses Thorne seemed to be in the grip of. Insofar as he was capable of benevolent impulses.

'Why would he want our photo?' Líria asked.

'I can't begin to imagine,' Esmeralda said, finally finding her voice again, and using it to lie smoothly, passionately. 'All I know right now is that you need to go outside and phone for help.' Her only thought was of protecting her daughter and saving Ben.

'I'm not leaving you alone with him.'

'I can see how much you love your mum, Líria,' Thorne said, and although Esmeralda thought, *You see fuck all about me and my daughter, and stop saying her name*, his face was so soft she couldn't help but be struck by how unlike himself he looked. 'So let me help . . .'

But Líria cut him off. 'I heard him talking before I came in. He said he's going to correct you. What does that mean?'

Thorne fell back as if he'd been winded. 'I shouldn't have said that to your mum,' he said. 'I didn't mean it. I wanted her to like me and I was sad when I realised she didn't.'

A distant part of Esmeralda recognised that he meant

this – that somehow, in his strange fantasies, he'd imagined her feeling genuinely grateful to him. Perhaps he'd gone so far as to convince himself that she would actually love him.

'This is not a film. We are not superheroes, Líria,' Esmeralda said. 'You need to go.'

'Your mum was about to put handcuffs on me,' Thorne said, 'so let's let her do that. I want you to see that she's safe, so you can leave like she told you to.' After a look at Líria so penetrating he seemed to be photographing her with his eyes so he could call on the image for the rest of time, Thorne rolled onto his stomach, turned his head sideways to face away from them, and placed his arms behind him, hands pressed together.

There is nobody else in the world he would do this for, Esmeralda thought. Only Líria, and she knew all too well why that was. She and Thorne both did. She would never know exactly how he figured it out, but she could guess with some confidence. Perhaps he saw that she had a child while spying on her. He'd reminded her only a few minutes earlier of his remarkable gift for faces, and she knew what he'd been implying, then. It would not have been difficult for him to see Líria and notice a resemblance that most people would miss, then work out her age and calculate the dates. He would have easily put it all together.

The syringe was still on the floor. She was weighing up whether to use it on him first and ask questions later. For all she knew, whatever he'd loaded it with could cause instant death. Her best guess was that it was a strong mix of tranquilliser and sedative, but she knew how dangerous a cocktail like that could be in the wrong dose, in inexpert hands.

As she approached him, she scooped the syringe up in one silent movement and dropped it into an empty pouch at the front of her utility belt where she could reach it if she had to. She knew that she had a profound dread of taking life, even in self-defence, and that this was down to what she had probably done to Hugo Green. Nor did she want Líria to watch her kill a man, especially if her daughter someday learned the truth about who this one was to her, though Esmeralda also knew she wouldn't hesitate to sink that needle into Thorne's flesh if he gave her the slightest excuse, even with the burner phone filming away.

She had a real terror that he would lunge. If he took her down that would leave Líria entirely unprotected. Despite her shaking hands, Esmeralda somehow got the rigid cuffs out of the utility belt and managed to lock them around Thorne's wrists. Up close, she was hit once more by the scent he'd left in her house. The room seemed to spin, an effect that she realised any proximity to Thorne had on her, but she couldn't afford to give into an attack of vertigo now.

'Mummy!' Líria's voice woke her up. 'Get away from him,' and Esmeralda startled in alarm when Thorne's upper back spasmed into a single, vigorous jerk, as if Líria's words had been a knife between his shoulder blades.

'Líria,' she said, trying to sound calmer than she felt. 'I can't risk him struggling to breathe. He could suffocate if I don't help him to sit up.' Which is more than he would do for anyone else, she thought, as she manoeuvred him into the upright position she'd practised in training. He thanked her quietly, then sat patiently with his hands behind him.

'What did you load into that syringe, Mr Thorne?'

When he didn't answer, Esmeralda looked hard at Thorne's face, trying to read him without meeting his eye.

'Get further away from him.' Líria seemed to know that this man haunted her mother's nightmares, and those of countless others.

Esmeralda took another step back. Did he have a time-bomb ticking away somewhere, about to explode and kill them all? She edged towards the doorway, still watching him. At last, she was beside Líria, who she risked another quick glance at, looking so achingly young and delicate in her school uniform and duffel coat, but brave too, and fierce, with her dark gold ponytail coming loose and her amber eyes shining in her pale face.

Esmeralda took Líria's hand in hers and gave it a quick squeeze. 'I need you to go upstairs now and call 999 like I said. I can't leave him alone in cuffs and it isn't safe for me to help him out of the house without assistance.' There was also the fact that she needed to open that hidden door as fast as she possibly could, fighting through her fear that she would find death behind it.

'I'm so sorry, Mummy,' Líria said, 'but you don't understand what I did.'

Esmeralda bit back the urge to scream. She said, 'There's nothing you could have done that I won't understand. We'll talk it all through later.'

'No.' Líria shook her head. 'You need to know now. I snuck out of school and came home to check on you. I was scared. Because of how stressed you've been lately.'

'Not your fault,' Esmeralda said. 'I shouldn't have let you see. That's on me, not you.'

'That's on Mr Whistler,' Thorne said quietly.

'But I looked over your shoulder this morning. I saw Folly View Cottage on your laptop. When I got home and you weren't there like you said you'd be, I called a taxi to bring me to this place. I put my phone on aeroplane mode so you couldn't stop me.'

'Right,' she said. 'That's a lot to take in.' She didn't have time to process the mix of admiration and pride and exasperation she was feeling. 'What did I just say to you, Líria?'

'I can't leave you with him. He's killed people. You might die.'

Thorne must have seen the naked horror and revulsion for him on Líria's face. 'Your mum won't die, Líria.' The sweetness in his voice made Esmeralda feel sick. 'I would never hurt you or your mum.' He quickly added, 'You believe that, don't you Esmeralda?'

If Thorne's words helped to dampen Líria's fear enough for Esmeralda to finally get her out of there, she was willing to use it. 'I do, yes,' she lied, knowing that she really was much better at it than he was. 'The best way for you to be brave and keep me safe, Líria, is to get to the garden where there's a signal, take your phone off aeroplane mode, and call 999. Tell them your mum is DC Avelar and she's with Jason Thorne on her own and there's potentially another victim in the basement. Have you got that?'

'Yeah.'

'Share your location and don't disconnect the call. Stay on the phone until they arrive. Hit speakerphone so you can be hands free if need be.'

'Okay. I love you so much, Mum.' And, at last, finally, Líria listened to her, and turned away, and was gone.

The Discovery

Esmeralda and Jason Thorne stared at each other. For the first time, she looked directly into his eyes. They were so beautiful, and so like the eyes she loved most in the world, it hurt too much to see them.

'Líria – your daughter – she's magnificent. She's all you.' He swallowed. 'I'm sorry, Esmeralda' – he broke off, looked at the phone camera, still recording – 'for – everything.'

'If you're really sorry then tell me how to open that door.'

His voice, when at last he spoke again, was hoarse. 'If I'd met you when I was a young man, everything would have been different. I would have been different.'

She shook her head, unable to stop the rage that she'd had to control in front of Líria. 'What you are is nothing to do with who you met or didn't meet, or how horrible your mother was, or your thinking Lucy rejected you. You made your choices.'

'You're the truest of all of my true loves, you know.'

She said quietly, 'Then you don't know what love is.'

He looked at her as if she'd slapped him. 'They said in the press that you're investigating a connection between me and Hugo Green. You believe me, don't you, that I never even met him? That I had nothing to do with what happened when you were fifteen?'

She slowly nodded. 'I believe that, yes.'

He seemed to collapse backwards. 'My great sadness and tragedy, the monster that I am to the public, means no child should have any association with me. But I protect children, however much I fail to control myself in other ways.' He closed his eyes tightly for a few seconds, then opened them again. 'It's truer now than ever. You can count on that.'

'I've learned to count only on your violence.' She started towards the hidden door. How the hell was she supposed to open it, especially when she had to keep checking that he wasn't about to spring on her? Was his knee really as immobilising as it seemed, or was he only pretending? Even with his wrists cuffed, she knew he could inflict serious damage in the time it took to blink. She should have overridden her qualms about killing him and stuck him with that syringe. 'Stop watching me,' she said, despite knowing he wouldn't.

She was running her hands along the side edges of the door, searching yet again for some sign of a lock or latch, but she couldn't find anything. 'If those noble declarations you've been making aren't a whole load of self-romanticising bullshit, then tell me how to open this bloody door.' She dreaded his pointing her to some mechanism she couldn't see, then having to get close to him to rummage in his pockets for a key.

He seemed to be counting silently, as if she were trying his patience. To her relief, he said, 'Just press against it, as close to the centre as you can judge.'

'If you come anywhere near me I'll stick you with that syringe,' she said.

He shook his head, as if in wonder at his own thoughts. 'I always knew getting to know you would be something special. I regret missing that chance.'

She was hardly listening to him. Her concentration was on the door as she pressed its centre, but nothing happened. Several times, she made slight adjustments to the position of her hands. On the fourth try, the door popped open and she swallowed back a gasp.

Strapped to an operating table, a gag over his mouth and a bandage on his temple, was Ben. Esmeralda was certain the bandage was not there because of Thorne's sense of a duty of care, but rather, because of his dislike of mess. The gag was identical to the one Thorne had used on Thomas Lederer. Thorne had cut Ben's jersey with surgical precision, leaving what was left of it beneath him. Although his torso was bare, he was still wearing the jeans he'd had on when he and Esmeralda parted in the botanic gardens the day before.

Ben's eyes were closed. Esmeralda didn't think he was conscious, but she thought she could see his chest moving. She double-checked to reassure herself that his abdomen really was lifting and lowering gently, in a regular motion. He really was breathing.

But why was he unconscious? Did the answer lie beneath the bandage? A blow to the temple could be especially dangerous. She continued to examine him, and noticed several pinpricks on his upper arm. Thorne must have shot him with multiple doses of something to control him. She tried to comfort herself with the idea that sleeping would be less frightening and stressful than being awake, and the drugs provided a more hopeful reason for his lack of consciousness than a head injury.

Against the opposite wall, in reach of the table, was a stainless steel trolley covered in sharp and shining instruments, stoppered glass vials of clear liquids, and syringes. Esmeralda moved towards it, so she could keep an eye on the door, but not before spotting two other things on that wall.

One was a circuit board, so now she knew how Thorne had cut the lights. The second was a series of monitors with live feeds of the basement rooms, all viewed from above, so she realised the cameras must have been installed in the ceiling. Thorne had been watching her all along, amusing himself with every step she'd taken, playing his favourite game, which was certainly cat and mouse.

Tenderly, she touched Ben's shoulder, smoothed his dark hair from his forehead. He was so cold. There was a stack of white towels on a shelf behind her. She shook them loose from their careful folds and covered him with all of them at once, to try to get him warm.

The strap around his neck was most urgent, given how tight it looked. Another horrifying thought occurred. As if there weren't enough of those. Had he lost consciousness because he wasn't getting enough air? She set about unbuckling the hideous thing, wincing when she saw the deep crimson ring it had left.

She removed the gag, then freed the first of his arms, which was restrained with three straps. She was concentrating on his other arm when she felt a hand in her hair and let out a cry, only to realise that the hand belonged to Ben, and his eyes had opened. His voice was hoarse when he said her name.

She tried to hush him with a gentle shush like the one she used to use on Líria when she cried as a baby. 'Try not to speak,' she said. 'Your throat – you'll hurt yourself if you talk.' When he repeated her name anyway she pressed her mouth against his and felt him kiss her back. At last, she pulled away and said, 'What else am I to do to keep you quiet?'

But Ben had turned his head. 'Door,' he said, his voice a warning.

Jason Thorne was standing there, wobbling as if he were drunk because he was trying to keep his weight on his right leg in order to minimise the load on his left knee. 'Step away from him.' Thorne spoke with furious calm, drawing out the second word.

Esmeralda reminded herself that Líria was outside calling for back-up. Nonetheless, and not for the first time, she calculated that even with his hands locked behind him and his balance off, his full weight and size, hurled upon her, could still be a lethal weapon. She needed to find a way to neutralise that weapon, but she also had a faraway realisation that he would not want to hurt Líria's mother. It was this last thought that made her say to herself, *What the fuck*, and to him, 'This man puts away *bad people*, to use your words. He isn't one of them. Unlike you.'

'He got in my way,' Thorne said, this time in what was more growl than language.

Something exploded in her head, in the pit of her stomach, in her throat. She rushed round the table, a cry of rage on her lips, aiming herself at Thorne like a rocket and pushing both hands against his chest with such force she nearly jumped at the electric shock that went through her fingers to the top of her scalp.

The momentum threw him backwards, so he landed hard on his tailbone with his legs straight out in front of him. His upper body followed, so that his spine and head hit the ground and he was almost flat, pinning his cuffed wrists beneath his own weight. His face contorted in pain and his mouth opened in a silent scream. He froze there, in the grip of spasms, too hurt and winded to move but not able to stifle his groans.

Weapon successfully neutralised, she thought as she returned to Ben, who was looking hard at her and managed a small nod of approval. She needed to deal with the multiple straps that were immobilising his body and legs. Ben tried to help but remained clumsy and slow. Gently, she stopped him, told him to stretch and shake his arms to get his circulation going. 'I can do this,' she said softly.

As she worked on the strap that had been wrapped over his waist, a piercing scream made her snap her neck and head up so violently she felt her nails go into Ben's skin. The scream was followed by a sound that was more cry than word – 'Mummy!' – and that sound went straight through Esmeralda's heart. It was coming from the garden above them, just on the other side of the wall.

The Mother

All in one motion, even as she was rushing towards Líria and away from Ben, Esmeralda was grabbing a pair of scissors and shoving them into his hand in case he needed a weapon, and she was dropping the loaded syringe by his side for good measure, but wordlessly, there was no time for words and she knew Ben would understand why she had given him those things and what to do with them if need be, and she was leaping over Thorne as if he were nothing more than a heap of old junk, flying out of the basement and up the stairs, along the hall and through the kitchen and lean-to, then bursting into the garden.

Líria was sitting on the ground, scooting herself backwards. Her spine hit the Queen's Enchantment Roses and their blanket of twigs, so that she couldn't move any further. Standing above her, a knife in her hand, was Elizabeth Thorne.

'Stop whinging,' said Mrs Thorne, pointing the blade from only a metre away, so that Líria swallowed back a sob.

Esmeralda took such a large gulp of air she felt her

lungs burn. The sound caught Mrs Thorne's attention, so that her eyes flicked briefly away from Líria.

'Of course it is you,' Mrs Thorne said, with her usual displeasure. She glanced down and Esmeralda followed her gaze. There, dropped in the grass, was Líria's phone, showing its wallpaper of a photobooth snapshot of Esmeralda smiling while Líria lifted a comic eyebrow.

Esmeralda took a step backwards, hoping Mrs Thorne would move with her, away from Líria. It didn't work. 'Please put down the knife, Mrs Thorne.'

'Certainly not.' Mrs Thorne held it up for emphasis, so caught in her parallel universe she seemed not to notice the sound of sirens, growing closer.

'Tell me what I can do to make things better for you.' Esmeralda took another small step back. This time, Mrs Thorne shifted a little with her, so there was a tiny bit of extra distance between her and Líria. 'You don't want to hurt a child.'

'You couldn't begin to imagine what I want,' Mrs Thorne said.

'Then tell me.'

'I want to make you suffer,' Mrs Thorne said.

'Why?' Esmeralda had to keep the conversation going until back-up arrived.

'You took away my son. You brainwashed him. You turned him against me.'

Esmeralda couldn't decide what response would be the least dangerous. To contradict might inflame things further. To agree would only confirm the woman's mad version of reality. To remain silent wasn't an option. 'I'd like to try to make things better for you.'

'You'll say anything to save yourself and your brat, but I have your measure.' Mrs Thorne snorted. 'My son is easily seduced by females. They always want me out of the picture so they can have him all to themselves. Did he invite you here?'

'No. I tracked him down. I'm a detective. It's what I do.'

Mrs Thorne shook her head. 'You're lying. He must have invited you or you'd never have found him. You used your female trickery and deception.' Her voice had reached a high pitch that Esmeralda hadn't heard in it before. 'Not that I pretend to understand what he sees in you. You've clearly been in some sort of a brawl.'

'Yes, Mrs Thorne. I have. With your son. He really didn't invite me here.'

'I'm sure that brat of yours must be very proud of her mother.' Mrs Thorne turned her sneer to Líria so that Esmeralda's heart began to thump even harder than it already was. 'Are you? Are you proud of your mother, brat?'

There was a shift in Mrs Thorne's stance, a new set to her jaw, and Esmeralda realised the sirens had cut out. Had they decided it was a bad idea to come in blazing?

'Answer me, girl,' Mrs Thorne said. 'I asked if you are proud of your mother.'

'Yes,' Líria said softly.

How far away was help? Were they still coming at all? Was Mrs Thorne oblivious, or asking herself these questions too?

'I knew the minute I met your mother what she was.

Using her body to get men to do what she wants. And you're not in the least bit ashamed of her?'

How long had it been since the sirens had gone silent?

Mrs Thorne waved the knife. 'Answer my question, you little horror. Show some respect. Are you ashamed of your mother?'

'No,' Líria whispered, and Mrs Thorne pounced.

Everything happened so fast it was like trying to watch the beats of a hummingbird's wings. Esmeralda leaped sideways to shield Líria, smashing a fist into the underside of Mrs Thorne's chin and grabbing at the wrist of the hand holding the knife to point it towards the ground. These actions threw the older woman off balance but didn't stop her from plunging the blade into Esmeralda's leg as Líria screamed and Jason Thorne ran towards them in his handcuffs, veering from side to side like an injured bull, making a guttural noise that wasn't language when he bent at the waist, then rammed the top of his already-bleeding head into his mother's upper abdomen with the full weight of his body behind the movement. Mrs Thorne seemed to lift and fly backwards like a doll before she smashed against the wall. There was the crack of bones breaking. The force of the momentum made Thorne bounce backwards from the blow and crash heavily to the ground for the third time that day. All the while, Esmeralda herself was slipping downwards, pouring blood into the earth, thinking that she could see her mother's face as her eyes closed and her head hit the bed of Queen's Enchantment Roses.

A Stay of Execution

Whistler had driven straight from the golf course to the taxi company's kiosk. It took him mere minutes to crush the owner's irritating adherence to data protection rules. Now, Whistler was running on blue lights to the address where the driver had taken Líria. He parked on a muddy verge in front of Folly View Cottage and jumped out.

Something was going on behind the house, and there was a terrible quality to the voices that made him certain it couldn't be anything good. He skirted the perimeter wall. When he came upon a heavy door that had been propped open, he smashed through the gap, with Isaac Avelar following close behind him.

The operational part of Whistler knew he ought to force Mr Avelar to stay back, but he was continuing to act under the instinct that being in the older man's company offered him protection against Jason Thorne, rather like garlic was supposed to keep away vampires. He propelled himself forward, huffing, vowing to get fitter if Thorne didn't kill him first, trying to assess what was unfolding before his eyes, feeling as if he were travelling in slow motion while watching a film where the actors were moving at super speed.

Esmeralda was wrestling with an older woman who was holding a knife. A young girl who he knew from photos to be Líria was on her hands and knees. A tall man in handcuffs, none other than Jason Thorne himself, was staggering towards them, moving with a pronounced limp but at extraordinary speed on extremely long legs, making Whistler think of wounded yet still-lethal animals, the type you saw on nature documentaries, continuing to fight despite mortal injury. Thorne hurled himself at the old woman with that visceral fury.

By the time Whistler reached the strange gathering, Esmeralda was on the ground. The old woman had crumpled a couple of metres away, and from the angle of her neck, and her open but unblinking eyes, she was beyond help. The knife was in the grass near the body, and Thorne was flat on his back. Although Jason Thorne, known brutal killer, appeared winded and was grimacing in pain, he seemed alert as he strained to watch Esmeralda with what looked like real worry, his hands behind his back.

When Thorne's eyes lifted and locked onto Whistler's own, the recognition passed between the two men and Thorne gave a barely perceptible but ominous shake of his head. Thorne's meaning was clear. If Esmeralda died he would hold Whistler responsible, and although Whistler knew Thorne would be incarcerated for the rest of his days, Thorne had shown with Adam Holderness that there were plenty of people he could encourage to kill for him, following his precise and terrible instructions to the JT letter.

Whistler tore his eyes from Thorne. Líria was crouching by her mother's side, saying the word 'Mummy' over and over again, but Esmeralda appeared to be unconscious. Whistler dropped to his knees beside them, ripping the already-sliced fabric of Esmeralda's jeans to assess her injury. 'Get the child out of the way,' he said, as her grandfather drew close.

Líria screamed her refusal. She locked herself into position like a much younger child in the grip of a tantrum.

'Pick up the knife handle using your fleece, Mr Avelar,' Whistler said. 'Get it away from the man. Watch him and tell me if he moves *at all*.'

The wound was in the upper part of Esmeralda's thigh. There didn't appear to be anything stuck in it, and Whistler couldn't see bone, but there was so much blood it was hard to be sure, and she was completely unresponsive.

What could he use? He flicked his eyes sideways and saw that Líria was wearing a navy wool coat. 'Lay your coat over your mum's upper body, Líria,' he said.

In seconds she'd shrugged it off and done as he instructed. 'How will this help her?' The child's voice was shaky but clear.

'Keep her warm.' He didn't add that he was trying to stop Esmeralda from going into shock but was worried she was already there. He was trying to press the gape in her flesh together with his bare hands but it was too slippery. There was too much blood.

'Here.' Líria clearly caught on quickly. She'd seen what was needed and shrugged off her grey jersey. Now, she was offering it to him.

Whistler nodded and took it. As his hands moved over the fabric to apply pressure to Esmeralda's wound, he looked briefly at the girl's face and saw that her lips were a straight line of determination that was exactly like her mother's.

The Secret

Ben had shakily freed himself of the remaining straps, all the while keeping the scissors and syringe in reach as well as an eye on Thorne. But Thorne had not so much as looked in his direction. Despite the pain he must have been in, and with his hands cuffed behind his back, Thorne somehow struggled to his feet, then lurched out of the room, crying Líria's name.

By the time Ben made his way out of the basement and up the stairs, light-headed from the drugs Thorne had shot into him, there was pandemonium in the garden. He clocked the victims on the ground, and that Esmeralda was one of them. Whistler was on his knees by her side, and Ben's first impulse was to knock him away. But as he drew closer, he could see that Whistler was working frantically to help her, and in a considerably stronger position to do that than Ben himself.

Ben staggered nearer, noticing how white Esmeralda's face was, and how red and wet Whistler's hands were, as well as the fabric he was using to try to staunch the blood. Ben blinked several times, trying to clear his head and keep himself alert, making sure of what he was seeing.

What Ben was seeing was Isaac Avelar, and he was standing only a metre away from Jason Thorne, who was lying on his back on the ground. Isaac was looking down at Thorne as if he'd been hypnotised. 'I have the knife,' Isaac said, and Ben saw that he was gripping the hilt with the blade aimed towards Thorne's chest, ready to plunge it downwards, while Thorne himself was looking up at Isaac with no expression on his blood-smeared face.

Somehow, Ben propelled himself to Isaac's side. Gently, his hand circled the older man's wrist. 'Come with me, Isaac, away from here.' Ben directed Isaac's attention to his granddaughter, who was crouched by her mother's side, shivering in her thin white school top. 'Do you see how scared she is? Líria needs you.'

Isaac's eyes moved over Ben, taking in the lacerations on his wrists, the red ring around his neck as if he'd been wearing a noose, which he practically had, the bandage on his forehead, and the fact that Ben was shirtless. 'What happened to you?' Isaac said.

Ben swallowed, his throat still feeling the constriction of the strap Thorne had circled it with. 'Long story.' He knew he wouldn't ever want to tell it, beyond to those who would absolutely need to know, and even then there were parts he would never disclose. 'How about you put the knife down in the grass here.' Isaac did as Ben commanded. 'Now you can go be with Líria.'

Isaac pointed to Thorne. 'What about him?'

'I'll watch him.'

Isaac swayed back and forth, as if all the energy that had filled him seconds ago had drained away. Ben felt something fuzzy against his hands and saw that Isaac was handing him his golf fleece. When Isaac said, 'Put this on,' Ben did so, and was glad of the warmth, barely noticing that it was tight on his shoulders.

He watched Isaac move towards his granddaughter, then put an arm around her, drawing her close against the cold. He heard Líria say in a low voice, 'Mum always says when I have a cut that it looks like more blood than there really is.'

Ben approached them. 'Your mum's right,' he said. But the more Ben looked the more convinced he became that in this case it looked like a lot of blood because it actually was a lot of blood. He caught Isaac's eye. 'Move back a little, Isaac,' he said. 'Just a metre or so to make some more room.' Isaac nodded and guided Líria a small distance away.

Worrying that the knife had nicked an artery, Ben fell to his knees beside Whistler, who was unbuttoning his collared shirt. Without looking up, Whistler said, 'So you're not dead.'

'Sorry to disappoint.' Ben could see the back of the man's white cotton vest was soaked with sweat.

Whistler was tearing his shirt into strips. 'What happened to you, Sachs?'

'Figured out this might be where Thorne was hiding and came to have a look around late yesterday afternoon. He saw me before I saw him.'

'That was careless of you. Not to mention stupid.'

Ben actually choked out a half-laugh, which hurt his throat. He could only say hoarsely, 'Right on both counts.' He touched Esmeralda's cheek, smoothed her hair back, away from her closed eyes, took one of her icy hands in his own.

Whistler pretended not to see, but he said, 'She saved you, didn't she?'

'She did,' Ben said, watching Whistler apply a tourniquet with a competence few would manage. It was a scary and dangerous move. 'Where'd you learn to do that?'

'After what happened to Nick, that knife on the stop and search all those years ago, they let me take the enhanced first aid training.'

'Module 5?' Ben asked. He couldn't decide if his sense that Esmeralda's bleeding had slowed a little was real or wishful. 'For firearms and public order officers?'

'That's the one,' Whistler said.

There was a crash at the front of the house, and Ben realised the emergency services must have arrived and forced open the gate. A minute later, police and paramedics alike were swarming around the man they'd hunted for so long, as well as the dead woman on the ground.

Ben watched Thorne's face through a gap, and saw him straining for the last hungry glimpse he would ever have of Líria. And he knew that Jason Thorne had somehow worked out the truth about who the child's father was, but would never tell.

SEVEN MONTHS LATER –
SUNDAY, 1 APRIL 2018

The Posy

Esmeralda and Líria were in the back garden. Líria was picking flowers, choosing them with care to make a posy. Esmeralda could see Ben and her dad on the other side of the glass wall, preparing Easter lunch while she and Líria wandered about in the fresh air and spring sunshine. Esmeralda was certain the kitchen discussion was serious and secret, because when she'd walked by to join Líria in the garden, there'd been a sudden hush.

'We've defo got things arranged the right way round, Mum,' Líria said.

'Defo.' Esmeralda repeated the word a little absently. 'It's way better out here.'

'Obviously, but I think I just died a little. Don't ever say defo again.'

'No promises, Líria,' she said, using her daughter's favourite comeback.

Esmeralda caught Ben's eye as he kneaded dough for the Easter cake he and Isaac were making from her mother's recipe book. The mysterious part of their talk appeared to be finished. Now, her father was miming the proper technique while Ben dutifully tried to follow instructions but somehow puffed a cloud of flour onto his clothes and into his face.

Esmeralda turned back to Líria, who was tying the flowers together at the stems with a gold and white ribbon, making a bow that was Líria-like in its symmetry and exactness. She handed the posy to her mum. 'Is it okay?'

'It's beautiful,' Esmeralda said. 'They're perfect.'

'So you like it?' It wasn't lost on Esmeralda how much reassurance Líria needed.

'I love it.' There were tight bright peonies of the most delicate pink, cornflowers of a starry strange blueness, and snapdragons pursing their crimson lips and looking like sea creatures. 'Thank you.' She kissed her daughter. 'I won't be gone long.'

Esmeralda was halfway along the path through the front garden when she heard the door open behind her. She turned to see that Ben was coming towards her with that loping walk of his that she loved.

When he reached her, he took her hand in his. 'Hello you.'

'Hello you,' she said back.

'Did you know the recipe for that cake is in Portuguese?!'

'It *is* a Portuguese Easter cake,' she said.

'Does the recipe really say that we're supposed to bury whole boiled eggs in it?'

'It really does,' she said.

'Blimey,' he said. 'I thought your dad was playing an

April Fool's joke on me.' He cleared his throat, then said, 'Are you coming back?'

'Here?' she said, trying to keep it light. 'To the house? I'll only be gone an hour.'

'Very funny,' Ben said. 'You know I was talking about the job.'

'I do,' she said quietly. 'It's that I still haven't decided. I'd have told you if I had.'

He nodded, then said, 'You know Whistler loves the idea that you owe him for saving your life? Says it makes him responsible for you for the rest of eternity.'

'Hurrah?' she said, making Ben laugh. She lowered her voice to a comical whisper. 'I willingly use his title these days.' But she was serious when she added, 'I do owe him thanks.'

'Well *you* are owed way more than thanks.' He kissed her. 'See?'

'DI Whistler is certainly not getting one of those,' she said.

'I find it extremely annoying that I can't hate him any more, but he really did stop you from bleeding to death.'

'He did.' Her attention had been drawn to a blue tit, flitting about in the hedge that acted as a boundary between the front garden and the pavement. After it flew off, flashing its bright yellow breast, she turned again to face Ben. There was flour on his cheek. She brushed it away. 'The doctors say I'm not quite ready to return to work yet. Not just the after-effects of the stab wound. The other stuff too.'

'Glad they're helping with the stuff.'

'Not sure they really are.' She rested one hand on his chest. In the other, she was still carefully holding Líria's posy. There was a flash of movement in the bay window of the sitting room, and she glimpsed Líria peeking out before disappearing again.

Ben had seen too. 'I woke last night, when you got out of bed to go to her. She was crying in her sleep again, wasn't she?'

'She's still having nightmares about Mrs Thorne.' Esmeralda smoothed the part of Ben's hair that always stuck up at the front, knowing it would pop back as soon as she moved her hand away. 'You never talk about what it was like for you, at Folly View.'

The shadow that sometimes passed over his face since his time in Thorne's secret room appeared. 'It was nothing. I was unconscious through all of it.'

She didn't believe him, and couldn't hide her frown. 'You have stuff too, Ben.'

'Esmeralda. I'm good.' He spoke with a firmness that made it clear the subject was closed, so she decided to leave it alone, at least for a little while.

Another movement inside the bay window drew their attention back to the sitting room. Líria was now standing with her grandfather, who must have gone in search of her, then coaxed her from the depths of a sofa or chair.

So much shared knowledge passed between Esmeralda and her father. While she was in hospital recovering from the stab wound, he told her in a low voice that he'd replaced the photo of Arthur Dalloway with an identical copy. Esmeralda's guess was that Thorne had burned the one he'd stolen. In any case, Líria never knew it was gone.

Esmeralda slid a speck of dough along a strand of Ben's hair, then let it fall from her fingers onto the grass. 'I do miss being a detective, you know. But I also miss teaching.'

'I've heard teaching can be pretty dangerous too. But you seem to have multiple lives. How many so far?' He was looking at her so intensely. 'Two? Or is it three?'

It depends how you count, she thought, and what you count. She imagined that sometimes a person escaped a death only narrowly and didn't even know it, though in her case there'd been a fair number of incidents that couldn't be missed.

She said only, 'Numbers are more subjective than people think.' She kissed him, then got into her car and drove away, knowing without looking back that like everyone else who loved her, he would watch until she turned the corner and vanished from his view.

The Land of the Dead

Lucy's headstone was bright white and new, a tablet of pure marble engraved with a simple cross at the top and her name at the centre. Her dates were heartbreakingly short.

Everything rushed back at Esmeralda in this beautiful land of the dead, this garden planted with lost women, because she knew that Lucy couldn't be the only one of those in this place. Her bed of earth was already covered in flowers, but there were no roses. Esmeralda had asked Líria not to include any. Nobody who loved Lucy would bring roses.

The forensic tests revealed that Lucy had been poisoned. The police were working on the theory that Mrs Thorne had lured her to Folly View Cottage before killing her and burying her in the grounds. Inside Lucy, like a tiny Russian doll, were the bones of her unborn baby. Esmeralda, who almost never cried, had wept to have her fear of this confirmed.

They would never know for sure how Lucy was captured, but Esmeralda imagined Mrs Thorne inviting her to a little tea party, persuading her not to mention it to Jason because it would be such a lovely surprise for him to turn up and find his mother and girlfriend had finally become friends and were having a happy time together. Before Lucy arrived, Mrs Thorne would have visited the golden building her son had built in Folly View's grounds, decanting exactly the right potions from her collection of carefully labelled jars.

Had Mrs Thorne known she wasn't only murdering Lucy, but her baby too? Esmeralda thought it probable. Mrs Thorne did not like to share. She was like the ogre mother in *Sleeping Beauty*, filled with remorseless hatred of any woman her son loved, and she extended her jealousy even to his future child. Nobody was surprised to learn that an identical poison to the one that killed Lucy was present in the exhumed body of Mrs Thorne's dead husband. Mrs Thorne didn't do co-parenting.

The police had tracked down the German importer from whom Mrs Thorne bought the seeds for her Queen's Enchantment Roses. That rose was her signature, her way of marking what she had vanquished and claiming what she believed belonged to her. She had planted the flowers in her own garden, where she made them thrive, and used some to decorate her husband's shaded grave, knowing full well they would never stick there.

No roses could thrive in such a place. In any case, Esmeralda had already guessed that Mrs Thorne would not spend her time weeping over her dead husband and tending the flowers she'd arranged over his body. They'd been a mere prop for the memorial service and Mrs Thorne's mournful photograph in her fashion-plate widow's weeds, posed beside her fatherless young son. Once that was done, the roses had served their purpose.

But the Queen's Enchantment fared better in the sun-soaked soil of Folly View, where Mrs Thorne buried Lucy and her unborn baby. Thorne had constructed the first of his giant playhouses there when he was only twelve, inside the walled gardens he'd inherited from his maternal grandmother, Charlotte Cavendish, who died soon after his father.

Esmeralda couldn't help but be struck by the amount of loss Jason Thorne suffered as a young boy. Folly View had been held in trust for him, but he spent as much time as he could there, avoiding his mother and trying to recreate the fairy tale chalet that had delighted him in the Georgian Pleasure Gardens where his grandmother had taken him for treats as a small child, just as Esmeralda's mother had once taken her. Before long, though, Mrs Thorne commandeered the little building to store her poisons. Thorne's response was to build a second playhouse in the grounds of his mother's haunted mansion, this time taking the precaution of adding extra layers of locks she couldn't possibly defeat.

Thorne had never before spoken openly to the police. Once he was released from hospital, though, he barely stopped talking. He began by explaining how he kidnapped and murdered the three women who'd been found in his freezers. He also confessed to what the press were calling *The Manosphere Murders*, recounting how he organised the torture and killing of Adam Holderness, kidnapped and murdered George Rossiter and Thomas Lederer, and planned to capture and kill Harold Whistler. Thorne also detailed his kidnapping of DS Ben Sachs when he found him in Folly View's grounds, acknowledging that he had committed grievous bodily harm with intent to cause serious injury to DS Sachs.

Late one night, as they fell asleep, Ben had whispered to Esmeralda, 'I'd have been dead by sunset if you hadn't turned up when you did.' Her only answer was to wrap her body as tightly around his as she could, and kiss him.

The police believed Thorne when he said he had nothing to do with Lucy's disappearance, and no knowledge of what had happened to her all those years ago. Without quite understanding the full extent of his mother's bitter jealousy, an instinct had made Thorne persuade Lucy to keep the pregnancy absolutely secret, even from her own parents. But that carefulness had not been enough to protect them from Elizabeth Thorne.

When Thorne learned that the photographs of Lucy with a lover had been faked, he admitted that he'd been foolish to believe his mother. The interviewing detectives also shared with Thorne that his mother learned of Lucy's pregnancy from the investigator she'd hired. After that, Mrs Thorne had no further need of his services. Nine years later, to try to win her son back, she'd hired a professional forger to create the counterfeit images.

Most of what Thorne said to detectives was factual, with little reflection or emotion. But when the detectives shared with Thorne that Lucy's body had been found at Folly View, mere metres away from where he'd been living for ten months, he put his head in his hands to hide his face. When he learned that the bones of a male foetus of five months gestation had been found with her, and that DNA showed he was the father, he pressed a fist against his mouth to stop any sounds from coming out.

The next day, detectives transitioned to the subject of Esmeralda herself. Thorne explained that he'd seen her for the first time at Ella Brooke's house and become fascinated, which was something, he confessed, that periodically happened to him with women. He recognised her as the girl from the Hugo Green case, he claimed. He had a funny little gift for faces, as they knew, and he had long been enraged by what Green had done. Hence the bulletin board that he kept in his basement, which included Esmeralda's school photo, and the drawings he made of her each year, to celebrate the idea that she had survived.

As Mary had worked out, Thorne formed The Actaeon Club himself, to lure in Thomas Lederer and George Rossiter after he encountered them online and learned that Ella Brooke and Harriet Sapphire were among their targets. When Lederer hacked Thorne during an online meeting between the two men and discovered Esmeralda's previous identity, Thorne regretted that he'd inadvertently exposed her. He'd been horrified to realise that when he'd taken those photos of Esmeralda in front of Ella's door, he'd given Lederer the tools to put her face in the game trailer and send her those *ugly* texts. Thorne killed Lederer, he said, to avenge Esmeralda, and to protect The Actaeon Club's other targets. A month earlier,

Thorne had taken care of another club member, George Rossiter.

Thorne was open about his wish to serve his past and future sentences in an ordinary prison instead of the secure psychiatric unit that he hated so passionately. He assured detectives he was perfectly sane, deeply remorseful, and absolutely clear in his intent to help his victims' families in whatever ways he could, in particular by taking responsibility for the things he'd done and answering any questions the police put to him. Wherever Thorne ended up, his incarceration would almost certainly be until death, so Esmeralda saw how important it was to him to get this right. The fact that he had defended her and Líria against his mother in front of witnesses was in his favour.

And it turned out that Mrs Thorne had known all along where her son was hiding. She'd hidden cameras in the grounds of Folly View Cottage that even he didn't know about. When Mrs Thorne saw Esmeralda enter the gardens, she drove straight over. Presumably she'd seen Ben too, the afternoon before, and watched her son capture him by plunging a syringe into his back near the lean-to door. But she hadn't been bothered about that.

'Though Thorne didn't know that she knew he was there,' Mary explained. 'Or he'd have left. Which is why she made sure he didn't find out. Make sense?' And Esmeralda said, 'Bewilderingly, it actually does.' She wasn't sure anyone had ever hated their mother as much as Jason Thorne hated his, or had more reason to.

If Jason Thorne formed The Actaeon Club as a lure

through which he could work against men who hurt women, then it had to be said that the enterprise was a success. All of Actaeon's data for *The Diana List* was gone. Thorne hadn't only protected the woman who made sure that Adam Holderness was put away for ever and the grieving mother who George Rossiter would have otherwise continued to torment, but also the girl who quite possibly buried a femur in Hugo Green's skull and the stalking victim who stopped Rhys Morgan's ugly heart. Esmeralda now knew that the latter lived a quiet life by the sea with her husband and their daughter, and she was happy to think that the little family would be left in peace.

The graveyard was so green and filled with light Esmeralda was dazzled. She arranged the posy carefully, tenderly, knowing Lucy's parents visited every day and that Lucy's terminally ill mother would soon be lying beside her daughter and unborn grandchild.

'I found you.' Esmeralda's voice was soft as she spoke to Lucy. 'I gave you back to your mum and dad. They know where you are now, and your little baby is with you.' She whispered that she would return soon and kissed the top of the stone.

As she walked away, Esmeralda pictured Lucy in that field of wildflowers, which was how she always saw her now. Wearing her denim shorts and pink sweatshirt, Lucy was radiant with the secret of her early pregnancy, and smiling in the spring sunshine.

Spring

When Esmeralda arrived back, Líria was in the front garden, sitting cross-legged on the grass and making a daisy chain. As she lowered herself into the pool of sunlight surrounding her daughter, Esmeralda breathed in the scent of her father's hyacinths. The pleasure of being above ground, her gratitude for it, never wavered.

She and Líria looked up at the perfect blue sky, and the puffy white clouds, and the lemon-yellow circle of the sun, and Esmeralda was reminded of the drawings Líria endlessly made when she was a toddler. These had quickly gained in a technical precision and imaginative artistic vision that nobody else in the family came anywhere near to sharing. Esmeralda preferred not to think about where that talent came from.

'Grandad and Ben still busy with the cooking?' she asked.

'I guess.' Líria's eyes were red and her cheeks were tear-streaked.

'Right. Good,' Esmeralda said. 'Anything you want to talk about?'

'No.' Líria was studying the near-finished daisy chain even more decidedly.

'Okay.' Esmeralda put her arms out behind her and leaned back.

After a few minutes, Líria burst out, 'It's my fault she stabbed you.'

Esmeralda sat up straighter. 'Why on earth do you think that?'

'Because I said I was proud of you. Because I said I wasn't ashamed.'

'That was my best moment.' Esmeralda was rewarded by a weak smile, though it was fleeting. 'Don't you know that she was going to use that knife no matter what you said?'

Líria could do no more than shake her head.

'She came to that house with the purpose of hurting me.' Esmeralda moved a strand of hair out of Líria's eyes. 'She saw me arrive on a camera she'd hidden.'

'I thought I did the wrong thing.' Líria was studiously concentrating on slitting the stem of a daisy with her thumbnail, then threading another through. 'That what I should have done was to lie so she didn't get madder. But I couldn't lie because I thought we were going to die and I didn't want that to be the last thing you ever heard me say.'

Esmeralda scooted closer and wrapped her arms around her daughter. Líria sniffled a little, then said, 'Is my face red?' When Esmeralda said no, Líria retrieved the daisy chain from where it had fallen beside her, linked the two ends, then arranged a crown on top of Esmeralda's head. 'You are the real Queen,' she said, stressing the words you and real.

'You are,' Esmeralda said, 'though I'll lock you in that Tower for the rest of your life the next time I'm arresting someone and you don't leave when I tell you to.'

'From now on,' Líria said, 'I will obey all of your commands instantly.'

Esmeralda pretended to faint.

'April Fool!' Líria said. 'No promises, Mum.' She jumped up and offered a hand to Esmeralda. Esmeralda gave her a look, then took the hand and let Líria help her to stand.

As she and Líria walked into the house, Esmeralda felt the sun warming her skin and seeping into her bones. The bright light was washing the autumn and winter away, and her two favourite seasons were before her. She thought again about choices between minor and major evils, and knew that the actions she took for her daughter were no kind of evil at all.

She remembered the sound of her mother's voice, telling her about hummingbirds. 'They are warriors,' her mother said. 'They protect their nests. They'll fight anybody who threatens those they love. Plus, their memories are wonderful. They don't forget a single flower they ever drank from. They're just like you.'

There were secrets Esmeralda would continue to keep buried deep. And though she knew there was always a risk they could be uncovered, she would deal with that if it happened. Those secrets were her absolute right. They belonged to her and her alone, because sometimes things happened that were never meant to be known.

Acknowledgements

This novel would not exist without my agent, Euan Thorneycroft, who made all the difference in so many ways, at so many times.

To have one tremendous editor is a great thing. I have had the exceptional support and input of two. Kathryn Cheshire and Jo Thompson are a joy to work with, and helped to make this novel infinitely better than it would otherwise have been.

I am grateful to the Art team at HarperCollins for the truly beautiful cover, to the Design team and typesetters for making every single page look so very pretty, to the Marketing and Publicity and Sales teams for everything they do, to Rhian McKay for her sensitive copyediting, and to Sarah Bance for her careful proofreading.

Lily's comments on the first draft of *Make You Mine* were invaluable and inspiring. Imogen gave me encouragement at the start, when I was in need of it. Violet helped when I was obsessing about the novel's opening lines. Richard's insights at a late stage were deeply important. Charlotte offered her own special forms of enchantment and wonder.

Because I am a bit of a referencing geek, I wanted to provide the full bibliographic details for the four epigraphs that appear in *Make You Mine*.

Giambattista Basile's fairy tale, 'Sun, Moon And Talia', appears in *The Pentamerone, Or, The Story of Stories, Fun for the Little Ones*. It was translated from the Neapolitan by John Edward Taylor and published in London in 1850 by David Bogue (Second Edition). The quotation can be found on page 364.

The excerpt from George Eliot's novel, *Adam Bede*, is taken from Volume III (page 17) of the 1859 edition published in Edinburgh and London by William Blackwood and Sons.

D. H. Lawrence's 'HUMMING-BIRD' appears in *Birds, Beasts and Flowers: Poems by D. H. Lawrence*. The collection was published in London by Martin Secker (Ltd) in 1923, and the poem is on page 146.

Lewis Spence's *The Mythologies of Ancient Mexico and Peru* was published in 1907, in London, by Archibald Constable & Co Ltd. The quotation itself can be found on page 15.